Something rustled and scanned the f( the garbage. I listened _ _

I lifted the top and threw in my garbage, then checked the sky again. Mars should be—

Another rustle, louder this time. I turned and made out a man-shaped figure in the shadows, moonlight gleaming off a cap and a shoulder...

Someone was staring at me from not ten feet away.

Moonlight glinted off something long and metallic in his hand...

A knife?

Suddenly he leaped toward me.

I let out a scream and ran—not the loping style of running I do every morning, this was a mad headlong dash at full speed toward my building's lighted entrance. I heard footsteps pounding on the grass behind me. Knowing it would slow me down, I didn't look back. I let panic push me to a speed I never thought myself capable of.

I pulled out my key card and had it ready when I hit the lit-up entryway. I swiped it and pulled open the door. As I slipped inside I turned and yanked it closed with every ounce of strength I had...

# Rx Murder

F. PAUL WILSON WRITING AS
## NINA ABBOTT

GORDIAN KNOT BOOKS

# AUTHOR'S NOTE

So...what's with the pseudonym, Wilson? Who's this Nina Abbott?

For the answer, we have to go back to 2003 when I've just put the finishing touches on *Crisscross*. If you remember the details of that very dark novel, great. If not, let me just say that I pushed the anti-hero motif to the limit, making Jack commit coldblooded first-degree murder (okay, the victim was a sadistic, murderous blackmailer, but still) and frame another killer for it. As I stepped away I felt the need for an anodyne to all the darkness and violence I'd just waded through.

So I sat down and wrote a light, cozy mystery about a young female family doctor practicing in a small suburb of Baltimore and...it simply didn't work. I mean it worked on cleansing and freshening my writing sensibilities, but not as a novel. At least not for me. Something was missing. So I put it aside and moved on to the next Repairman Jack on my contract.

Sixteen years later I retired from my medical practice just in time to go into lockdown for the COVID pandemic. With extra time on my hands, I pulled out my old cozy. After all those years lying fallow on my hard drive, maybe it would read better now. Nope. Still needed something. So I added a ghost and *voila!* It all came together. I liked it so much I blasted off a sequel.

Despite the paranormal aspect, this is by no means the kind of book my readers expect from the author of *The Keep* and *Midnight Mass* and *Sibs* and such. The *Rx* novels are much lighter in tone and content. So I decided on a pseudonym...one that began with an "A" because as a lifelong "W" I get tired of winding up on the bottom shelf all the time.

So, hey, everybody...meet Nina Abbott. I think she tells a pretty good story. I hope you'll agree.

# TUESDAY

# 1

I awoke expecting this to be like any other Tuesday: Early hospital rounds, the rest of the morning and afternoon seeing office patients, then closing the day on call until the next morning.

Good thing I'm a doctor, because I'd make a lousy psychic.

This morning I'd experience the first shot across the bow of a week that would prove to be one of the best and worst and strangest of my life.

Best... because I'd reconnect with an old flame.

Worst... because I'd be hit with my first malpractice suit, a beloved patient would be murdered, and someone would try to do the same to me.

Strangest... because I'd encounter a real, live ghost. Okay, so "live" probably isn't the best word here, but I'm talking about the genuine article.

And it would all begin around lunchtime.

But first: me. Let's get me out of the way.

They call me Doctor Norrie.

Trust me: That wasn't my idea. My first name is Noreen and I've been called Norrie all my life. My surname is Marconi—you know, like the guy who supposedly invented the radio, although some say Tesla was first. I'd prefer the first to be Marconi, but I'm prejudiced.

How does someone with Marconi for a last name wind up with Noreen as a first? Long story. One I won't inflict on you now. Maybe later.

The "Doctor" part comes from my MD degree; I'm board certified in Family Medicine.

I'm part of a three-doctor family practice group in Lebanon, Maryland, a smallish town at the crossroads of Route 206 and Interstate 70, about a dozen miles west of Baltimore's city limits. The other two docs, Sam Glazer and Ken Lerner, are full partners in the mini-corporation. I'm the new kid—two years in as an employee and hoping to start on the partnership track in one more. Together we make up LFPA—Lebanon Family Practice Associates, LLC.

As for my looks, I stand about five seven, my eyes are blue and my hair light brown with red highlights; I don't like to fuss with it so I keep it straight, chin length, and tuck it behind my ears to keep it out of the way. My skin is fair, I blush easily, and my face freckles in the summer. I'm a month shy of my thirty-second birthday and, in my less critical moments—which are few—I'll admit that I'm not terrible looking. No raving beauty, but no bow-wow either.

I'm not the dress size I'd like to be—I've spent most of my life in "plus size" clothing—but I'm getting there. I was roughly the size of Asia when I entered college. Okay, not quite that big, not yet ready for *My 600-lb Life*, but I was squeezing into size eighteens—mostly (surprise!) peasant dresses and jumpers—and it got to the point where even those were too tight. On my twentieth birthday, when my years matched my dress size, I realized I had to take control of myself.

Six years later, when I started my family practice residency, I was down to a twelve. I've heard that Marilyn Monroe was a twelve, but if that's true, I wasn't her kind of twelve. Nowadays I'm a ten—not in the Bo Derek sense, unfortunately—and slaving toward the unreachable four, but I'll gladly settle for an eight.

This morning my size ten consisted of slate-blue Banana Republic slacks and a matching shell. Yes, I dress monochromatic. No surprise there.

Now, about that lunch…

# 2

"What kind of a lunch is that?" Sam Glazer said, eyeing the paper plate I'd placed on his desk.

Sam's consultation office contained a bookshelf, a desk, a high-backed, swivel chair for the doctor, and two conventional armchairs for the patients. The walnut-paneled walls were studded with diplomas and Physician Recognition Awards.

Sam has been in practice in Lebanon for about as long as I'm old. He started the group. He and I hold the fort on Tuesdays, and I'd stopped by his consultation room after completing my morning callbacks. I'd brought my lunch along.

As for Sam, if you can picture a very thin Albert Einstein sans mustache, you've pictured Sam Glazer: same wild gray hair, same twinkling dark eyes, same bushy eyebrows.

I love the man. He's become an uncle. Whenever I run into a diagnostic or therapeutic dilemma, I bounce it off Sam. After thirty years in practice, he's seen just about everything. Hard to find a situation where he hasn't been there, done that.

But it goes beyond his experience. I wasn't here long before I realized that Samuel Glazer is one amazing doctor. This man knows *everything*. He's obsessive with his journals and his continuing medical education, and it shows. He could have been a top cardiologist, nephrologist, pulmonologist, any sort of subspecialty you can imagine, but instead he chose to be a family practitioner, a lowly grunt on the front lines of medicine.

I asked him about that once and he told me he liked the intimacy, and especially the variety of primary care. Said he'd go nuts in a specialty, be bored out of his skull treating the same organ system day in and day out.

Sam and I are on the same page as far as that goes. In fact we see eye to eye on a lot of things.

I'd had a long, long morning. Hospital rounds had chewed up more time than usual due to an emergency admission: Amelia Henderson, one of my first patients here, had arrived at the ER weak, feverish, and short of breath. X-ray showed a left lower lobe pneumonia. In a younger person I'd treat something like that as an outpatient, but Amelia is eighty-three with type-2 diabetes. She's frail on her best days. I thought it best to keep her.

I wrote the admitting orders, patted her arm as they wheeled her toward the elevators, then jumped into my Jeep Liberty and raced the whole two blocks to the office.

I barged through the back door at 9:20 and got to work. On Tuesdays my patient schedule starts at 9:00 sharp, so already I was behind. I ran late all morning. I hate to be kept waiting, so I tense up when I have to keep others waiting. Very undoctorlike, I know. Just one of my crosses.

Then lunch hour arrived—finally. I'd thought I'd been hearing the rumble of distant thunder. No, that was my stomach. I was famished.

I held up part of my lunch for display. The aroma of the horseradish mustard wafted around me.

"This?" I said.

Sam squinted at it. "Yes, that. I've never seen anything like it."

"I call them turkey-Swiss roll ups."

They're one of the staples of my diet. I take a slice of Swiss cheese, top it with a slice of smoked turkey breast, add a little mustard, and roll it up. I make three of them every morning, stick them in a plastic bag, and store them in the office refrigerator among the suppositories and vials of vaccines.

Turkey-Swiss roll ups with a can of Diet Pepsi. That's my lunch pretty much every workday. Boring? Not to me. I kind of like it.

"Want one?"

I prayed he'd say no. My stomach felt ready to digest itself.

"They're not exactly kosher."

I laughed. "Neither are you. You ordered lobster salad for the last meeting. I don't know much about kosher, Sam, but I'm pretty sure lobster isn't on the list."

Once a month we order sandwiches and extend the lunch break to two hours while the three of us gather in the waiting room to discuss practice-related issues.

He smiled. "Guilty. So, let me put it another way: They don't tempt me."

"Okay. The important thing is they've got no carbs."

"Still on that Atkins thing?"

I shrugged. "Not really. My own version."

As a doctor I'd never thought much of the Atkins diet. Too much fat. But when I saw my patients losing weight on it without their cholesterol shooting up—going *down* in some of them—I decided to give it a try. I figure if I avoid saturated fats, there's not much of a downside—except in pounds.

"How's it working out?"

"Not bad. Slowly but surely the scale is heading in the right direction. I did the low-fat, calorie-counting thing for years and got nowhere. Now I count carbs instead."

"Seems like a lot of trouble."

"Easy for a skinny guy like you to say." I leaned left and patted my ample right butt cheek. "I want this to be history."

"You look fine, Norrie. In fact you look great. Take my Jessica. She's so thin sometimes I think she might be bulimic."

I'd never met his daughter. She was married to a Navy man and lived in San Diego.

"I've never been bulimic. My problem was always hemi-bulimia."

Sam frowned. "Hemi—?"

"I do fine with the gorging part, but then I forget the throwing-up part."

His smile was tolerant. "You're not fat. You're what—five six?"

"Seven."

"Whatever your weight, you carry it well. A woman should be rounded, not angular."

"I know all about rounded, Sam. I grew up with an Italian father who loved to cook and never made a pasta I didn't like.

Did I ever tell you my high-school nickname?"

"No."

"Macaroni."

He *tsk*ed and shook his head. "Kids can be cruel."

"I don't think cruelty was behind it. Just a play on my last name. It's a cosmic certainty that a fat girl with the last name Marconi is going to end up Macaroni Marconi."

"Didn't it hurt your feelings?"

"It stung a little at first, but I got used to it. Truth be known, there was something to be said for having an identity, even if it derived from your weight. I guess I was somewhere else when they were handing out the self-pity gene." I laughed. "Probably had my head in the refrigerator, looking for something to eat!"

Sam laughed too.

I remember it being anything but a laughing matter back then. I had many a good cry over my blimp shape. But the tears came from frustration rather than feeling sorry for myself. As a child I was, believe it or not, rather svelte. At least until my teenage years. The pounds started packing on right after my first period. It seemed like someone had hooked me up to an air pump. I ballooned. And no matter what I tried—dieting, exercise, even fasting—I couldn't lose a pound.

Weighing 200-plus and wearing a size sixteen is okay for some adult women—not okay in the health sense, because you won't live as long as you should—but in a sense that a lot of women can carry it off and look pretty damn good. A teenager, though, is a whole different story. For a teenage girl, where body image is critical, where even size fours think they're fat and ugly, being size 16 or 18 can be devastating.

At least I had brains. As a straight-A student, number one in my class, I could cling to a certain intellectual self-esteem. But—excuse the expression—fat lot of good it did for my body image. Things could have been a lot worse, though. How would I have felt with C's and D's?

I see now that my home environment had a lot to do with it. For my father, everything revolved around food. Between his cooking and my mother's sweet tooth, you couldn't turn around in my house without running into leftovers or a full candy dish.

College took me away from that. I started losing pounds when I could structure my own environment.

Even so, it's been a long, long road to where I am now, and I've still got some traveling to do.

"So I've done the 'rounded' thing, Sam. I'd like a shot at angular, just to see how it feels. Anyway, diets aren't on my mind at the moment."

Sam stifled a yawn. Not—I hoped—because I was boring him. Sam was looking tired and a little more wan than usual. I'd gathered early on that his health was behind the cutback in his schedule, but I'd yet to learn the diagnosis. I was sure Ken knew, but neither of them had shared it with me.

I had my suspicions, but I itched to *know*. Not out of morbid curiosity, but because I didn't want it to be anything that would take him away from us. Not a malignancy. Please, not a malignancy.

He dropped a napkin and when he bent over I lined up the three pens and the scattered reports on his desk. I like orderly.

Just then Giselle's voice came over the intercom.

"Is Doctor Norrie there?"

"She sure is," Sam said to the air.

"The ER is on two-four. Doctor McIver wants to speak to her."

Sam hit the blinking button and handed me the receiver.

"*Norrie!*" said the familiar voice of the county hospital's ace ER doc.

"Hi, Joe. What's up?"

"*Patient of yours… let me see… Harris… Margery Harris.*"

I knew Marge. Knew her well. I'd sort of inherited her from Sam. I say "sort of" because Marge and I go back a ways and she switched over to me soon after I joined the practice. It gave me a little glow to know she'd named me as her doctor.

"Sure. What's up?"

"*Anaphylactic reaction. Arrived in shock. Almost didn't make it. But we've got her systolic back up to a hundred now and she's awake and alert. Going to need admission, though.*"

Marge Harris… almost didn't make it… the words killed my appetite for the last roll-up.

"I'm on my way. What set her off? Bee sting?"

*"Nothing so exotic. I'll tell you when you get here."*

I handed the receiver back to Sam. "Got to go."

"I'll man the ship till you come back."

I hurried for my car. Admitting Marge would take some time. Looked like I was going to be starting my afternoon appointments late too.

# 3

Carson County Community Hospital—"Three-C" to us locals—is hardly a university medical center, but it serves its community well. I flashed my hospital ID badge as I breezed past the security guard at the emergency room entrance. I went straight to the nursing station where I found the doctor in charge leaning against the counter as he two-finger tapped on a keyboard.

"Hey, Joe."

He looked up. Joe McIver, MD, is on the short side, maybe five eight or nine, with a many-hours-at-the-gym build. He has these piercing blue eyes and black—not dark brown, I mean *black*—hair that he wears back in a short, neat ponytail. He's the kind who's got five-o'clock shadow at noon. Maybe that was why he'd recently decided to grow a beard. With said beard and ponytail he looks like he should be riding a Harley instead of running an emergency room.

"Hey, Norrie. Your valuable prize awaits behind curtain three."

As I headed toward the treatment bays he fell into step beside me, stroking his newly hirsute cheeks.

"Coming in nice, don't you think?"

Despite his fur, Joe is a good-looking guy, so burying his handsome face beneath a black rug wasn't a good move. I decided that as a friend, colleague, and former lover, I should let him know that the beard wasn't working. But I should do it gently, with compassion and concern for his feelings.

"If you're going for the Bigfoot look, Joe, you're almost there."

He laughed. "That's my Norrie. Always hiding her true feelings. Come on. Tell me what you really think."

"You want my advice? Unless you want your patients wondering if evolution might have started running in reverse, lose the beard."

"But then I have to go back to shaving two, sometimes three times a day."

"Trust me, Joe, it's worth the trouble. Now, about Marge Harris: What happened? What kicked off the anaphylaxis?"

"Would you believe peanuts?"

I nodded. I believed. Allergic reactions to peanuts were getting more common, and could be fatal. I remembered a patient in one of the clinics I worked during my residency who'd break out in hives if he got downwind from a peanut.

"Ever happen to her before?"

"She says she's been allergic since she was a kid. I've got her epied, cimetidined, Benadryled, and Medroled to the limit now, but it was touch and go for a while. If her cleaning girl hadn't been around to use the EpiPen, she wouldn't have made it."

"The EpiPen wasn't enough?"

"Apparently not. She must be *super* allergic. IgE out the wazoo."

He gave my shoulder a squeeze and headed back to his charts.

Joe McIver is a great ER doctor. I don't say that lightly. He knows his stuff—can make an accurate diagnosis like lightning and immediately set the best therapy in motion. Dexterity-wise, he can insert a central line, even set a temporary pacemaker when the cardiologist on call is taking too long to get in. And he's a whiz with a needle and thread. He can suture like a plastic surgeon.

So I was pretty taken with him during my first year here. He's four years older and single. We started off talking over coffee, then going out to dinner, then we graduated to the bedroom—sometimes his, sometimes mine.

I'm not sure what we had—I do know I was on the rebound and vulnerable at the time—but whatever it was, it ran out of steam after four months or so. I can't say exactly why. The sex was good, but we didn't seem to connect on a deeper level.

We never really called it off. We sort of let it die by attrition, with each of us finding other things to do besides going out together.

It ended with no hard feelings. We'd had a good time, but it was over and we still remain close friends.

# 4

I pushed back the curtain and found Marge lying on a gurney. She had an IV running into her left arm and a green plastic oxygen mask stuck over her mouth and nose. Her face was the color of uncooked bread dough.

She pulled off the mask and gave me a weak smile as she reached out a trembling hand.

"Norrie... I'm so glad you're here."

I took her hand. Her skin was cold.

Marge Harris... not simply a patient... a very special someone in my life.

She'd been Margery Scarborough back when I was twelve and she about twice that. She had an education degree from Notre Dame of Baltimore but, with no openings for teachers in the local school systems, she'd made do by living at home, substitute teaching, and giving piano lessons.

Margery was gentle, sweet, and patient, and I looked forward to the moment she'd arrive for my weekly lesson. To my teenage eyes she was beautiful, intelligent, graceful, poised, and charming—everything I longed to be. She became a sort of big sister. She hadn't minded my size, commiserated with my fruitless efforts to lose weight, cheered me up when I was down. During some lessons we'd just sit and gab and laugh and do very little piano playing. She was just the person I needed at that time in my life.

The piano lessons and the visits stopped when she got married and moved away to Lebanon. I'd been brokenhearted then. But she'd been there for me, and I'll never forget that. I owe her.

Later on, before I left town myself, I heard she'd had a baby. A little boy.

Marge was now a matronly brunette in her forties; one of those empty-nest ladies who turn all their nurturing instincts outward.

Tragedy had prematurely emptied her nest when, years before my arrival in town, her only son had been killed in a car crash.

So Marge volunteered her time and effort to just about every charitable cause in Carson County. She was one of the good people. Always had been. One of the first patients in the practice to refer to me as "my doctor." She had faith in me, heeded my advice—gave me props, as they say.

Life is strange. Marge had been my hero. Now she was looking at me as if I was hers.

"How'd this happen, Marge? You never told me you were allergic to peanuts."

"Well, it's been so long since I had a reaction, I guess I didn't think to mention it. I mean, you weren't ever going to prescribe peanuts, were you?"

I smiled. "No, not likely. What happened? Couldn't resist a Snickers?"

"Lord, no." She frowned. "I always check ingredient labels— I've been doing it so long it's automatic. The strange thing is, the only thing I've eaten today is a banana and a breakfast bar—you know, one of those Havermill power bars—and they're nothing new. Stan and I have been eating them for months."

I'd gobbled more than a few Havermills in my day. High protein and low fat, they're supposed to help you lose weight. Never worked for me. Of course, eating a dozen a day might have had something to do with that.

"Maybe they changed the ingredients."

"Could be. I'll have to check later when I get home."

"That won't be today, I'm afraid. We're going to keep you overnight."

"Oh, no! I have to get back! The Children's Concert is Saturday and there's still so much left to do. I can't—"

"You can," I said in my no-nonsense tone. "You're in no shape to go home today. We've got to make sure your blood pressure is stable before we let you go. By tomorrow you'll be a lot stronger."

If I sent her home now I could see her BP plunging as she got out of bed or tried to maneuver a flight of stairs. She could break something, or worse.

"But I hate hospitals. I want—"

I was still holding her hand so I gave it a little extra squeeze. "You almost *died*, Marge. Doctor McIver told me if the cleaning girl hadn't found you, you wouldn't have made it."

"Alison? I don't remember. Alison saved me?"

"That's what I'm told."

"God bless her!"

"Looks like we're going to have to get you a double set of EpiPens."

"Why?"

"Well, the one Alison used didn't do the whole job."

She gave me a sheepish look. "Oh. That. Well…"

I had a pretty good idea where this was going.

"How old was it, Marge?"

"Old," she said.

"*How* old? Are we talking the Truman presidency? Or maybe when Hannibal crossed the Alps?"

She smiled. "Even older. *Very* old."

I shook my head. Anyone with a severe allergy to anything—bee stings, penicillin, peanuts—needs to keep an EpiPen within easy reach. It auto-injects a dose of epinephrine that can mean quite literally the difference between life and death. But if it sits around too long, it loses potency. Using a "very old" EpiPen like Marge's was probably equivalent to injecting water.

"First thing you do when you get out of here is get a new one. I'll give you a prescription—"

"Marge?" said a male voice behind me.

A good-looking, middle-aged man in a dark brown business suit swept through the curtains and stopped at the far side of the gurney. His longish brown hair was thinning and receding along his temples; horn-rimmed glasses gave him a professorial look.

"Marge, are you all right?"

Mr. Harris, I gathered. The one who'd taken Marge away from me. I'd never met him but knew he was Lebanon's go-to guy for insurance.

"I'm fine, Stan, really." She didn't look overjoyed to see him.

"I got the call at the office and got here as soon as I could."

"I'm sure you did."

I felt the temperature around the gurney drop about twenty degrees. Any colder and our breaths would be fogging.

"I thought you were dying!" he said.

"That's what they tell me, but I'm going to be fine now that Norrie's here."

I couldn't let Joe go uncredited. "Don't forget Doctor McIver. He's the one who saved you.

"Yes, but *you're* going to *keep* me safe."

"Oh, and your cleaning girl deserves a raise."

"Alison?" Mr. Harris said. "Oh, right. It's Tuesday. But why...?"

Since Marge didn't seem to be in any hurry to introduce us, I extended my hand across the gurney.

"I'm Dr. Marconi."

"Stan Harris," he said. "Glad to finally meet you. Marge talks about you all the time."

I repeated what Joe had told me about the cleaning girl's part in the rescue, and answered his questions about what had happened, mentioning the power bar.

"A Havermill?" he said. "We've both been eating them." He pulled something in a bright yellow wrapper from a jacket pocket. "Here's one. But there's no peanuts in them."

"May I see that?"

He handed it to me and I scanned the ingredient list. He was right. No mention of peanuts.

Stan leaned toward Marge. "Did you eat anything else?"

She gave him a cold look. "Of course not."

Definite disharmony in the Harris house.

Stan looked puzzled. "Then how—?"

Marge ignored him and turned to me. "I've read where some food manufacturers run different products through the same production line and sometimes there's cross contamination."

Stan reached his hand toward me. "May I see that again?"

I handed it back and watched him read the label. He looked up with a gleam in his eye.

"If there's peanut contamination in this, they'll hear from me. Damn well better *believe* they'll hear from me."

I could almost see phrases like *product liability suit* and *big settlement* scrolling across his forehead.

The American way.

I did a quick exam, then entered a history and physical and admitting orders into the computer. Stan was still hovering by Marge's side as I said good-bye.

She grabbed my hand. I saw tears in her eyes. "Norrie, please don't make me stay."

"I can't *make* you do anything, Marge. All I can do is advise you as to what I think is best. You can take it or leave it. If you want to walk out, we'll ask you to sign a release, but I can't stop you."

Her eyes went wide. "You can't?"

She acted as if this was some sort of epiphany. People seem to equate a hospital with a prison: Once you're in, you can't leave until we let you. But it's nothing like that. You can always sign yourself out AMA—against medical advice.

"Then that's just what I'm going to do."

Stan said, "I don't think that's wise, Marge."

She ignored him and sat up, but before she could swing her legs over the side, her already gray face went two shades paler. She groaned as she dropped back, her head bouncing on the pillow.

"What's wrong with me?"

"Your blood pressure's way down. It's going to take a while before it stabilizes."

She grabbed my hand again. "But I'm *scared.*"

"Of the hospital?"

She nodded.

Hospitals feel almost like home to me, so sometimes I forget how scary they can be. The loss of autonomy has to be the worst—the knowledge that people you barely know or have never met are making decisions about what you wear, what you eat, how far you can walk, whether you get to use a toilet or a bedpan. They're sticking needles in your arms and pumping God-knows-what into your veins. They're shoving tubes into every orifice you've got. Plus they have these sterile rooms where they take you and rob you of your consciousness so they can slit you open and rummage around in your innards.

Terrifying. Truly terrifying.

I gave her hand a squeeze. "You'll be fine, Marge. You have my personal guarantee. No one's going to so much as take your temperature without checking with me first."

That seemed to have the hoped-for effect. She relaxed her death grip on my fingers but didn't let go.

I told her, "I'll be back after office hours to check on you again. Until then, hang in there. Everything's going to be fine."

I extricated my hand and headed for the exit.

# 5

A long the way I spotted a good-looking, dark-haired man talking to McIver. He wore the light brown shirt and dark brown pants of the County Sheriff's Department. His shirtfront was splattered with dried blood and he had gauze taped above his left eyebrow.

Something familiar about him.

Just then a thin, angular young woman, mid-twenties, rose from a chair and touched my arm.

"Are you Doctor Marconi?"

She had a whiny voice and smelled vaguely of ammonia. Despite her outfit of worn gray sweatsuit and battered sneakers—her work clothes, no doubt—she was cute in a hard sort of way. She wore her hair very short and bleached, with black eyebrows. Kristin Stewart as Jean Seberg.

"Yes. Can I help you?"

"How is Marge—Mrs. Harris—doing?"

"Are you related?"

"I clean her house. I was there this morning when—"

"You must be Alison. You saved her life."

"Really? She's gonna be okay?"

"Really. Thanks to you."

"Oh, I didn't do nothing."

"Sure you did. You knew enough to use her EpiPen to—"

"You mean that needle thing? She told me what to do. I heard this noise in her office and I come in and she's on the floor sounding like someone's choking her. First thing I did was call 9-1-1 but I didn't think she was gonna make it. I mean, what with her like turning blue and all. But she's pointing to one of her desk drawers—she couldn't talk, know what I mean?—and so I open it and start pulling stuff out and showing it to her and she keeps shaking her head. And then I see the needle and I know right off that had to be it, so I grab it and hand it to her. She takes it from me but couldn't hold it and I knew I was losing her, so I jab it into her arm"—she pointed to her left deltoid—"just like my doctor did to me when I was a kid. It was really weird, feeling the needle go through her skin. Anyways, I pushed the plunger and she seemed to get a little better, but not a whole lot."

"You wouldn't happen to have it with you," I said.

"Yeah. I brought it along."

As she leaned over to fish through her bag, I noticed a blackened area on the nape of her neck. I realized it was a tattoo—a Chinese ideogram. I wondered what it meant. I wondered if she knew. And I wondered if it meant what she thought it did.

"Here it is."

She handed me the used EpiPen. I checked the expiration date—seven years ago. No wonder it hadn't had much effect.

"I never gave nobody a shot before. Kinda creepy."

"You did fine." I stuck out my hand. "You're a hero."

She looked down as she hesitantly shook my hand. "I ain't no hero. Anybody'd do that."

She was probably right, but I didn't want her to minimize it. Alison didn't look like she had much going for her.

"Maybe anybody would *want* to do it, but not every anybody *could*. And you did. So be proud."

"Think she'll be needing me?"

"Her husband's here and—"

"Yeah, I saw him come through, but he didn't see me."

"Well, she'll be staying the night, but I expect to send her home tomorrow good as new." I patted her on the shoulder. "Nice to meet a hero. Do you want to go in and say hello?"

She backed away. "Oh, no. I'm a mess."

She turned and hurried toward the visitors door.

# 6

I realized I still had the used EpiPen in my hand. As I headed for the nursing station to dispose of it in the sharps receptacle, I spotted the injured deputy again.

The dark hair, the blue eyes, the slightly lopsided twist to his mouth... it all looked so familiar.

He looked up and caught my stare. Our eyes locked. His puzzled look vanished as he smiled. I knew that smile.

Travis Lawton.

"Macaroni? Is that you?"

I wanted to kick him. Nobody at the hospital knew my old nickname.

McIver looked at up and saw me. "*Macaroni?*"

I looked past him and said, "Travis? I don't believe it!" I thrust out my hand. "How *are* you?"

"Look at you," he said, smiling and giving me the up and down as he shook my hand. "Look at *you!* You look absolutely *terrific!*"

I let loose the breath I'd been holding. I'd half expected him to say something like, *Where's the rest of you?*

"Thanks, Trav. You're looking pretty good yourself."

And still he stared. "Where'd the rest of you go?"

I forced out a laugh that sounded pretty scary. I could have said, *Same place as your old pimples,* but bit it back.

Not only was the acne gone—no surprise there, considering his age—but so was the baby fat. He used to have a soft, almost puffy face; now it was all planes and angles; his former long, scraggly hair was cut close to his scalp. A slim, vertical, one-inch scar ran lateral to his right eye, added character to his features. I wondered how he'd come by it. And his body... well, from the look of his shoulders he'd obviously been working out. Travis Lawton was no longer a shlub. Far from it.

Good for you, Trav. We've both taken control.

I ignored his rest-of-you quip and searched for a way to turn the focus away from me. I pointed to his bandaged head.

"Is that what brings you here?"

"Oh, I'm here a lot anyway because of my father."

I was trying to remember what his father did. Something in construction, I thought.

"He works here?"

"He gets dialysis here."

"Oh, sorry to hear that."

"Yeah, me too. He's not a happy camper about it. I volunteered a kidney but I wasn't a match."

I knew Trav was an only child so that meant his father was added to the long national transplant waiting list.

"And the bandage?"

He gingerly touched the gauze with his forefinger. "This is courtesy of a car thief I caught in the act. He swung his slim jim at me and tried to run."

I didn't keep up on Carson County politics or law enforcement. "Are you the sheriff?"

Trav laughed. "No. Just a deputy."

"And this car thief... you catch him?"

McIver looked up and said, "He sure did. The guy's behind curtain number seven, waiting to be patched up. He's going to need a bit of work." He turned to Travis. "Have that looked at in a couple of days, okay? Just to make sure there's no infection."

Without thinking I blurted, "Stop by my office tomorrow afternoon and I'll give it a quick look."

That appraising stare again. "Yeah, I heard you came back a doctor. I appreciate the offer, Norrie, but since this is work related I've got to see Doc Hansford. He does all the county comp."

"Just a thought." I glanced at my watch. I was late. Really late. "Got to run. Maybe we can catch up sometime."

He smiled. "Love to."

# 7

Iwas halfway to my car when I heard a voice call out behind me.

"Doctor Marconi!"

I turned and saw Marge's husband hurrying toward me.

"Yes, Mr. Harris?"

He smiled. "Call me Stan."

I nodded but said nothing.

He took off his horn rims and wiped them with a tissue. Patches of scalp, lit by the high bright sun, peeked through his thinning hair.

"I'm worried about Marge."

"She had a close call."

"I'd like to talk to you about her."

I glanced at my watch. "I have patients waiting at the office. If you want, I can call you tonight after hours."

"Can we meet instead. Say for dinner? I'd prefer to talk in person."

I stared at him, trying to get a read. Was he that worried about Marge? Was he coming on to me? Or did he want to sell me insurance?

"I'm sorry. This is my night on call."

"Some other time then?"

I stayed one-hundred-percent professional. "If you want to make an appointment some time, fine. But be aware that I'll only listen. Marge may be your wife, but unless I have her permission, I can't discuss anything in her medical records."

I have this strict policy about patient privilege: Nothing said or done in my office while under my care goes any further— not even to a spouse—without the patient's signed consent or a court order. And maybe not even with a court order.

His smile looked forced. "All right then. I'll do that."

I nodded, said, "Nice meeting you," and turned away.

I'd taken a quick turn on Stan Harris. And I *had* to get back to the office.

# 8

Thoughts about Travis Lawton flitted through my head along the way. I didn't have much choice, what with Natasha Bedingfield's "Unwritten" thumping from the car's speakers via my phone's songlist. Most people's favorite songs are from their high-school years, and so mine are from the early aughts. The song took me back in time to when teen-aged Macaroni Marconi had a humungous crush on Travis Lawton.

But grown-up Norrie had forgotten all about him.

Until today.

With his thick waist and bad skin, Travis had *not* been the heartthrob of Carmel Memorial High. But he'd been mine, though he never knew it.

He'd been on the football team, second string. Maybe third. The only time he got to play in senior year was when the Carmel Cougars were beating another team—for the life of me I can't remember its name—by something like 60 to 7. He was put in for, at most, a whopping five minutes, but I gnawed off all ten fingernails while he was on the field, scared to death he'd get himself hurt.

We had a one-sided love affair and a two-sided friendship. We both took piano lessons from Marge and every so often she would gather some of her students for an informal recital. That was when we became acquainted and I learned he was a lot smarter than he let on. It wasn't cool, after all, for an aspiring jock to get A's and volunteer answers in class. Since he lived only a couple blocks away, we started to hang out now and then, study together now and then, do some homework together now and then, even practice piano together now and then. Now and then never provided enough together for me.

The hardest part had been listening to him tell me about other girls he had a crush on—like I was his sister! He was shy and always asking me how to meet them and talk to them.

I always made sure to give him bad advice.

Guys are so dumb.

Trav was especially enamored of Diana Robinson. That baffled me. My face was twice as pretty as hers. Of course I was twice her weight too. She was a lean cross-country runner, with slim, muscular legs I'd have killed for. My legs, on the other hand, were modeled after Stonehenge.

By senior year Trav and I had sort of drifted apart. During the year he reduced his waistline and his pimple count. I guess he managed to wear down skinny Diana Robinson because they started going out together.

I, on the other hand, through fancy footwork and artful dodging of the myriad suitors pounding on my parents' front door, managed to remain unattached all the way through to the end of senior year.

I graduated first in my class. The principal wanted me to be valedictorian but I refused. No way was I standing on a stage wearing a graduation gown that was tight around the waist. Okay, the XXXL size turned out to be not tight at all, but it made me look like a bright blue Hindenburg. One spark of static electricity and I might burst into flame.

Oh, the humanity.

A couple of weeks after the ceremony I put Carmel Memorial High behind me and headed for New York. I had a full-ride scholarship to NYU and no intention of looking back.

During the eleven years I was gone—and through the two since my return—I don't think I gave a single thought to Travis Lawton. Now I was back, and he'd never left. He looked better than ever to me. Maybe a spark still remained in the ashes of my burned bridges.

But as for that spark growing into a flame... I couldn't see it. We'd spent years apart and became adults in two different worlds. For all I knew, he'd turned out to be a creep.

One thing I did know: I wasn't Macaroni Marconi anymore. I'd never be Macaroni again.

# 9

The practice occupies its own building, a clapboard-sided, single-story structure within sight of Carson County Community Hospital. Driving into the office parking lot I felt my usual little blip of pride as I passed the *Lebanon Family Practice Associates, LLC* sign with my name following Sam's and Ken's.

I like this practice. I like being in this town. I just hope I can stay here.

Two years ago, as I was nearing the end of my family practice residency at University of Maryland Hospital in Baltimore, I began looking for a place to hang my shingle. I found an ad in the back of an issue of *JAMA* placed by a family practice group "convenient to Baltimore" that was looking for a third doctor.

I called and learned that "convenient to Baltimore" meant Lebanon. I wasn't sure if this was good luck or bad. My widowed mother still lived in our old family home in Carmel, the next town west of Lebanon. That was the upside. The downside was I'd grown up in Carmel.

This presented a dilemma. I didn't want to practice medicine where I'd worn white anklets and patent-leather Mary-Janes, if you know what I mean. If the practice had been in Carmel, the answer would have been a quick, emphatic no.

But Lebanon... I would still run into people I'd grown up with, but not that many. And I'd be close to my mother. Close enough to ease some of the guilt trip I'd been on since Dad's death.

So I sent in my résumé and received a callback from a Dr.

Sam Glazer, inviting me for an interview. He sounded interested.

I made the short trip out from Baltimore, visited my mother, then met with Sam and his younger partner, Ken Lerner. Ken was heavier than Sam, verging on dumpy, and younger looking despite his receding hairline.

We met after hours, the staff had gone home, and the three of us seated ourselves in the deserted waiting room. I remember Sam as warm and friendly from the get-go, but Ken seemed aloof, almost cold, saying very little. At the time I figured that was just his personality. Turned out I was wrong. That doesn't mean he's a warm-fuzzy teddy bear once you get to know him—not even close—but he had his reasons.

Months later I learned what those were.

Sam led off by explaining that he wanted to reduce his workload, but he didn't say why. I thought it strange that a relatively robust-looking guy in his late fifties or early sixties would be cutting back, but figured maybe he had other things to do with his life: Golf, fishing, travel, or maybe he wanted to get into research.

After about an hour of discussing everything from current events to politics to sports, and discovering that my expectations of what I wanted from family practice were pretty much in line with the way things were done here, we adjourned to the Lebanon Golf and Country Club for dinner.

Sam's and Ken's spouses awaited us there. Sam's wife, Sofia, was short and the size I used to be; together Sam and she looked like Mr. and Mrs. Sprat. Allie—Ken's second wife—was the size I longed to be and she didn't fit with him. Ken was kind of squat and she was a tall, leggy blonde. Someone less kind might call her a trophy wife. I took one look at her very big, very blonde hair and dubbed her Barbie.

Really, it wouldn't be fair to expect me to resist that.

Sofia was as warm and welcoming as Sam. Barbie—I mean Allie... I was going to get myself in trouble if I wasn't careful—was as distant as her husband, but that didn't stop her from letting me know that *they* were members of the club, not the Glazers.

I survived dinner despite the one bottle of Chardonnay

divided between five people during a four-course meal. I'm half Irish on my mother's side and grew up sneaking swigs of my dad's jug of barbarone; if I'd been ordering for the table it would have been a different story. But Ken had put himself in charge of the wine, and didn't offer anyone a second glass.

Two weeks later Sam called and said they wanted to make me an offer. Would I like to come by and we'd all sit down and talk about it?

Of course I would.

We met again—same time, same place. The offer wasn't quite what I'd been looking for. As a matter of fact, it was a long way from what I was looking for. Most of my fellow residents who'd accepted positions with groups were set to receive a fairly decent salary with a few performance incentives. Sam and Ken were offering a low base salary and anything I'd make over that would be on a strict productivity basis.

I thought Sam looked a little uncomfortable; Ken looked anything but.

I later learned the reasons behind their expressions. Ken had insisted on the low base as a condition before he'd agree to hire me. Sam had wanted to be more generous but Ken wouldn't budge. Nothing personal. He simply didn't want a third doctor in the practice, period. He didn't think there'd be enough volume to support me. He feared it would lower his take-home pay.

How shall I put this about Ken? Let's say that he's the kind who never tips a waitress more than fifteen percent, and even then he rounds *down*. The kind who, even on a cold night, will self-park at a restaurant and leave his overcoat in the car so he can avoid tipping the valet and hat-check girl.

Get the picture?

As for me, I was worried about my take-home pay too. I wasn't naïve. I knew how a small medical group worked: All the expenses are subtracted from the gross revenues, and the doctors split whatever is left over. In order to get a third of that pie—or even a sixth—I was going to have to account for a proportionate part of the income.

The productivity part didn't bother me. One thing I'm not

afraid of is work. I'll toil as long and as hard as anyone else—longer and harder, even. I was just coming out of a residency where eighty-hour weeks were routine. The schedule I faced here at LFPA would be a cakewalk in comparison.

The problem was that I didn't have a practice—no patient base to keep me running. It takes time for a new kid in town to be accepted. I could wind up taking home that low base pay and nothing more. And that wouldn't be enough. I'd borrowed my way through medical school and had Godzilla-size education loans waiting to be repaid.

I voiced these concerns but Sam reassured me that his cut in office hours would create an overflow that would end up on my appointment sheet.

That sounded a bit iffy. I said I'd think about it and returned to Baltimore.

I knew I could easily do better. Much better. But money wasn't the only consideration. Lebanon was near my mother. After high school I'd moved away from home and hardly ever looked back. Between undergrad, med school, and residency, I'd been gone over a decade. Not that I disliked my folks or had issues with them, I'd just wanted out—*far* out—of Carson County, Maryland. I visited them on holidays and such, but mostly I took it for granted that they'd be there whenever I got an itch to see them.

Strange… during your medical training you see death all the time, sometimes slow, sometimes out of left field with no warning. But you don't think of it striking close to home. That happens to other people's parents.

Well, in my fourth year of med school a clogged left anterior descending artery in my father's heart—they call it "the widow maker"—provided me with a brutal reality check. Dad collapsed carrying someone out of a burning building and was DOA at Hopkins ER.

I was devastated. NYU Med cut me some slack, but they could allow me only so much time away from my clinical rotations. I visited as often as I could but felt terrible about not being there for her more. At least she had my brother Sean, but he had his own life.

That was why I took my residency in Baltimore. To be near, to be available—just in case. A secondary gain from that allowed me to reconnect with Sean who lives and works in the city.

My mother seemed to be in good health, but who knew how much longer she'd be around?

One day my father had been there, the next he was gone. I'd seen little of him during the last years of his life and now I'd never see him again, never get to say the things I might have said if I'd been around. I didn't want that to happen with my mother.

So I called Sam and made a counteroffer on the base pay; we split the difference, and I signed on.

The deal was I'd spend three years as an employee. Then, if my professional performance was up to snuff and both Sam and Ken approved, I'd start the partnership track, which would make me a part owner of this little limited liability corporation known as Lebanon Family Practice Associates. During the following three years as a junior partner, my equity would grow equal to Sam's and Ken's, making me a full-fledged partner.

Could be I've told you more of the business side than you want to know, but I'd like to debunk the too-common misconception that a person goes through med school, does a some post-graduate training, then hangs out an MD shingle and watches the money roll in.

Wish it were so, but that's not how it goes in the real world.

It's *hard* to go into solo practice. The hurdles are daunting. It seems almost every patient belongs to some sort of managed care plan—HMO, PPO, IPO, POS, etc.—and in most cases those organizations require you to sign a contract before you can treat their members. I've seen some of those contracts: You need an MBA and a law degree to make sense of them.

So I joined a group practice to fulfill my dream: To have enough autonomy to practice my own style of medicine and still have enough time for a life.

That second part is as important as the first. I'd spent years shedding the old Norrie and recasting myself in a new mold. But my headlong pursuit of a new me *and* a medical degree had left little time for rose sniffing. Sure I went to art museums—the

Hopper show at the Whitney still resonates—and Off-Broadway shows and poetry readings, but those were brief cultural pit stops along an ever rolling, seemingly endless highway of texts and tests and labs and dissections.

I created a new me, but just who is that person? I'm not sure I know. But I'm going to find out. And for that I need time. Group practice affords that time.

Anyway, things seem to be working out. A lot of Sam's overflow has stayed with me, and I even picked up a few of Ken's patients—guess who was not happy about *that*. Plus, my razor-sharp clinical acumen, in unison with my sparkling personality, led to good word of mouth that brought in new patients. And being female didn't hurt either.

But I haven't reached the point where I can say I've made it. My morning schedule tends to be full but my afternoons are light.

I need more people. When my three-year employee period is up, Sam and Ken will sit down and decide whether or not I start on the partnership track. I'm pretty sure which way Sam will vote, but Ken... Ken might not want his stock position to drop from fifty percent to thirty-three and a third. If, however, by decision time I'm a performer, such an asset to the practice that my leaving would be damaging, he'll have no choice but to vote me in.

That's where I want to be this time next year.

As it is, money is tight. I'm not saying I'm ready for a shopping cart and the street—I'm earning enough to cover my bills and stay on top of my education loan payments—but as they say, there's too much month left over at the end of my money. Lucky for me my needs have always been simple.

The most important thing to me is practicing medicine the way I want to: Not treating Fred's heart or Jane's depression, but treating Fred who happens to have heart disease, and Jane who happens to be depressed. If you think that's just word play, think again. There's a world of difference between the two approaches.

# 10

I pulled into the packed office parking lot and jerked to a halt in one of the *Doctor's Only* spots. Yes, we know about the apostrophe. A helpful sign maker had added it and no one could be bothered arranging for a replacement. I killed the engine and dashed inside.

Being the only female primary care doctor in a medium-size suburban town has its advantages. Women are more comfortable bringing their emotional issues to me and coming in with gynecological problems that won't wait the two or three weeks it takes to get in to see their OB-Gyn. The same holds true for teenage girls whose mothers will allow them to be alone with me in the examining room where they can ask me questions about and birth control. And mothers, for some reason, seem to feel more comfortable bringing their younger kids to a woman doctor.

Harriet Baxter, RN, stepped out of Room Three and said, "All set to go."

Harriet has been with the practice a long time—since the last Ice Age, I think. She looks like she could play Nurse Ratchet, but she's got a good heart.

I ducked into Sam's consultation room to tell him about Marge, then hurried back to Room Three.

All four of the office's examining rooms are the same: white-walled cubes with white cabinets. One corner houses a sink, a lazy Susan, and a Formica counter. The paper-covered, upholstered exam table sits center stage; a blood-pressure cuff and diagnostic set adorn the wall to its left. The examining rooms are divided into sets of two, with a small consultation room between each pair.

A fourteen-year-old girl awaited, complaining of a sore throat and trouble swallowing. She had enlarged lymph nodes in her neck and a thick white coating on her swollen tonsils. I knew a test would prove mono.

And so began my Tuesday afternoon.

Hours later, at five thirty, I'd finished for the day after seeing people of ages ranging from eight to eighty and treated them for bronchitis, strep throat, diabetes, hypertension, anxiety, depression, abdominal pain, fatigue, lightheadedness, high cholesterol, and sciatica. A typical day. And as good an explanation as any as to why I chose family practice: the variety. How can you get bored with such a diverse mix of people and diagnoses? A cardiologist opens the door to an examining room and knows he's going to see a heart problem. A pulmonologist knows he'll be seeing a lung problem. Me? I'm like a contestant on *Let's Make a Deal*. I have no freaking idea what awaits behind doors number one, two, or three.

After finishing my charts, I signed out to the answering service and headed for Three-C. The hospital has a number of hospitalists, a more permanent form of what were once upon a time known as house doctors. They manage admissions and take care of medical situations that arise overnight, but I like to take one last peek at my inpatients before I call it quits for the day.

Amelia Henderson wasn't looking much better. I had a gram of ceftriaxone running into her twice a day plus a daily piggyback of half a gram of azithromycin. It's a rare community-acquired pneumonia that can stand up to that pair. And she hadn't been here even twelve hours.

Amelia wasn't alone. Her daughter Beth, prim, proper, forty-something, and single, sat at her bedside. She wore the same house dress I'd seen her in this morning when she'd brought her mother to the ER. Gray showed through her tinted hair and she looked haggard. Probably hadn't been home since this morning. A devoted daughter.

I nodded to her. She was one of Sam's regulars but I'd seen her on occasion.

"How's Marge Harris doing?" Beth said.

I'm always surprised how fast news travels in Lebanon, but not surprised that Beth knew. She'd long worn the crown of Lebanon's Queen of Gossip. She had a reputation as an obligate, nit-picking busybody who'd been known to elicit loud groans from the town council whenever she rose to speak at a meeting.

"How do you know about Marge?"

Her thick eyebrows lifted, making her look like Miss Gulch from *The Wizard of Oz*. "We live less than a block away. How could I not notice the racket of the ambulance and police cars there this morning?"

Even if they hadn't made a sound, she would have known. Beth was rumored to spend most of the day at her windows, keeping tabs on the neighborhood.

"She's doing fine," I said.

"What happened to her?"

"I'm sorry, Beth. I can't discuss that."

The patient privilege thing again.

Beth narrowed her eyes. "Did that husband of hers have anything to do with it?"

My antennae went up. "Mr. Harris? What do you mean?"

"I'm sorry, doctor," she said with a haughty lift of her chin. "I can't discuss that."

I almost laughed. She wanted to trade gossip for privileged medical information.

"If you want to know about Marge, why not pop into her room for a visit and ask her? But as for her husband… we're not talking about spousal abuse, are we?"

The thought of Stan or anyone battering Marge made me queasy.

That haughty look again. "Why don't you ask *her*, doctor."

This was getting nowhere. Besides, I hadn't detected a single bruise on Marge during her admitting physical.

I told Amelia that I was going to start getting her up in a chair tomorrow. I'm a firm believer in early mobilization, especially for old folks.

Then I said goodnight to both of them and headed for

Marge's room—only one floor down, so I took the stairs. Beth's insinuations about Stan Harris followed me through the echoing stairwell. He'd wanted a tête-à-tête with me and I'd witnessed the chill between them, but couldn't see how it mattered medically.

# 11

Stan was in Marge's room, sitting by her side; they were both watching TV in silence.

"Can I go home now?" Marge said.

I'd checked the chart. Her BP was still erratic.

"Not yet, Marge. I need to be sure we've suppressed the reaction to the point where your blood pressure remains stable."

"But they've had me up walking about."

"How did you feel?"

"Fine. I—"

"You were dizzy and almost fell when I helped you to the bathroom a moment ago," Stan said.

She shot him a hard look.

"That's what I'm talking about," I told her. "Lying down, your blood pressure's fine. But in the upright position, it will have a tendency to drop."

"But I hate being here, and I hate the food. I want my own bed."

"Tomorrow," I told her. "Just hang on till tomorrow."

"I found the power bar she was eating," Stan told me. "Looks like she only had a couple of bites before the reaction. Tomorrow I'm going to find a lab that can check it for peanut residue. If they come up with anything... well..."

He let it hang, but clearly he was hoping they would.

He looked at his watch. "Speaking of which, I'm going to go home and start searching the Internet for the right lab. Maybe I'll cut the bar in two and give it to a couple of labs. If they both find peanut residue, there'll be no doubt."

He gave Marge a peck on the cheek and hurried out, barely glancing at me as we passed. She didn't look sorry to see him go

"A man with a mission," I said.

Marge made a sour face. "But not with the Internet, I'll bet."

I waited for her to say more but her eyes drifted back to the TV. I couldn't see the screen from where I was, but the laugh track told me it was a sitcom.

"Anything wrong?" I said.

She shook her head and kept her eyes on the screen. "I'm trapped in a hospital with a needle in my arm and my doctor won't let me go home." Now she looked at me, her eyes imploring. "Norrie... for old time's sake... couldn't you please—?"

"Tomorrow, Marge. I promise"

I beelined for the hall. I didn't want to play the bad guy anymore, especially with Marge. I was pretty sure I could send her home in the morning, but you don't have to be in practice very long to learn that there are no guarantees in medicine.

I'd just stepped out of the door when I heard a sob behind me. I hesitated on the threshold. I hated to leave her like this, but how deep could I pry without seeming nosy?

Marge was more than a patient, but I *was* her physician—her *family* physician—and if some family problem was causing depression, I needed to act. She'd helped me through some rough times as a teen; I wanted to return the favor if I could... if she'd let me.

But I couldn't address the problem if I didn't give her a chance to tell me about it.

I stepped back inside. She saw me and quickly wiped her eyes.

"Marge, are you crying because I'm not sending you home, or is there something else?"

"It's nothing," she said in a quavering voice. "I'm fine."

I waited a long time before replying. Then I stepped closer to the bed.

"Is that really true? If it's something I can help with, tell me. If it's something you find embarrassing, then give me a thumbnail sketch. I'll close the door and it will never leave this room."

She sighed and looked up at me with red-rimmed eyes. "It's

a lot of things, Norrie. None of which you can help me with, I'm afraid."

The thought of her being so unhappy twisted something inside me.

"Don't be so sure. I can—"

She waved her hands. "All I need it to get back to my house and my routine. I'm much better when I'm keeping busy."

Workaholism is the way a lot of depressed or anxious people cope: Keep yourself too busy to notice how awful you feel.

"Why don't I just set you up with a therapist, someone you can talk to?"

"No-no!" she said quickly with an alarmed expression. "I don't need a shrink. I just need to get home."

"Soon, Marge." I couldn't very well grab her by the shoulders and shake her until she told me what was up. "But if you ever decide you could use a little tea and sympathy, you know my number."

Her smile looked forced. "Thank you, Norrie. But I'm fine, really. I'm handling it."

Like hell, I thought as I said goodnight and left her.

At least this time no sob followed me.

# 12

Next stop was my mother's place. She still lives in the old family home in the neighboring town of Carmel.

I took the back roads—Route 70 is quicker but my way is shorter—and arrived in front of my old homestead, a tidy little three-bedroom ranch, built in the 1950s but still in good shape. Long ago my father had lined the half-acre lot with about a million arbor vitae. Okay, maybe not a million, but it must have been a Herculean task considering the linear footage he had to cover. The resulting twelve-foot-high wall of green gives the property a ton of privacy.

I grabbed the pills I'd brought for my uncle, crossed the awakening lawn, and bounded up onto the little front porch. I've never had to knock, so I pushed through the door and stepped into the living room.

"Hello!" I called. "Just me!"

A skinny, white-haired fellow was sitting on the couch, diddling with his phone. Uncle Timmy is my mother's first cousin on her father's side; he's ten years older and lives a block and a half away. Mum was at a loss in so many ways after Dad died—he used to take care of everything. I'm not even sure she knew how to write a check. Timmy, a widower for years, stepped in and acted as handyman and financial advisor. Sean and I have thanked him countless times and his reply is always the same: I've got nothing better to do with my time.

I stopped on my way through. The couch sat near the old upright piano where Marge used to give me lessons.

"Hey, Tim."

"Norrie! Good to see you. You just missed dinner."

They often ate dinner together. Better than each eating alone.

"I had a late lunch," I said—a white lie. "How was the meatloaf?"

"Delicious, as always."

See? I didn't have to ask what they'd eaten. I knew today was Tuesday, and that was enough. Growing up, Sean and I never needed to ask what Mum was making for dinner, all we needed to know was the day of the week. Here's how it went:

Monday was pork chops with applesauce, red cabbage, and mashed potatoes.

Tuesday was meatloaf with baked potatoes and peas.

Wild Wednesday—wild in the sense that we could expect one of three possibilities. Most often it was minute steaks—does anyone still cook minute steaks?—with string beans and mashed potatoes, but sometimes we'd have beef stew or a clove-studded baked Polish canned ham, which meant ham sandwiches for lunch the next day or two.

Thursday was always hot dogs—boiled Thumann's hot dogs only, because no other brand will do. And Tater Tots, of course. I have such fond memories of Tater Tots.

And because Vatican II never happened for Mum, Friday was either sandwiches—invariably tuna salad or egg salad—or creamed tuna and peas over toast. I shudder now at the memory.

Dessert was always, *always* bananas with milk and sugar.

Except on weekends...

Weekends were a different story: That was when Dad would take over the kitchen; dinner on Saturday night would be like dining out in Little Italy. And Sunday was always spaghetti and meatballs with Sunday gravy.

"Say, Norrie," Timmy said, "do you have any extra money?"

"I wish." I knew he wasn't looking for a loan.

"Too bad," he said, tapping his phone. "Cobdica Industries is ready for a big jump. New product coming from their pharma division. You should be getting in now. Next week might be too late."

"That sounds like just a rumor."

"You know the rule: Buy on rumor, sell on news."

Timmy watches Fox Business News and CNBC like most people his age watch the Weather Channel. I'm sure he has a stock-quote crawl running along the bottom of his dreams. He's a retired civil engineer who's become quite the financial analyst, amazingly adept at picking winners. He's managed my mother's finances, parlaying the payout from my father's life insurance into a tidy piece of change.

Unfortunately I wasn't going to have any investment income next week either.

I handed Tim a Ziplok bag containing blister-pack samples of his blood-pressure pills.

"The sales rep dropped these off today."

He grinned as he took them. "Ah, you're a good niece, Norrie."

His pills were the first reason I was stopping over. The second was a question I wanted to ask. Mum might have the answer.

As I turned to go, I noticed the living room's landscape painting—one of those generic bucolic long shots of trees and bushes and sky and a waterfall—was tilted. I straightened it but it still looked off. Oh, well. Not my problem.

The living room segues into the dining room. I passed through there and through the arched doorway on the right wall that leads to the kitchen. That was where my mother would be.

Mum has aged since my father died. She used to be more active, now she mostly sits. I know she misses him. At least she's got Timmy to keep her company, but I know she's lonely without Dad. And I know I can't live here. I love her dearly but she's too set in her ways.

"There she is!" she said and gave me a big hug.

The former Kate Fogarty has a round, red-cheeked Irish face and dyes her own hair to hide the gray. She can well afford a beauty parlor these days, but has always been a DIY type. Which goes back to being set in her ways.

She wanted to fill me a plate for dinner. She makes a great meatloaf but the bread and potatoes that always go with it were not on my diet.

I begged off, saying I wasn't hungry.

"I was about to open a stout," Timmy said as he wandered in. "Want one?"

Stout didn't exactly fit with my diet. And the name alone would be enough to have it declared anathema.

"Wish I could but I'm on call." I decided then to hit them with the question that had been nagging me. "And speaking of on call"—a poor segue but the best I could come up with—"you'll never guess who I ran into in the ER today. Remember Travis Lawton?"

"Of course we do, dearie," Mum said. "He's a deputy sheriff. He used to be your boyfriend, didn't he?"

"Boyfriend." I felt myself redden—it doesn't take much. "Not even close. One school dance. Not exactly going steady."

She shrugged.

I tried to sound casual. "What's he been up to since I left—besides joining the sheriff's department?"

"Oh, he married that one from high school... what's her name...?"

"Diana Robinson?"

"Yes! That's her." She lowered her voice. "Had to, if y'know what I mean." She returned to normal volume. "I hear they had a little girl."

I hid my disappointment. "I see."

Oh, well.

"They split up about four-five years ago, I think." She lowered her voice again. "Divorce, you know." Mum doesn't approve of divorce.

I felt my mood brighten and didn't like myself for it.

"Really? Any idea why?"

"Well, I haven't the foggiest, but I do know the wife got awfully fat while she was carrying, and kept getting fatter and fatter afterwards."

Timmy nodded. "Looked like a prize heifer, she did."

"Diana Robinson... fat?"

"Very," Mum sad. "Haven't seen her in years, though. She might have slimmed down by now."

Timmy, always helpful, added, "Or she might be the size of a house."

I fought off the grin that a burst of glee pushed toward my lips.

Never said I was perfect.

"Oh, my. That's too bad."

And then a thought struck. My uncle's roaming territory was usually limited to his place and my mother's and the short walk between. I looked at Timmy.

"Where did you see her?"

"At the Safeway."

That figured. The only exceptions were to accompany Mum when she went food shopping. It wasn't so much to help her with the groceries as to check the labels of everything in the basket before it came into the house—to prevent her from being poisoned.

Uncle Timmy sees conspiracies everywhere, and one of the most insidious has to do with food additives. I once asked him to explain it to me and regretted it: I got a migraine trying to follow his lines of reasoning.

Suffice it to say that "they" are trying to poison us.

# 13

I headed home to my second-floor, two-bedroom, one-bath apartment in a condo cluster just north of the interstate. The cluster calls itself Holly Ridge, but if any holly ever grew there, it's long gone. And there's no ridge either. The buildings sit on land as flat as a mannequin's cardiogram. I suspect the property was a cornfield before the developers dug it up. If they'd been honest they'd have called it "Corny Meadows," but that lacks the marketing magic to lure the lemmings from Baltimore.

Holly Ridge consists of four three-story buildings arranged in an arc, with parking along the outer rim and a lawn in the convexity.

I bought my place six months after I started with LFPA and it's plenty for me. I use the second bedroom as a little office where I keep my computer, my medical journals, my old Casio portable keyboard—I still put Marge's lessons to use now and again. I don't want the hassle of a house. I don't know if I ever will.

The furniture is a hodgepodge of pieces from Mum's and Uncle Timmy's overstocks, some mahogany, some walnut, some oak. I've managed to arrange it all into a coherent configuration that's comfortable and functional. I've hung half a dozen art prints on the walls, everything from van Gogh to Mondrian. My taste in art is almost as eclectic as my taste in food.

I grabbed a can of Diet Pepsi from the fridge and a can of tuna from the pantry. As I was saladizing the tuna with mayo and pepper—no carbs there—I spotted the blinking red message light on my answering machine. I pressed *PLAY* and cringed when I heard the voice.

"*Hi, Norrie. It's Ted. I really need to speak to you. We—*"

I hit *STOP*. Three years since I broke it off with Ted Houchens and still he called. Nowhere near as frequently as he used to, but every so often I guess he gave in to the urge to find out how someone could manage to resist his charms. Could I be the only one in his life who wound up being the dropper instead of the droppee?

Ted was this fortyish hotshot orthopedist on the staff of Maryland U Hospital where I did my residency. During my first year he consulted on a number of patients I was following. I guess you could say he took a shine to me. The relationship went through the usual stages. We segued from coffee in the doctors' lounge to lunches in the caf, which led to dinners out, which led to a weekend away at a CME course in Tampa.

I'm not proud of the fact that I knew he was married and didn't care.

You've got to understand that although I wasn't a virgin, I wasn't exactly on anybody's speed dialer. So I was a sitting duck for loving attention from this suave, good-looking, accomplished surgeon. It blindsided me—in the argot of my teenage patients—like totally. This was the first time in my life I'd felt *attractive*. I was wanted and needed, a heady brew that kept my conscience in suspended animation for about a year and a half.

Then I met Mrs. Houchens.

It happened at a reception to celebrate the opening of a new surgical suite at the hospital. While I was dipping some punch from the big crystal bowl, this attractive brunette in a black Donna Karen came up and stood beside me. I poured her a glass and we got to talking. Somewhere along the way she introduced herself as Anna Houchens.

I don't remember much more about the reception. All the Catholic guilt I'd locked up burst free and settled around me like a fog. Mrs. Houchens was no longer a vague, shadowy figure in a faraway place. She was right here and she had a first name and a face and seemed like a nice person.

And I was sleeping with her husband.

All the good feelings I'd had about the affair—about *me*—shattered. I saw it for the tawdry thing it really was and I felt dirty. Some folks might see that as an overreaction. Maybe it is, but that was how I felt.

I broke it off the next day. He hounded me for a while—after all, I was the one that got away—but then found someone else. After I finished the residency and moved out to Lebanon, he tracked me down and started calling. I've yet to call back.

If you want to know what heads my list of Things I Wish I'd Never Done, it's having an affair with Anna Houchens's husband.

My least proud moment. But I'd learned from it, and I'd put it behind me. It doesn't always stay there, though. Every time Ted calls it sneaks up and bites me on the butt.

The memory made me want to take a shower, so I did.

Afterward I checked myself in the mirror as I always do. I know I'm the trimmest I've been in fifteen years, but those love handles, those thighs...

Got to keep after them.

I headed for the kitchen.

The answering service called my cell phone as I was chopping up some celery. A medication question from a patient Sam had seen today. They put the caller through. It took less than a minute to resolve.

I added the celery plus mayo and a dash of Old Bay to the tuna, whipped it up, and had myself a tuna salad sandwich on imaginary bread. I imagined a nice thick Kaiser roll.

After that I went to my study and checked my email—pardon: my spam. For some reason the Internet equivalent of telemarketers has me profiled as a small-penised, impotent male in need of life insurance, a new mortgage, and Viagra.

After deleting these, I ventured out onto the wonderful world of search engines. I remembered reading something somewhere in a journal about a treatment for peanut allergy. I did a little surfing and discovered a program at Johns Hopkins where they were treating people like Marge with an anti-IgE antibody. It didn't cure them of their allergy, but it did raise the reaction threshold—people who'd started out reacting to half a peanut got to the point where they could tolerate nine.

That sounded like just the thing for Marge.

After bookmarking the site, I quit the computer and settled myself on the living-room couch. A little surfing through the high-number channels yielded *Better off Dead*—yes, I know it was made before I was born, but John Cusack was cute back then and that paper boy always makes me laugh. Despite Bert Castanon's recurrent car-hawking appearances in the breaks— he and his family are patients at the practice—I stuck with that. I love screwball comedies, old and new.

I warned myself that if I don't pace myself, I could easily burn out from the mad tempo of this high-flying lifestyle.

# WEDNESDAY

# 1

I awoke to a pounding noise that seemed to come from everywhere in the bedroom. I sat up, blinked, and looked at the clock's LED display: 5:32. Then I focused on the sound. When I realized it was coming from behind me, I knew what it was. And who.

Janie Ryan.

Her bedroom shares a wall with mine. The sound was Janie's headboard. Either she and her boyfriend du jour were having at it like sex was going to be outlawed tomorrow, or she'd exchanged her bed for a pile driver. The wall was thick enough to muffle whatever cries of "Yes!" or "Oh-God!" might be echoing on its far side, but not the slamming headboard.

I wondered what position they were using, and that started a yearning tingle in my pelvis. My body said it wouldn't mind a little of that—but my head said not with the strutting peacocks Janie favored.

Janie's other name is Poochie Sutton. She told me she derived it from her first pet and the street she grew up on. So Janie Ryan, who grew up on Sutton Avenue with a mutt named Poochie, becomes Poochie Sutton when she steps on stage at the various Baltimore strip clubs she works.

We don't bump into each other that often because she tends to be asleep when I'm up and I'm asleep when she's up, but we've hung out a little on the landing and gotten to know each other. I like her. She's very up front about how she earns her living and how much she earns. No surprise: She makes lots more than I do, much of it tax free.

I stretched and knew I was awake for the day. Might as well get up and get going.

A little after six I was out and into my jog. To my right the sun was just clearing the horizon, the full moon heading for bed to my left. I loped through still morning air laden with touches of low-lying fog. I wore my dark-blue sweatsuit today; the other is gray. Both oversized.

You didn't really think I'd squeeze these thighs into running tights or bicycle pants, did you?

I try to run thirty-forty minutes at least five days a week. I'm constantly preaching the benefits of regular exercise to my patients, so I figure I should practice it to set a good example. I keep looking for the endorphin high they say running gives you. Maybe I don't run hard enough or long enough, but the only physical sensations I experience are air hunger and sore muscles. The only pleasure I feel is when I'm able to stop and know I won't have to do this again for another twenty-four hours.

When I get sick of listening to music or podcasts on my iPod, my morning run becomes a time for introspection. Like: Who am I? Where am I going? What do I want out of life?

I know where I am, and I like it. I just wish I knew if I was going to be able to stay here.

As for the rest, I don't know.

I'd certainly like a man—an *unmarried* one—in my life. Something serious and permanent. I don't want to fall into a pattern of one "serious" relationship after another—a parade of Joe McIvers. Maybe that's okay when you're young like Janie Ryan, but I'm a grown-up now, and serial monogamy doesn't appeal to me.

Besides, I'm not exactly invisible in Lebanon. Anything but. And I'm increasingly conscious of the fact that I'm becoming a role model for a lot of young girls around here. That's an honor, but it's also a burden, one I never looked to shoulder.

I could say screw it, it's my life and how I live it is nobody's business but mine.

In principle I don't disagree, and I think that's fine if you're a voice coming through a speaker, or an image jittering in a music video, or playing a part on the screen. Or even a Janie Ryan.

But I'm their family doctor. I can't ignore that. What I do away from the office *does* matter, because it affects how I'm perceived when I'm in it. I don't need my younger female patients discussing who Doctor Norrie is shacking up with at the moment. These girls ask me questions they don't feel they can ask their parents. Too many of those parents provide nothing in the way of guidance, no moral compass, nothing to look up to.

So they look to me. For their sake I need to stake out the high ground and stay there.

Role model... never asked for it, never even saw it coming. But I'm stuck with it, so I try to live up to it.

As my father once told me on a completely different subject: You know the right thing. Now go do it.

I'm giving it my best shot, Dad.

# 2

Ijogged into the business district that straddles the highway, past the "Welcome to Lebanon" sign emblazoned with the logos of all the local lodges—Kiwanis, Moose, VFW, Masons, and so on.

Behind that loom the two towers—water, not Tolkien. The old one is a metallic four-legged oil-can, used mostly as a cell tower now; the new is a huge white drumstick proclaiming "Lebanon" to the world in big black letters.

Directly below and between them, a dilapidated red-sided barn with a roofless silo reminds you of the area's not-so-distant agricultural past.

The Shell, Exxon, Mobil, and Sunoco stations are clustered south of the interstate. And just north of it, two shopping centers face off across 206.

Carbon monoxide wafted from the interstate as I cut under the overpass and through the deserted Ames parking lot to the low-rent residential district beyond.

Lebanon is a Baltimore bedroom community; only a dozen miles west of the beltway, but light years away in culture and sophistication.

If you don't drive a pickup here—even most of the rich hill-siders own one—you drive a Chevy suburban. On the whole these folks are good, solid, salt-of-the-earth types, but the town still has its share of the drug, alcohol, and domestic-violence problems plaguing every community.

Your socioeconomic status in Lebanon is relative to latitude and altitude. The further up you live in the hills north of the freeway, the higher your income. The folks with more modest paychecks live in the flat country on the south. Beyond that it's all farmland. Hill and dale.

Our practice treats more south-side people—sometimes called "dale-dwellers"—than "hillsiders." I guess that's because a lot of the well-to-do feel they're too good for a primary care doc. If they have a sinus problem they go to an ENT specialist; for an upset stomach, it's a gastroenterologist. And God forbid they'd see a *local* specialist. Only someone in Baltimore—which we natives pronounce "Bal'more"—will do.

But when they wind up in the CCCH emergency room with chest pains or a broken bone, guess who's there for them?

I passed some early birds heading for the highway and their jobs in Baltimore. A few of them recognized me and waved. A homey, friendly place, Lebanon.

I really do want to stay here.

# 3

April may be the cruelest month, but May can be schizo-phrenic. I decided to risk wearing my brown cotton mid-calf skimmer, but took along the matching sweater just in case.

A word about my clothes. If it were up to me, I'd go to the office in a sweater and jeans. But I have to look professional. I'm not sure what that means, but I know it's not popping into an examining room dressed like you're ready to mow the lawn. So I dress a little older than my thirty-two years. With my young, mid-twenties face, I have to. More than one sep-tuagenarian has asked me if I'm old enough to have a medical degree.

On my morning rounds at the hospital, I learned Amelia wasn't responding as quickly as I'd anticipated. I'd left orders to get her out of bed and so I found her sitting in a chair, wrapped chin to toes in a blanket. Her nurse reported that she'd com-plained of shortness of breath despite the oxygen, so I ordered another chest X-ray.

"When's Harry coming?" she said, looking at me with watery blue eyes.

"Is Harry your son?"

"Oh dear no. He's my husband."

I knew Amelia's husband had been dead for about ten years. Beth had quit her job in Baltimore then and moved back to care for her mother.

"I'll check on that," I told her.

This wasn't uncommon with elderly inpatients. Plop them in an unfamiliar environment and they become confused. I've learned not to argue with them. When they get back home they return to normal.

When I reached Marge's room I found her fully dressed and pacing the floor. Her husband Stan sat on the bed, watching the morning news on the TV.

Her IV had come out during the night—with a little help maybe? The floor had called me about it and I'd told them to leave it out for the time being. I'd checked her chart on the way down the hall. Her blood-pressure readings were stable and all her vitals looked good.

Marge charged toward me as I crossed the threshold. "Can I go now?"

I couldn't see any reason to keep her.

"As soon as I give you a couple of prescriptions and some instructions, we'll sign you out."

She grabbed my hand. "Oh, thank you, Norrie, thank you!"

Stan rose from the bed and approached. "Do you think that's such a good idea, doctor? Less that twenty-four hours ago she was almost dead, and now you're sending her home? Pardon me if I'm out of line, but that seems rather reckless."

"Concern for a loved one is never out of line," I said, slipping into silver-tongue mode, "but clinically she's fine, chart-wise she's back to normal, and she's up and about and wants to go. I can't find a medically sound reason to keep Marge an extra minute."

"But I've got to go to New York—I've got a round of meetings with underwriters I can't miss—and Marge'll be home alone all day and all night. I won't be back till tomorrow. If something happens—"

Marge said, "I'm going home, Stan, whether you like it or not." Her tone was just a hair shy of a snarl.

He reddened and looked away.

I scribbled a note about the dose of Benadryl I wanted Marge to take, then gave her prescriptions for a new EpiPen, plus cimetidine and prednisone; she'd get a heavy dose of the latter for the first three days. Barring any complications, I'd taper it off over the next week or so.

"Take these as directed and don't miss any doses. They'll

keep any residual effects at bay. Take it easy and eat a bland diet until you see me in the office Friday. I'll be in all afternoon. When we've got you straightened out, I want to see about enrolling you in a program at Hopkins that will reduce your peanut sensitivity."

"That would be wonderful. Anything to keep this from happening again."

I adopted a stern tone—so strange to be giving Marge orders—and told her, "And when I say 'take it easy,' I mean hanging around the house and maybe a little light shopping if you get cabin fever, but nothing more. Are we clear on that?"

"Yes, doctor," she said with a wry smile as she held up the scripts. "Take these, take it easy, and see you on Friday. Got it. Can I go now?"

"I still don't like it," Stan muttered.

I should have listened to him. Marge had less than twenty-four hours left to live.

# 4

I was ahead of schedule this morning, so I poured myself a cup of coffee in the doctors' lounge and sipped it as I sifted through the lab and X-ray reports in the group's mailbox. After that I headed for the office at a leisurely pace, turning up the volume when Gnarls Barkley's "Crazy" came on.

You see, Sam takes off Mondays and Wednesdays and so on those days I spend the entire workday with Ken Lerner. Not that we see that much of each other; once I get rolling, going from patient to patient, I enter a sort of Zen state where there's no outside world beyond the examining rooms, and my focus constricts to the sick or hurt people within them.

As soon as I arrived, I ducked into Ken's consultation room and caught him between patients. The only thing we ever talk about is the practice, because that's about all we have in common. Since he'd be on call tonight, I updated him on the inpatients under our care.

He made a few notes, then said, "Looks like you and Sam had a good day yesterday. A few hefty AR payments came in too."

I sensed the rubbing together of mental hands. He always knows to the last penny what we take in every day.

I don't know much about Ken except that he's in his forties, divorced and remarried to Barbie, and been with the practice a dozen years. He seems very impressed with being a doctor. It defines him. That's all fine and good. Whatever floats your boat.

But for me, a little Ken goes a long way.

Not that he exhibits open hostility. Far from it. He's never less than polite, but he's never more than cool. I don't think he dislikes me. He might even *want* to like me, but he can't because he thinks I'm costing him money. Maybe when I started here my presence lowered his paycheck for a while, but I'm holding my own now. He simply can't seem to get past his temporary pay cut.

I suspect he and Allie might be living a bit above their means. He's into status clothes, drives a Lexus LS, belongs to the country club—all the upper-class trappings. He's on the status treadmill and he's running as fast as he can. Plus he's got alimony and child support payments from his first marriage.

That would explain his thing about money.

Sometimes I think the only reason he acquiesced to hiring me was because I'm not Jewish—that way they wouldn't have to close the office on Yom Kippur and Rosh Hashanah.

I can't say Ken isn't a hard worker. He's a trouper. And I can't say he's not a good doctor, because he's a very good one—an excellent diagnostician who keeps up to date on the latest therapies.

But personality-wise, he's a drip. At least as far as I'm concerned. Maybe he uses up all his charm on his patients and there's none left for me. Or for the staff here. He always seems ticked about something. And he's *so* competitive, always counting everyone's visits to make sure he sees the most patients per week.

Speaking of patients, he has this proprietary attitude toward the people who see him regularly, as if they belong to him. You'd think they'd been stamped with a *Ken Lerner, MD* bar code. Which may explain why he grumbles whenever one of them decides to see me instead of him. Does he think I'm *stealing* them?

I'm making him sound like an ogre. Yes, he has some trollish features, like a squat body, thick lips, beady eyes—okay, not beady eyes; I don't even know what that means—but he's not an ogre.

He's just… Ken.

Harriet stuck her head into the room. "Your next patient's ready," she told Ken. "Lenore Jefferson."

His face fell. "She's back? But… she was here just last week."

Harriet gave a casual shrug, but I could tell she was loving this. "Must be your appreciation of fine art."

We all attract our share of weirdoes. One of Ken's was Lenore Jefferson. I've seen her on occasion. She isn't an official Patient From Hell, but she's a strange one and dealing with her can be trying. She's harmless, a sweet old thing with nary a mean bone in her bony old body, but she's weird.

Harriet grinned. "New art work! I can't wait!"

Lenore Jefferson is a former executive secretary who lives in the local retirement village. Soon after moving in she enrolled in an art class and discovered she had a real knack for watercolors. She exhibits her work in some of the local restaurants. For the public she does landscapes and still life. But in private she does special paintings, ones she shows only to her doctors.

Lenore, you see, has a bowel fixation. On each visit she presents with a dozen or so life-size watercolors of her bowel movements, ones that "didn't seem quite like the others." Each, she swears, is the exact same size and tint of the original stools.

I've occasionally wondered about the technique she uses to get such, um, lifelike paintings, but never had the nerve to ask.

Every encounter consists of close examination of the details of each painting as she questions about caliber, color, and consistency. Her visits last the usual fifteen or so minutes, but they can be some of the longest minutes of a doctor's life. You step out of the examining room expecting to look ten years older.

Try to look on the bright side, I wanted to tell Ken… as an alternative she could save the original subjects of her art and display them in plastic bags. But instead I said, "Gotta run."

I waved and followed Harriet out into the hall. She half turned and spoke out of the corner of her mouth.

"Some days I just love my job."

So do I.

# 5

We had a lunch scheduled with Cobdica Pharma. The rep, Donna Wegener, wanted to introduce us to Tezinex, the company's new weight-loss med. Donna was, like so many of the pharmaceutical reps these days, a stunner. A shapely blonde with big brown eyes and a dazzling smile. Not a dumb blonde by any stretch. First off, she's not really blonde, and secondly, she is easily the smartest person in any room, no matter who's there—Ken and me included—though she's learned to hide it. I've liked her since her first visit to the office, but then I've always liked smart people.

A simple lunch was delivered from the local Chick-fil-A—chicken strips, chicken nuggets, waffle French fries, sweetened and unsweetened iced tea. We locked the front door and hung a note to say we'd reopen at two o'clock. Ken, Giselle, Harriet, Tammy Franklin—one of the part-time clerks—and I dug in while Donna gave us the low-down on Tezinex. The regimen was simple: one pill every morning, watch a two-minute online motivational video, and follow its dietary recommendations for that day. The clinical studies looked good with no signs of habituation or insomnia; no significant side effects except substantial weight loss when compared to the control subjects.

"Sounds promising," I said, "but that name is awful. How am I going to remember Tezinex?"

She laughed. "We take no responsibility. The FDA is naming prescription pharmaceuticals now. If it were up to me I'd call it 'LardAway' or 'ShrinkyWaist.'"

She invited Ken and me to a dinner in Baltimore Monday

night where the company planned to introduce "revenue incentives" to participating practices. Ken's attention suddenly focused but Donna played coy, telling us that all she could say was that the incentives were guaranteed to be legal and ethical. The dinner was going to be at Morton's by the Inner Harbor.

I begged off—a big steak dinner didn't fit with my diet.

Ken went upstairs to check on what today's mail had contributed to the accounts receivable, while the others went about their business. I stayed with Donna for a while. Tezinex was sounding interesting and I thought I might want to try it myself sometime, but decided to hold off pulling the trigger.

# 6

When I came back upstairs and was congratulating myself on maybe getting a head start on the afternoon schedule, I found Ken waiting for me in the hall. He waved a thick legal-size envelope and pointed to my consultation room. His expression was grim.

"I think you'd better open this in there."

When we were both inside he closed the door and handed it to me.

"What's going on?" I said.

"Certified mail from an attorney's office. Never a good thing."

I ripped it open and unfolded the papers within. Words from the top sheet leaped at me...

*Edward Stark, Esq.... Superior Court... Carson County... Docket Number... Civil Action...* Summons...

Malpractice?

Me?

I felt my blood draining toward my feet. I dropped into the chair behind the desk...

"I'm being sued."

"I knew it!" Ken snatched the papers from my cold fingers and scanned them. "Oh, hell. It's Stark the Shark."

"Who?"

"An ambulance-chasing leech from Carmel."

"Eddie Stark?"

His head snapped up. "You know him?"

"*Knew* him. High school."

My stomach constricted to a tight knot. Eddie Stark... he'd

been a weasel and a slimeball as a teenager. What was it they said about leopards and spots?

Ken looked down at the summons again. "Plaintiffs are listed as 'Theodore E. and Mary C. Phelan.' Know them?"

My brain was stalled in neutral. *Phelan... Phelan...* and then it clicked.

"Ted Phelan! *He's* suing me?"

"And his wife."

"I've never *seen* his wife! At least not that I remember."

Ken flipped through the pages. His mouth twisted and he shook his head.

"Check out the second count. Never fails."

I scanned some legalese, then reached a part that read: *As a direct and proximate result of the negligence of the defendants, the plaintiff, Mary C. Phelan, has been deprived of any and all services which would have been performed by her husband and has been deprived of his care, comfort, companionship, society and consortium...*

"What?"

"It's standard practice for the spouse to join these suits—motor vehicle, product liability, whatever—it's another hand to stick out."

Something in what I'd just read bounced back at me: *defendants...* that was plural.

I returned to the front page and saw a list of names: Dr. Leonard Saxton, Dr. Mark Collins, and my own, plus *John and Jane Does #1-50, presently representing unknown healthcare providers, including but not limited to, doctors, nurses, technicians, radiologists, etc.*

I looked up at Ken. "Is this a joke?"

He shook his head. "Stark's casting a wide net. That John-and-Jane-Doe thing lets him add defendants later."

Lenny Saxton was a pulmonologist, Mark Collins was an internist over in Carmel. What was this all about?

I intercommed downstairs to the chart room and asked for the Theodore Phelan file. While waiting I scanned over the first count. It repeated the defendants' names, then went on to say that as a result of our *professional negligence, the plaintiff was caused to suffer severe and permanent injuries, resulting in pain and suffering, limited activities, medical expenses, loss of wages and loss of ability to work* and on and on.

I felt my cheeks burning. Negligent? Me?

It added that *the conduct of the defendants, jointly and/or severally, was grossly negligent, wanton, reckless, and intentional.*

The words were knives through my heart.

Wanton… reckless… intentional… he was talking about me.

"But it doesn't say what I did wrong!"

"It doesn't have to."

Tammy popped in with the chart and I tore through it.

"Ted Phelan was here just last week! This thing has to have been in the works for months, but he never gave the slightest hint anything was wrong. Why would he keep coming to a doctor he thinks is negligent?"

Ken shrugged. "I gave up trying to figure out this suit-happy world a long time ago."

I thumbed back through the chart to refresh my memory. I remembered treating him for a stubborn bronchitis. I found an X-ray report and it all came back to me. The films had been grossly abnormal… arteriovascular malformations suspected… confirmed by CT of the chest… referred to a specialist…

"The only thing Phelan has wrong with him are pulmonary A-V malformations, but I'm not taking care of him for that. Lenny Saxton is."

"Nothing else wrong with him?"

I scanned again. "He sees me every three months for mild hypertension, but that's controlled."

"Then it has to be the AVMs. And my guess is that Lenny is the real target."

"Then why me?"

"Stark's covering all his bases, and hoping that when he deposes you he can get you to say something damaging about Lenny."

"He doesn't have to sue me to question me."

"It's common practice. Costs Stark nothing to add your name to the defendant list, so why not?"

I looked at him. "Sounds like you've been through this before."

Ken rolled his eyes. "Show me a doctor in practice for any length of time who hasn't. You've just joined the club, Norrie."

"But why? I identified the AVMs. I recognized them as beyond the scope of my expertise, and I immediately referred him to a board-certified specialist in that field. I did everything *right*! Why am I being sued?"

Ken fixed me with a watery stare. "Welcome to the wonderful world of American liability law, doctor."

I leaned back in the chair. I felt sick. Someone was accusing me of being a negligent doctor. Worse: wanton, reckless, and *intentionally* negligent. But I wasn't, damn it. Anything but. I care about my patients, worry about them, wake up in the middle of the night thinking about the really sick ones.

I glanced at the chart and saw Theodore E. Phelan's phone number on the tab. I picked up the receiver.

"I'm going to call him and find out just—"

Ken jammed a finger down on the plunger. "No. Never call the plaintiff. And never, *never* call his attorney. The only time you speak is in a deposition or in court—*never* without your own attorney present."

"Why not?"

"Because you may say the wrong thing. You may say the right thing that's interpreted the wrong way. Remember the warning about 'Anything you say can and will be held against you in a court of law'? Don't forget it."

"But I didn't do anything *wrong!*"

His smile was thin and sour. "Since when does that have anything to do with a lawsuit?" He shook his head. "You must have done *something* to tick him off."

"That's why I want to talk to him. I want to know why he's still a patient here if he's suing me."

"I'm telling you that's a no-no. From now on the only one who speaks for you is your lawyer."

"But I don't have one."

"The malpractice carrier will get you one. *That's* the call you need to make. And today."

I sat in silence with a chaotic mix of emotions roiling through me. I felt sad, angry, betrayed, afraid, embarrassed, and hurt.

Yeah, hurt. Big-time hurt. I thought I'd had a pretty good rapport with Ted Phelan. Now I had his knife in my back.

"You know what this means, don't you?" Ken said. "Your malpractice premium will be going up." He lowered his voice to a mutter. "Shit."

"But I wasn't negligent!"

"Doesn't matter. A suit is a suit. It costs an insurer to defend the innocent as well as the guilty."

I could see him calculating the increased overhead from my escalating premium and the impact on his paycheck. Another black mark against me when partnership time came around.

Thanks for the support, Ken, I thought.

Where was Sam when I needed him?

# 7

I was pretty damn certain I hadn't been negligent as far as Ted Phelan was concerned, but as for the rest of the patients I saw that day, who could say? Throughout my afternoon hours I felt distracted and impatient, barely half there. The rest of me kept asking why-why-why?

Considering how much time and attention I usually put into each visit, some of my regulars probably felt I was giving them the bum's rush. And in the back of my mind I couldn't help wondering with each patient I encountered, *Will you sue me too?*

I pointed the last patient toward the front of the office, then called our malpractice carrier. I was a little annoyed that the woman I spoke to was so matter of fact about this, as if it was an everyday occurrence. And then I realized: To her it was just that—many times a day, no doubt.

But to me it was devastating.

She wanted a copy of the summons and a copy of the chart which I promised to send to her. Then Giselle buzzed me on the intercom.

*"There's a policeman here to see you. Says it's official business."*

My heart rate shot up a good twenty beats per minute. Now what?

"Send him back."

I sat behind the desk in the consultation room, gnawing at a cuticle as I waited. It had been a rotten day, one I'd assumed could not get any worse. I prayed I wouldn't be proven wrong.

When Travis Lawton stuck his head through the door and grinned, I could have cried.

Then when he said, "Hey, Macaroni," I could have killed. "Lose the 'Macaroni,' okay, Trav? Hit the DELETE key in your brain. Macaroni is gone and she's not coming back."

That probably came out harsher than I'd intended, because I saw him blink, saw his smile drop ten degrees of warmth.

"Sorry," he said.

I sighed. "No, I'm sorry. It's been a long, long day."

"Something wrong?"

Did he know about the malpractice suit? Possibly. I had to figure he was in and out of the courthouse every day, and with the way people talk around here, he could have known before I did.

Even so, no way was I going to talk about it.

Me... negligent... wanton... reckless... so humiliating.

I shook my head. "No. I'm okay." I turned the subject toward him. "So, what brings you to Lebanon Family Practice Associates?"

He pointed to the bandage on his forehead. "You said to come by for a look-see."

What was going on here? Had he been passing by and given in to an impulse, or had he decided to use the injury as a chance to see me again?

Interesting... and flattering either way I looked at it.

"I thought you had to see Doctor Hansford."

"I'm supposed to, but I wanted to check out your bedside manner. If it's a problem—"

The last thing I wanted to do was chase him away.

"Absolutely no problem at all."

"I probably should have called for an appointment but—"

I popped from my chair and came around the desk.

"Don't be silly. We bend the rules for old friends and members of the constabulary. And you're both." I pointed to an empty examining room. "Let's go in here."

I waited till he'd settled himself on the examining table, then I pulled off his bandage. I used a small, illuminated magnifier to take a look.

The laceration was maybe three-quarters of an inch long, running vertically above his left eyebrow. Joe had done his usual plastic-surgeon-grade repair. As I checked out the fine, closely placed sutures that held the edges together without undue pressure, I became aware of how close we were—close enough to smell the lingering traces of Trav's aftershave. Woods, maybe? I noticed an animal magnetism about him that hadn't been there when we were teens. Or maybe I'd sensed it without identifying it. Hence the crush.

I stepped back. "Looks great. Good closure, no sign of infection."

He put on a mock-anxious expression. "Am I going to be sc-sc-scarred, Doctor?"

"As a matter of fact, yes." I wrinkled my brow and pointed to the horizontal lines there. "The lines of cleavage over the eyes are mostly horizontal. Your cut runs across those lines. When that happens, you scar. So in the future make sure you get cut *along* the lines of cleavage, not across them."

He laughed. "I'll try to remember that next time someone takes a swing at me."

I pointed to the fine white line lateral to his right eye. "Same thing happened here. What's the story behind that one?"

He suddenly looked uncomfortable. "Nothing that interesting."

Which meant it was most likely very interesting, but I didn't press.

I put a fresh bandage on the wound, then gestured around at the examining room.

"I guess you can figure pretty well what I've been up to since high school. How about you?"

"Got an associate degree from C4, got married to Diana—"

"Robinson?" I said, pretending the marriage was news. I hadn't known about C4—the local name for Carson County Community College. I'd always figured him as university material. "I guess it wasn't just high-school puppy love between you."

He shrugged. "We had a kid. Her name's Madison—we call her Maddy—and she's..." He smiled. "She's the best thing that ever happened to me."

I liked the way Trav's eyes lit when he spoke his daughter's name. Every little girl should have a daddy who feels that way about her. I know I did.

"Who does she look like—you or Diana?"

"Diana, luckily." His smile faded. "With a baby on the way I couldn't stay in school so I joined the sheriff's department. Diana and me split about five years ago."

"I'm sorry to hear that."

I meant it. Really. A divorce is hard on everyone, especially children. What did make me happy was how up front he was about it. He didn't seem to be playing games.

"Yeah, well... probably the worst time of my life."

I resisted asking about Diana's current dress size.

He glanced at his watch as he hopped off the table. "Got to run. They're making some sort of public relations film about the sheriff's department. I think they're planning to run it on local cable." He smiled. "Got to remember to keep my bandaged side away from the camera."

"Is it scripted or cinema verité?"

"Cinema very what?"

Cinema verité... I realized he had no idea what it meant.

And suddenly I was aware of the culture gap between us. I'd become a city mouse and he'd remained the country kind. Not that that made me the better person, it just meant our frames of reference weren't going to be on the same wavelength. I'd gone to countless art galleries and museums, hung out with fringe folk, seen too many obscure films—many of them deservedly obscure—at the Angelika, and spent the first semester of my junior year in England at Oxford. Trav had stayed here, but I'll bet he'd witnessed his share of violence, maybe committed a little himself, and had seen a lot of the slimy things crawling under the human rock of Carson County.

"It means someone will come in with a camera and film your regular routines."

He shook his head. "I don't know how much of a script there is, but I can't see Don Hincher letting—"

"Hincher?"

"The sheriff?" he said with a how-can-you-not-know? tone.

"Oh."

I probably should pay more attention to local politics.

"Anyway, I can't see him letting someone come in and just

wander around his department with a camera. No way." He reached for his back pocket. "Where do I pay?"

"You're kidding, right?"

"Well... I don't like to be on the receiving end of freebies."

"It's not free. You have to buy me lunch sometime."

Now where had *that* come from?

Trav smiled. "You've got a deal."

"Those will be ready to come out on Monday. Stop by when you can and I'll yank them."

He winced. "Yank... don't know if I like the sound of that. Will it cost me another lunch?"

I laughed—my first of the day—and it felt good.

"No. You're covered."

He gave my forearm a friendly squeeze as he passed. "See you Monday."

I realized that while I'd been with Trav I'd forgotten about the malpractice suit.

# 8

I finished my patient calls, then I made one for myself. I needed to talk to someone about this malpractice thing, so I called Sam's house. After four rings the answering machine picked up. I didn't leave a message.

I headed for my mother's. I knew she couldn't give me much in the way of advice. She'd never sued or been sued, and I'd bet the only time she'd ever spoken to a lawyer was about Dad's will. But at least I could count on a friendly ear.

Or so I thought.

Timmy was there and I was glad for that. He's more of the world than Mum. I sat both of them down in the living room where that landscape still didn't hang straight, and told them about the summons and some of the details of the case—all without naming names, of course.

Timmy grumbled and Mum patted my knee. "Anyone can make a mistake, Norrie. It's human nature."

I felt my jaw drop. "Weren't you listening? I *didn't* make a mistake."

"But you must have."

"Thanks a lot, Mum."

"Oh, I feel for you, love, but maybe you missed some tiny little thing. Lord knows they can't sue you for nothing."

"Of course they can. And they are."

She looked shocked. "But that's… they can't *do* that."

I should have expected this. My mother is someone a defense attorney would least want on a jury. Her mindset goes something like: If they arrested you, you must be guilty. If you're innocent, they wouldn't have bothered with you because the police have too much else on their plates to be wasting their time with innocent people.

She has this thing for authority figures. Loves them. The ultimate authority is, of course, God. And the ultimate human authority is the Pope, because God speaks through him.

She *loves* rules. Ten commandments aren't nearly enough. I'm sure she wishes there were twenty, thirty, a hundred. The more the merrier.

"Well," I said, "they *can* do that and they are."

"It's all part of the plan," Uncle Timmy said. "They're looking to drive out good doctors like you, Norrie, and leave us without medical care."

Mum said, "Now Timmy—"

"It's true, Kate, and you know it. Do you think you'll ever hear of that quack Hansford being sued? Never."

"Don't you talk about him like that. He's a good doctor."

My mother goes to a doctor only when she's got no choice. One foot in the grave? *Maybe* she'll seek medical advice. She started with Dr. Hansford when she came to town and has stuck with him ever since. He hasn't killed her yet.

"He's a quack," Timmy said. "That's why they want him in practice and a real doctor like Norrie out."

I knew I shouldn't ask, but I had to. It's like coming upon a button labeled *Do Not Touch.* Some of us simply *have* to press it.

"Who's 'they' this time, Tim?"

"The usual suspects: the Internationalists at the UN."

My mother rolled her eyes. "Don't start with that rubbish again."

"Not rubbish. It's a truth no one will admit to, one that will not stand the light of day. And it's no secret. The UN is controlled by the Masons, who're also controlling the legal profession. They're all Masons, you know. *All* of them. The trial lawyers take the heat, but the defense lawyers are right there all cozy with them in the same bed. And why not? Every time one ambulance-chasing lowlife files suit, the poor victim has to hire another lawyer to defend him. One hand's always washing the other, you see."

"Not all lawyers are bad," Mum said.

Timmy nodded. "Right. Some are dead."

I said, "But what's all this—?"

He held up a hand. "Let me finish now. The Internationalists, the New World Order, call them what you will, they've had their covetous eyes trained on the US for more than a century now. Plan after plan to bring us down has failed. That COVID virus almost succeeded but our doctors saved us. This malpractice scheme is their latest: Sue the good doctors until they can no longer afford the insurance premiums, driving them out of practice, thus leaving the country defenseless against the next pandemic they launch. When the hospitals are overflowing and we're dying in the streets, they'll step in to 'save' us. But that'll be just a smoke screen to hide their real purpose: Taking us over so they can run our country like they run the rest of the world."

Timmy's theory was one of the most ridiculous things I'd ever heard, right up there with Princess Diana being abducted by aliens just before the car crash.

And yet... I found it somehow attractive. A part of me wished it were true. Maybe because emotionally I could more easily handle the idea that I was a pawn in a game fixed by a huge, shadowy international cartel or coalition; at least if someone eliminates or defeats that group, everything will return to normal.

The truth was more discouraging, more difficult to deal with: I could do everything right and still be sued. And even when—*when*, not if—I was exonerated, my malpractice premiums would rise, not because I'd been negligent, but merely because I'd been sued. And at no point would the lawyer or the plaintiff be liable for a cent.

This is the way the system works—the way it was *designed* to work. And it isn't going to change. Because the reforms necessary for change have to come from the legislature. And ninety-nine per cent of legislators are—surprise—lawyers.

Might as well ask a shark to limit its feeding to certain times of day and only around certain reefs.

Mum was shaking her head. "Maybe you should think again about this doctor thing, Norrie. If you got married and settled down with a husband and had babies, you wouldn't have to worry about being sued."

Doctor thing?

"I'm only thirty-two, Mum."

She pointed at me. "Your clock is ticking away, and you know what I mean. I'd like at least one grandchild before I go to my grave. Heaven knows, you and Sean are cut from the same cloth. He should be the father of three by now."

Timmy glanced my way at her mention of Sean. We both knew my brother would not be bringing any children into the world.

Mum wasn't finished. "Two children who don't want children! What did I do to deserve this?"

"I do want children, Mum. I just don't want them *yet*."

She shook her head and I leaned back and closed my eyes. I'd come for some bucking up but now I was only more depressed.

I fended off Mum's offers of food—she'd gone the beef stew route tonight. I'd skipped lunch because the summons had stolen my appetite, but I still wasn't hungry. And even if were… I never did like Mum's beef stew.

I did accept a cup of coffee, then headed for home.

# 9

On the way, my playlist shuffle perversely decided I needed to hear "Bad Day."

But I made it back to the apartment where I picked at the left-over tuna salad as I fanned through my mail. I felt exhausted, as if someone had pulled a stopper and drained off all my energy. I hadn't worked harder today than any other, so it had to be the suit.

I pulled out the summons and read half way through it again before tossing it aside. Why was I torturing myself? It wasn't going to change.

I realized I was letting this get to me. I was obsessing on it. But I'd never imagined myself in this position. Malpractice suits happened to other doctors.

I also realized I was in a useless state, so I figured I might as well—as my dad used to say—call it a day and hit the hay.

A quick shower, lights out, and under the covers...

...where I lay wide awake.

Exhausted as I was, sleep wouldn't come. Whenever I closed my eyes I saw Ted Phelan pointing an accusing finger at me.

And I had to wonder: Was it possible I'd missed something? Had something turned up on later exams that I'd overlooked? Could I—*should* I have done something different?

I had to get past this. I had to maintain confidence in my ability. But the truth was that even if I'd done everything right—and I was sure I had—Mr. Phelan was convinced I hadn't. Didn't matter that he was wrong, the fact that he thought of me as negligent throbbed like an open wound.

I threw off the covers and got out of bed. Sleep wasn't going to happen.

I went to the kitchen and pulled a bottle of merlot from the wine rack.

I don't know much about wine but I like a glass of red now and again. I have a hard time telling a cabernet from a merlot, so I tend to buy whichever Corky's Liquors has on sale.

I popped the cork and poured myself a glass. Then I reached way back in the pantry for the secret stash of little dark chocolate squares called Dove Promises. I keep them there for special occasions and emergencies. Screw the carb count, this was an emergency.

I took the wine and the chocolate to the living room where I caught the last half of *An Affair to Remember*. I had myself a good cry at the finale. I always puddle up at the end, but tonight I bawled like a baby.

Maybe something more than a movie was behind that.

Me... wanton... reckless... *negligent...*

I was sure I couldn't feel any worse, but tomorrow would prove me wrong. Tomorrow a patient would die.

# THURSDAY

# 1

I woke up at around quarter to nine and found myself on the couch with some noir-ish old black-and-white film running on the TV. I never sleep this late, but then I rarely stay up as late as I had last night.

Good thing I have Thursdays off. That meant no office hours today, but not necessarily no hospital.

I didn't feel up to a jog, so I showered, dressed in my casual Ralph Lauren black knit warm-up, and made the bed. I always make the bed. The idea of leaving it unmade for the day is, well, unthinkable. I tried it once and found I couldn't concentrate. I had to drive back and make it.

My serum caffeine level was in the cellar so I stopped at the Dunkin' Donuts along the way for a cup of high octane. The glazed crullers beckoned from the display case…

*Oh, come on, Norrie… just one of us… how much could it hurt?*

I fled to my car. I'd messed up last night with the chocolate. Had to get back on track today. I wondered about that new diet drug. What was it called again? Tezinex. Would that fend off these cravings?

I thought again about trying it. Why not? I should be willing to dose myself with anything I might prescribe for my patients. And if it worked for me with no downside, I could be more confident it would work for them.

I arrived at the hospital. I have this thing about my inpatients: I feel personally responsible for them. Even on my days off when either Sam or Ken make rounds, I like to pop in and say hello and check the chart. The older more experienced docs tell me I'll get over it as soon as I get a life.

Truth is, this *is* my life. At least for now.

I accessed Amelia Henderson's chest films on the computer. The reray showed a slight regression in her left lower lobe infiltrate. The pneumonia was on the mend, but taking its own sweet time.

Next stop: the lady herself.

"But that other doctor was already here," Amelia said as I stepped into the room.

She was sitting beside the bed with a frilly pink robe draped over her shoulders. An IV ran into her left arm. Her green oxygen line ran under her nose. She'd yet to be weaned off it.

"Doctor Lerner. Yes, I know, but I was just passing by and thought I'd stop in to say hello."

A white lie. What could it hurt?

"He said I'm not ready to go home."

I agreed.

"You've still got a ways to go. First we have to see more clearing of your pneumonia, and then you have to be off the oxygen."

I wondered about her mental state. She looked depressed. Was she still waiting for her late husband to show?

"Did you have many visitors yesterday?"

She shook her head. "Just Beth." I saw tears rim her eyes. "She told me Harry's dead. I didn't remember. How could I forget something like that?"

"It happens in hospitals, Amelia. Maybe it was the medication in the IVs." It wasn't, but I wanted to give her something to blame besides her aging brain. "Do you remember now?"

She nodded. "Now, yes. But I shouldn't have forgotten. It's not right."

I sat with her for a few more minutes of reassurance. When I left she was in better spirits and checking out what was on the tube.

I now felt I could call the rest of the day my own. Well, except for the office meeting at one o'clock.

# 2

I was chugging through the ER, aiming for the daylight beyond the sliding glass doors, when Joe McIver flagged me down.

"You know your peanut lady?" he said.

I slid to a halt. "Marge Harris?"

He nodded. "Looks like she did it again. First aid's bringing her in and it doesn't look good."

The ceaseless bustle of the ER seemed to slow around me. Marge...?

"How bad?"

"EMTs responded to a 9-1-1. They just called in. Looks like deep shock. Want to hang?"

I nodded. Yeah, I wanted to hang. I couldn't *not* hang.

I rubbed my suddenly cold hands and waited. Marge... my patient... had I somehow let her down?

The ambulance's siren began as a high-pitched whisper that graduated to a tortured wail. I heard the rig screech to a halt outside. Seconds later the crew was rushing a wheeled stretcher through the doors.

Vonne Hayes, one of the RNs, directed them to a rear corner where Joe and I waited with the crash cart. One of the first aiders was pumping air into her while another thumped her chest, and still another held an IV bag aloft, all on the run.

I bit my upper lip when I saw her. Oh, God... Marge looked dead.

I grabbed an oxygen line, hooked it to the Ambu, and took over the bagging; Hayes took over the chest compression while another nurse, Sarah Martinez, hooked up EKG leads as Joe flashed a penlight into her eyes.

"Pupils barely reactive," he said. "So barely it might be my imagination."

The heart monitor glowed to life. Ronnie paused compression so we could see what was going on.

*Nothing* was going on.

Joe looked at me. "Flatlined. I don't think there's anything left."

"We've got to try, Joe. Please?"

The ER was Joe's ship and he was captain. If he said no, then it was no.

Tugging on his beard he hesitated a heartbeat, then said, "Okay. We'll give her ten minutes. If we can't get anything going by then…"

He didn't need to say more.

When Joe had the laryngoscope ready, I removed the bag's mouthpiece from Marge's face so he could intubate her. He pried open her jaws with the scope and slid the ribbed plastic tube toward her larynx. But he couldn't pass it.

"Shit! Laryngeal edema. Trach tray!"

Martinez brought the tray, and within seconds Joe had a hole punched through the flesh of Marge's throat and into her trachea. After the initial whoosh of air Joe fitted a tube into the opening, then I hooked the Ambu to that and started pumping oxygen directly into her lungs. Martinez began handing Joe the meds he called out for.

We kept this up for ten minutes, Joe doing intracardiac injections between Hayes's runs of compressions, pausing every so often to check the monitor and let Joe flash her pupils. We used every tool except the defibrillator which is useless in asystole.

Finally, he shook his head. "Non-reactive." He glanced at the still flatlined monitor, then at the clock. "I'm pronouncing her dead at 10:32 a.m."

"No…" I didn't have breath for anything more.

Joe gripped my arm. "Norrie, we all loved her, but she's not coming back."

I released the bag and looked down at the corpse. Marge lay

limp and pale before me, mouth slack, eyes glassy and staring, naked from the waist up, breasts drooping to the sides, punctures in her chest wall where Joe had shot meds straight into her heart… nothing dignified about this kind of death.

Just yesterday morning she'd been so bright and perky and… alive.

Joe looked at me. "Damn shame. No cleaning girl around to save her this time, I guess."

I couldn't speak. My throat was locked. I felt as if my chest were about to explode. I waited till Martinez had disconnected the leads and lines, then I pulled the sheet up over her.

My body felt leaden as I turned away. I'd been on autopilot during the resuscitation, but now the reality hit me: Marge would never again volunteer for any of the hospital fundraisers or local charity functions. The little town of Lebanon, Maryland, had lost a good friend. And I'd lost a big sister.

Only in her forties… she could have had another four decades ahead of her. Now she didn't have even a minute.

I felt tears pool along my lids, then spill over.

What had happened? Another reaction? I'd told her to keep to simple foods, basic and natural, the less processed the better. And how could she have such a catastrophic reaction while on the Benadryl and cimetidine and the big dose of prednisone I'd given her?

It didn't make sense.

I saw a sheriff's department uniform walk in. I realized it was Travis Lawton. I wiped my eyes just before he spotted me and came over. He looked grim.

"Hey, Norrie. Where's Joe?"

I looked around and didn't see him. He could have been in any of the curtained treatment spaces.

"I don't know. We just finished a CPR—"

He straightened. "Marge Harris?"

"Yes. How did you know?"

"Where is she?"

"She didn't make it, Trav."

I saw sadness in his eyes as he muttered, "Shit!"

We both observed a spontaneous moment of silence.

"Remember her piano lessons?" he said finally.

I nodded. "She was so patient with me. You, at least, had some talent."

"I still tickle the ivories now and then. But she was everywhere. She just ran a fundraiser to supply the department with more Kevlar vests." He shook his head. "We just lost a good one."

His expression seemed troubled as well as sad. I knew he didn't show up every time someone was rushed to the hospital, even someone like Marge.

"Something wrong?"

He didn't make eye contact. "Could be."

I had a crawly feeling at the back of my neck. "What are we talking about here?"

"Just something I heard. Have you seen her husband?"

"Stan? He's in New York."

"You're sure?"

The crawly feeling became cold, clutching fingers. "Well, no. But that's what he told me yesterday. Some kind of business trip. He wanted me to keep Marge another night."

"Too bad you didn't."

I knew Trav didn't mean anything by it—just stating the obvious—but still it stung. Marge *would* be alive now if she'd remained an inpatient.

"What did you hear? Something about Stan?"

"Not sure. It was on the 9-1-1 call."

"What was?"

He fidgeted and looked away. "I can't talk about it now. It may be something or nothing. I'll let you know when we straighten it out."

His two-way chirped. He pulled it off his belt and wandered toward an empty corner as he started talking. I thought I heard a snippet that sounded like, "This just became a coroner's case."

Marge… a coroner's case?

What was going on?

# 3

I somehow made it home from the ER. Devastated, I plopped on the couch and stared out the window wondering if I'd failed Marge.

*Should* I have kept her another night? The answer to that seemed pretty obvious now. But there'd been no medical reason.

After maybe an hour of moping I forced myself up and got moving. Sitting here all day wouldn't bring Marge back. I changed into an ancient Outkast T-shirt, denim overalls, and dirty sneakers. I was feeling down—way down—and needed therapy.

So I headed for my garden.

The condo association had put aside a southern-exposed area where owners so inclined could stake out little vegetable gardens. My father always had a garden in our backyard where he'd grow the usual Italian staples: tomatoes, peppers, eggplant, zucchini, veal. He used to drag Sean and me out to help him weed, and along the way I discovered I had something of a green thumb.

Just kidding about the veal, by the way. My father's favorite joke. We heard it every single spring.

I hadn't been near a vegetable garden since I was a teen, but last year I decided to give it a try. I wasn't going to take the easy way with tomatoes and such. Oh, no. My plot was going to be the envy of the other gardeners: I was going to bring in a crop of broccoli.

The sky had clouded over by time I got outside. I hated weeds—they did *not* belong in my garden—and wanted to pull them weeds before the forecasted rain. I stood among the neat rows of Green Comet cultivars I'd planted about three weeks ago—broccoli doesn't do well in the heat of summer so you set it in early. The little plants were coming along with no sign of wilt or insect damage. A low fence kept out the rabbits.

I knelt and started digging out the weeds and crabgrass with my trowel.

I like weeding. Call me strange, but I like washing dishes too. The condo came with a dishwasher but I rarely use it, preferring to clean my plates by hand. Simple manual tasks put me into some hazy state where the problems of the world—malpractice suits, dead friends, mysterious 9-1-1 calls—recede to a safe distance.

I worked quickly and was just about done when I spotted a pair of purple sneakers at the end of my last row. I looked up and saw they were connected to Janie "Poochie Sutton" Ryan.

Janie appears to get her fashion tips from Larry Flynt. She wears her raven hair long and banged, giving her a sort of Bettie Page look.

How do I know about Bettie Page? I never would have heard of her if not for this undergrad gay guy I knew at NYU. He'd lined his room with old black-and-white photos of her—*crazy* about her. But when I asked him why a guy who likes guys would go bonkers over a 1950s pinup, he had no answer except he thought she was beautiful. Go figure.

While Bettie went for the natural look, Janie didn't. She'd mascaraed her brown eyes to the max and painted her lips a bright vermilion. She's a pretty girl who doesn't need any of that. But then again, in her profession...

An ankle-length black vinyl raincoat covered the rest of her.

"What's up, doc?" she said, waving as she smiled down at me.

I noticed that her fingernails were the same shade as her lips. Mine were safely hidden away inside my work gloves. I was overdue for a manicure and intended to remedy that this Saturday.

I smiled back. "Not much. Just killing weeds." Like I was going to discuss my malpractice situation with her? "What's up with you?"

"Just on my way out and spotted you. What're you growing?"

"Broccoli."

She made a face. "Yuck."

"Just get up?"

She yawned. "Yeah. Figured I'd hit the gym for a while. Got to keep the bod in shape, you know."

"Working tonight?"

"Yeah. I was thinking about taking off, but after last night I changed my mind."

"Oh?"

"Eight Uncle Bens—on a Wednesday!"

"You've lost me."

"Ben Franklin—he's on the C-note."

"The C...?" And then I got it and gasped. "You made eight-hundred dollars last night?"

She nodded, grinning. "Eight-thirty-two, to be exact. Still don't know where those two singles came from but, hey, money's money. Not bad for five hours at the club and less than an hour and a half total onstage."

I shook my head. "What kind of place pays you that kind of money? I mean, I don't want to get too personal, but what do you do for that sort of money?"

"I go between the Hustler Club and the Shark Tank down on the Block. I take off my clothes and shake it around, and collect tips. Right now there's some kind of cop convention down at the harbor and are they ever ready to spend." She looked at me, cocking her head left and right. "You ever decide to do the ecdysiast thing, let me know."

"You mean stripping?"

"Hey, you know the word. Bet you're surprised I do."

"Well..."

"Just cause I strip doesn't mean I'm stupid. You should play chess with me some time. Mate in twelve moves, tops."

I smiled. "Next you're going to tell me you strip just to put yourself through grad school for a masters in physics."

She laughed, a musical sound. "That'll be the day! High school was such a drag. But I do read a lot." She gave me an appraising look. "Seriously though, you'd probably do okay on the pole."

I stared at her. "You're kidding, right?" I slapped my rump. "Baby got back—too much of it."

"No way. You got back, but you got front too. What size cup are you?"

I couldn't believe this. I turned my attention back to the weeds.

"C."

"Figured. I used to be a B till I had a boob job. Now I'm a D. But I'm not kidding. Mako's lookin' for—"

"Mako?"

"Vladimir Makovei—the Ukrainian guy who owns the Shark Tank. Mako... Shark Tank..." She gave me an exaggerated wink. "Get it?"

"Got it." Wow.

"Anyway, Mako's old but thinks he's a stud, but the only long, hard thing he's got is his name. Anyway, he's looking for a coupla bigger, older women—"

"*Older?*"

She laughed again. "Hey, no offense, Norrie, but you're what, early thirties?"

"That's not old!"

"In my job it is. And Mako's looking to add a couple what he calls 'strong, mature women' to the lineup. So what do you say?"

I could have told her that even the threat of violent death and/or dismemberment would not get me naked in front of a roomful of men.

You get to see a lot of naked flesh in medicine—a *lot*. Some of it is worth a look, but the vast majority is not, and by the time you finish training you truly appreciate the concept of clothing.

Most anthropologists theorize that early humans didn't start wearing clothes until they migrated from Africa to cooler climes. I'm convinced it happened much earlier than that. I can see a bunch of early hominids—say, half a dozen Australopithecines—confronting one of their number and telling him that, for the good of the tribe, he had to cover up.

I think Leviticus said it best: "Cloak thy nakedness for it causeth lamentations of pity and woe from Heaven and Earth alike."

No, wait. That wasn't Leviticus. That's from the *Book of Norrie*.

I said, "Obviously you've never seen me dance. Two left feet."

"C'mon," she said, drawing out the word. "You'll be good at it. Besides, I get a bounty if I bring someone in. I'll split it with you."

I laughed. "You'll be split from your job if you walk in with me."

"All right." She sighed. "I tried. Don't say I didn't give you a chance." She started to turn away. "Off to the gym."

"What do you do there?"

"I start off with a spin class. Ever do one?"

"One. And only one."

It had taught me that you don't have to die to go to hell. You can find it right here on earth at something called a spinning class. It's like some bizarre satanic rite: A dark room lined with people puffing and sweating and straining on stationary bikes, heavy metal music turned up to 11, and a body Nazi screaming "Faster! Faster!"

Never again.

I pointed my trowel at her super-long raincoat. "You're going to spin in that?"

She turned back to me. "No, silly. In this."

She pulled open her coat to reveal her workout duds: a two-piece ensemble with a halter top and shorts the same vermilion as her lips and nails. She had a narrow waist, gently swelling hips, all sheathed in smooth, evenly tanned skin.

She wiggled her hips. "Faked and baked and looking *good*."

I knew what that meant: breast implants and a tanning booth. By reflex I opened my mouth to warn her about too much UV exposure, but snapped it shut. Like she'd listen.

Her outfit didn't hide much. In fact it looked barely legal. Her halter top would have been right at home on a teeny bikini, and the shorts… well, to call them skimpy would be like saying the Kardashians like to be photographed now and then. And tight? Paint would have hidden more. From my low-angle view I could see the outline of her labia.

"Doesn't that, um, cause a stir in the gym?"

She winked and grinned. "Ooooh, yeah. Especially when I get on the weight circuit. I like to watch the guys trip over their own feet as they pass, or position themselves on machines that'll give them a good ogle angle."

"You're going to give some poor old guy a heart attack."

She laughed. "Now *that* would be cool."

She closed her coat and waved as she strolled away.

Every now and then I meet someone like Janie, so at home in their skin, so comfy and offhanded about their sexuality, and I envy them. Not that I'd ever want to be a stripper, even if I looked like her. I was raised with the notion that sex is an important step, not to be taken lightly. But I couldn't help wondering what it would be like to treat sex so casually, so lightly, like... like buying a candy bar.

But then, I don't take candy bars lightly either.

I had to smile at the thought of her trying to recruit me as a "strong, mature" stripper. Me. Stripping. Hah!

But eight-hundred dollars for a few hours work... I could pay off my student loans in no time...

Kind of a fun thought, but that was all it would ever be.

Back in the real world I finished off the last of the weeds just as the first drops started to fall. I ran for shelter and a change of clothes...

And found out that all the time I'd been outside, it had been raining inside.

# 4

When I opened my front door I heard water dripping. Had I left the sink running?

No, the ceiling in my bathroom was running. The wallboard had bulged downward and then cracked open. A small waterfall was pouring through. I let out a scream, then ran and got the only bucket I had and shoved it beneath the torrent.

I had the property manager on speed dial from when I first moved in and all sorts of things were wrong with my place. I pulled out my phone and hit the 6 button—1 and 2 were the office and the ER, Mum was 3.

The bucket was already full by the time he answered. I emptied it in the bathtub and kept up that routine until he showed up. He took one look and dashed upstairs.

About fifteen minutes later he reappeared. Tom was late forties with a trim body and trim beard.

"Someone left the tub running in the Harleys' place."

"Idiots!" I said, fuming. "Look at this!"

"I turned it off. This should stop soon."

"Not soon enough."

"You've got tenant's insurance, I hope."

"Of course. I'm not stupid."

He grimaced. "Hey, I didn't leave the tub running."

I realized I'd raised my voice. I hadn't meant to.

"I'm sorry. I'm not blaming you. It's just that this is so unnecessary."

"I hear you. First thing to do is get on the horn to your insurance company and have them send an appraiser ASAP."

If I could find my policy.

"Got a mop?" he said.

"No."

"I can find you one. Then I'll bring the wet vac."

"Thanks."

Good. Because a mop wasn't going to help the carpet in the hallway.

# 5

The first Thursday of every month is office meeting day at LFPA. Always a Thursday. Guess whose day off is Thursday. Uh-huh.

Despite the flood, I didn't want to miss it—I was sure they'd talk about me.

So after the waterfall stopped and I'd mopped up what I could, I headed for the office.

Sam had finished a little early and I caught him in his consultation room. I told him about Marge's death—she'd started out as his patient.

He shook his head. "Nice lady. Too bad."

He looked so tired I hesitated broaching the subject of the suit, but Ken had already told him. I handed him the Phelan chart and gave him a capsule version of the case.

He thumbed through the sheets, then looked at me.

"How do you feel?"

"Heartbroken about Marge. As for the suit, I think 'crushed' sums it up pretty well."

He looked at me with his soft brown eyes. "You're having a bad couple of days, aren't you."

"I've had worse."

Like the day I heard Dad was dead. No day could be worse than that. But these last two were up there.

"Don't let the bastards get you down, Norrie. You've got to look at a suit like everyone else who deals with the public: part of the cost of doing business."

Business? I preferred to think of myself as a physician, not a businesswoman. Sam must have read my mind.

"Sure, medicine's a calling, but it's a business too. If we don't make money we can't buy supplies or pay our staff or lease our fancy cars. And it's a fact of life that as soon as you put yourself out there, you become a target for lawyers. It's the way it is."

"It's not the lawyer who bothers me—I knew him as a kid, by the way. It's the patient. Someone in this practice thinks I let them down—and I didn't."

"Don't take it personally Norrie. You—"

"How *else* can I take it?"

"Hear me out. We've become a culture of victims—it's always somebody else's fault. Even with an inherited disease like this, *somebody's* got to be at fault. Add that to the lottery mentality that goes with liability suits—you've got a helluva better chance of winning a suit than Mega Millions—and everybody starts suing everybody else."

"I wish I could say that makes me feel better."

He leaned forward. "But there's a more important reason not to take this personally: It can affect the way you practice, and it can erode your effectiveness as a doctor."

"I hope not."

"It will if you're not careful. You'll start approaching every patient as a potential malpractice plaintiff."

That jolted me: I'd begun to feel some of that yesterday afternoon.

"It's one of the subtle, subversive effects from frivolous suits that the public never sees. Even when you're finally vindicated, the process of interrogatories and depositions changes you; sometimes you can't go back to the doctor you were. You no longer have confidence in your intuition, and intuition is the unsung strength of the best doctors. Without that you become a plodding automaton, shipping patients off to medical centers at the drop of a hat, or ordering tests you know are unnecessary but you order anyway because you can hear some lawyer's voice saying, 'And now doctor, please enlighten us as to *why* you decided Mrs. So-and-so did not deserve a PET scan of her left buttock.' I don't want to see that happen to you."

Sam sounded as if he'd been down that road.

"Don't tell me you've been sued too."

He shrugged. "Of course."

"What?" I couldn't believe it. This was the best, smartest, sharpest doctor I'd ever met. "How many times? When?"

"Once, very early in my career. For medication side effects. And you know why I was sued? Because of another doctor. We've got some real arrogant jerks in our profession, Norrie, and they cause almost as many problems as the ambulance chasers. This one was a psychiatrist who wound up seeing a patient I'd been treating with Haldol. She was a wreck when he saw her, shaking, quaking, urinary incontinence. He immediately blamed it on the Haldol, and on me for prescribing it. According to him only a psychiatrist should prescribe Haldol, not some lowly family practitioner."

"The son of a bitch."

"You've got that right. So the patient and her husband sued me. It came out in the discovery phase that my records clearly showed she was a shaking, quaking, incontinent wreck the day she first walked into my office. If the psychiatrist could have put aside his arrogance and asked her about her symptoms, he would have known that they'd all pre-existed her first Haldol tablet. But no, he preferred to get on his specialist high horse and shoot his mouth off."

"What happened?"

"The insurance company wanted to settle. The plaintiffs would go away for seventy-five-hundred bucks, a fraction of what it would cost to go to trial, even though a trial would have been a slam-dunk victory for our side. Unfortunately I agreed."

"No!"

He shrugged. "I was young and the whole idea of going into court scared the hell out of me, so I gave them the go ahead. I've regretted it ever since. A settlement, even for a paltry sum, is viewed as a black mark on your insurance record. Don't you make the same mistake."

I knew what he meant about being scared—I was terrified—but no way was I going to settle.

# 6

When the last patient had departed, we began the meeting ritual: After locking the office doors, the five of us—the three docs plus Harriet and Giselle, our only full-time employees—moved into the waiting room where we helped ourselves to a platter of sandwiches from the Moonstruck Deli, then settled into a rough circle.

The impassive, hulking Harriet presented a list of needed supplies—vaccines, paper goods, and so on. Giselle, short, thin, and fidgety as a sparrow, went over the latest billing issues—which insurance companies were paying, which were delaying. All this was discussed, decisions made, and then Harriet and Giselle were cut loose.

Now came doctor issues. My suit was raised briefly, and then we moved on to an always touchy issue.

Sam said, "Giselle asked me when she could get a raise."

"Forget it," Ken snapped. "We can't afford it."

"We can afford a token amount for her and Harriet. Another dollar an hour isn't going to kill us. That totals eighty bucks a week."

Ken shook his head. "It's a matter of principle. They should be glad they've got jobs at all in this economy."

I crossed my arms and bit my lip. I wanted to scream but it wasn't my place. I had no vote—not until I became a stockholder.

Sam said, "Come on, Ken, they're good people, hard workers, and things aren't getting any cheaper. They haven't had a raise in two years."

"And you and I haven't had a raise in *four*! No one gets a raise until *we* do."

Sam turned to me. "What do you think, Norrie?"

Don't do this, Sam, I thought. Please don't do this.

Ken shook his head. "She has no say in this."

Yes! For once I was on Ken's side.

Sam kept his eyes on me. "She works here, she sees what's going on, she's an intelligent person... I'd like to hear what she has to say."

Ken made a dismissive wave. "Okay, okay." He turned to me. "What's your take on this, Norrie? To raise or not to raise, that is the question."

How was I going to put this without making him even more unhappy about my being in the practice? I had to say something.

"Well... as I see it, the downside of giving them a raise is an increase in overhead, and our overhead keeps climbing even without giving raises."

Ken looked surprised for a few seconds, then nodded. "Thank you. Exactly my point."

"The downside of *not* giving a raise is the risk of losing a valued employee. With Harriet, I don't see that as a problem. She's loyal to Sam, plus her husband makes a decent living from the Post Office. She'll stay no matter what."

Ken was nodding again.

"Giselle, though," I said, "is another matter. She runs this office. She knows all the ins and outs of our billing system, she knows exactly who to call at the insurance companies when we've got a problem. She's priceless. But she's divorced and this job is her only source of income. I'm afraid if she starts to feel unappreciated here she might go test the waters elsewhere. And if she does I think she'll soon find someone willing to pay her not just a dollar more, but *plenty* more than she's earning here."

Now it was Sam's turn to nod. "Couldn't have said it better myself."

Ken said, "I think you're overestimating her importance—way overestimating."

Sam leaned forward. "Let me lay out a little scenario: Giselle finds another job and gives two weeks' notice. What do we do?

Within the span of ten working days we'll have to find someone who can multi-task like Giselle, and then train that someone to do all she does. How do we do that?"

For a moment it looked as if Ken was going to admit he hadn't the faintest, but then his eyes lit.

"We can hire Allie to do it!"

*Office Manager Barbie?* No-no-no-no!

I glanced at Sam. I'd been wondering if his health problem might be heart related, but this sort of proved that it wasn't: If he had coronary artery disease, even a mild case, the thought of Allie Lerner managing LFPA would have had him clutching his chest and keeling over in cardiac arrest.

Sam coughed once into his fist, then cleared his throat. "As I remember, Ken, we agreed from the start that no wives would be involved with the group."

"Yes, but..." Ken probably saw from the look on Sam's face that this was a dead end. "Just a thought... as an interim measure."

The meeting ended with Giselle and Harriet each receiving a seventy-five-cent raise—Ken was adamant about not going all the way to a buck.

As soon as we adjourned the meeting Ken gave me a quick, angry look, then made a beeline for his consultation room and closed the door behind him.

My foot ached from the hole I'd just shot through it.

# 7

The rain was still falling as I headed home. I stopped at the Everything Store to buy some cleaning supplies. While there I passed a cage full of not-quite-baby chicks, probably left over from Easter. I stopped and listened to them go *cheep-cheep-cheep*. How about that? They were talking about Ken.

I'd called the insurance company and they'd said they'd have an adjustor out this afternoon. Sure enough, when I returned to the condo, he was waiting by the door. It felt like a swamp inside. My feet squished on the carpet. I hung around till he'd taken his photos and made his notes. He said the company would get back to me soon.

When he was gone I looked around and knew I couldn't stay here. I hated to do it, but I hit 3 on my speed dial. I told my mother the story and she was delighted to have me stay. She'd get my old room ready for me right away.

"Thanks, Mum. And I'm going to fix you and Timmy dinner tonight. Steaks on the grill."

After turning down Donna's invitation to Morton's Steakhouse yesterday, I'd developed this huge craving for red meat.

"Oh, you don't have to do that. You've enough to deal with as it is."

"I want to do it. I'll bring all the fixings, you just save your appetites."

"Well... all right, if you really want to... but I'll do dessert."

"You've got a deal."

I packed a bag of basics and essentials from my closet that I hoped would hold me. Tom showed up with the wet vac as I was leaving. That would help some.

At the Safeway I picked out a big London broil—I had a new marinade I wanted to try and a new way of cooking it I'd seen it on the *Cooking Channel*—I watch it like some men watch porn— that had looked delicious.

This was going to be good. When someone hands you a lemon, make lemonade, right?

# 8

The rain had stopped but I stayed in my warm-up and arrived with my suitcase and a full grocery bag. Timmy was there and took the suitcase to my old room at the rear of the first floor. I found my way to the kitchen, set the bag on the counter, and pulled out the steak to oohs and ahs from Mum. Steak had never been my father's thing. Not a lot of steak in Italian cooking.

His name had been Rocco and everyone called him Rocky. Except me. I called him *Babbo*. A big, barrel-chested guy, with thick black hair, thick eyebrows, and a thick waist.

I remember a time when I was about ten years old: We were all at a funeral at St. Catherine's and Dad was outside, wearing his only suit and his dark glasses, standing with his arms crossed across his chest as he scanned the street. He looked like a bodyguard. One of the kids at the funeral asked me in a hushed tone if my dad was "connected."

As a member of the Baltimore City Fire Department, mostly working the day shift, he got home around six every night and had to eat my mother's cooking. I don't know how he did it, because Dad was a super cook. I guess that's what love is about.

But on weekends, once the odd jobs and yard work were taken care of—and you've gotta know our lawn was *perfect*—he'd hit the kitchen.

I remember coming home Saturday afternoons to a house redolent of sautéing garlic and onions, bubbling tomato sauce, and frying meat. I'd go to the kitchen and there would be Dad, this big man wearing a tomato-stained apron, hovering over huge, steaming pots of spaghetti sauce—he called it gravy—that he'd pour into quart containers and freeze for later.

His stints in the kitchen were always peppered with Italian curses. He emigrated from Italy as a child and grew up in a bilingual house, so he often broke into Italian when he was mad or had cut himself.

Sometimes now, when I visit, I can stand in the kitchen and still hear him yell *Stunad!* at himself.

Dad's meatballs were his *pièce de résistance*. He must have shown me half a million times how he made them—double-ground beef, a little ground veal, a little ground pork, an egg, a pinch of oregano, a smidgen of garlic, breadcrumbs, a dusting of salt and fresh-ground pepper—the man wouldn't know a teaspoon or a measuring cup if it hit him in the head—and bada-bing, bada-boom, there you'd have it.

Well, there *he'd* have it. No matter how many times I've tried to duplicate Dad's recipe, I can never get my meatballs to taste like his.

Maybe that was because he'd fry them in lard. Yes, lard. I think that was a big part of the secret. He'd cook them until they were just a tad crispy on the outside and soft and juicy on the inside. On Sundays he'd add a couple to a plate of capellini topped off with his homemade gravy and fresh-ground Romano... *mama mia.*

Is it any wonder I wound up a *balena*?

I'm sure those meatballs were a big part of why Dad's heart quit pumping at age sixty. Might as well inject fat directly into the coronary arteries.

But God they were good.

I looked up and found Timmy staring at me.

"Thinking about your dad?"

I nodded, suddenly tight in the throat. "I wish he was here."

Timmy nodded as he went to work pulling the cork on the big bottle of cabernet I'd brought along. "A good man, Rocky. We got into such a row when I learned he'd asked Kate to marry him. I wasn't going to allow some guinea bastard to marry my cousin. We almost came to blows." He shook his head. "What a dumb-ass I was. He was the best thing ever happened to her. What laughs he and I used to have together. A shame he's gone."

Laughs... yeah, I remember my *babbo* being such a happy man. He had his wife, his kids, his house, and Corrado, his best friend from the old country who was also my godfather. But somewhere around when I was twelve or thirteen or so, he changed. His buddy Corrado ran off without a word, abandoning his sick wife and his daughter and it crushed dad. He felt betrayed that his best friend would do such a thing. He never forgave Corrado. Wouldn't even speak his name after that.

I still have dreams of my father. I still hear my mother's voice telling me how he cried the day I left for New York... cried for a week, she said.

I remember how she got on my case about how I could have had a scholarship to any college, how I could have gone to Johns Hopkins right there in Baltimore. But I couldn't have. They'd have expected me home every weekend, and I'd have felt guilty if I didn't go. I'd have no breakaway, and I'd needed the break.

Then he wasn't there anymore...

I didn't trust myself to speak—what was going on with me?—so I grabbed a bottle of olive oil and poured some over the steak.

"What are you doing?" Mum cried. "That's a steak, not a salad!"

"Just trust me, Mum. This'll be great."

I then took the wine bottle and poured about half a cup onto the meat.

"Wine! Will you look at this, Timmy. My little girl's gone daft! She's drowning the meat in wine!"

"I wouldn't mind drowning in wine myself," Timmy said, then wandered back to the TV to watch *Business Center* on CNBC.

I added pepper and rosemary and salt, then turned the steak over and did the same. I covered the dish with aluminum foil and put it aside.

I had some wine, then lit the grill outside. I helped Mum make a chopped salad, then took the steak to the fire. After searing it on both sides, I caused more consternation in the kitchen by putting it in the oven for a few minutes. But it turned out delicious. Everyone thought I was a genius.

Dessert was Mum's traditional bananas and sugar, followed by coffee generously laced with Bailey's.

I wasn't driving, so why not?

# 9

After dinner I felt a bit tipsy, so I decided to turn in early. My old room... I never thought I'd be back here. The dresser was the same mahogany monstrosity I'd used from the time I could remember till the time I moved out.

The memory of Marge's pale dead face had receded during dinner, but it sidled back while I was getting undressed, leaving me chin deep in melancholy. On my way to the bathroom I stopped by the family's old upright piano in the living room—right next to the never-straight landscape painting. I remembered all those hours of lessons and Marge sitting beside me, coaching me.

I sat down and played a few soft chords, then played very sloppy versions of "Fur Elise" and "Au Clair de la Lune" from pure muscle memory. I appreciated more than ever how she'd touched my life... was continuing to touch me through the music I could still play.

I crawled into bed and pulled the covers up to my chin. Tears began rolling down my cheeks and I had myself a good cry.

Before falling off to sleep, I saw this faint, misty glow, maybe three feet high and a foot wide, hovering beside my bed. And I thought I heard a voice speaking to me.

*Norrie... don't you recognize your Babbo?*

Babbo? That was the name I called my father as a child.

It's the wine and the Bailey's, I thought, and then I was gone.

# FRIDAY

# 1

I began the day with an achy, foggy head. I have a fairly effi-cient liver, but I challenged it last night. I'd hallucinated a glow in my room, and all through the night I kept thinking I heard a voice whispering my name.

I forced myself into a quick jog to clear my head, then headed for the hospital in a black pantsuit with a white blouse. Mum had yet to show by the time I left.

I have Friday mornings off, so I could have stayed in bed, but I wanted to check on Amelia Henderson myself.

I'd much prefer to work the morning session on Friday and have the afternoon and evening off, but that wasn't going to happen for the one with least seniority.

The size of the LFPA office is such that only two doctors can work at once. We divide each day into two sessions: an early—eight to one—and a late—two to whenever. Ken and I each work seven sessions a week and alternate Saturday mornings. Sam works five sessions a week and no Saturdays. All three of us rotate weekend call. The only time we don't have two doctors working is Friday's late session. That's mine alone.

Of course, when one of us gets sick or goes on vacation, we shift around and work extra sessions to keep everything covered.

I found little old Amelia Henderson sitting bedside, dressed in her pink frilly robe and pink slippers, but she still needed her oxygen

Beth perched on the edge of one of the chairs, her purse clutched with both hands atop her locked knees.

Both Amelia and Beth were looking better. The former had more color in her cheeks and the latter more color in her hair. Beth looked more rested, and better dressed. She'd traded the house dress for tan slacks and a checkered blouse. And she'd had her nails done—something I desperately needed. I guessed she'd taken advantage of having no one to care for to get a little care for herself.

Even the most devoted daughter needs a break now and then.

"You're here early," I said to Beth.

"I was hoping to take Mom home."

Now here was an optimistic lady.

I turned to Amelia. "You're looking better this morning, but as long as you need that oxygen, I can't let you go."

Her face fell. "Oh."

Always quick with the platitude I said, "Better safe than sorry."

"Yes, Mom," Beth said. "Another day or two won't hurt."

As I was typing the progress note into the hospital tablet, Beth said, "Terrible about poor Marge Harris."

My fingers stopped on their own. Yes, poor Marge. I'd done some heavy thinking about her during my jog. I still didn't understand how she'd had a second major reaction in the space of forty-eight hours.

"Tragic," I said.

Beth lifted her chin. "Well, at least she was spared the humiliation of learning that her husband has been making a fool of her."

So there it was, right out in the open. Or was it? Stan had asked me out to dinner, but...

"Do you know that for a fact, Beth, or is it just something you heard?"

She sniffed. "I assure you, I am not in the habit of spreading gossip."

Like hell. Beth was the town crier.

"Then how—?"

"When you see a married man driving out of the parking lot of the Starlight Motel with a woman beside him, and that woman is not his wife, I think it's a safe assumption that he's up to no good. Wouldn't you agree?"

"Yes, I would. Did you recognize the woman?"

She shook her head. "No, it happened too quickly."

That probably meant someone from out of town. Not many people in Lebanon on whom Beth didn't have the proverbial skinny.

"What I can tell you," she added, "is that she most definitely was *not* Marge Harris." She sighed. "I'm just glad the poor woman never knew. But it would have been only a matter of time before she did."

She was right about that. The Starlight was a small single-level motel a ways south of town on 206. If Stan had been driving in and out of nearby motels with his paramour, Beth Henderson certainly wasn't the only one to know.

But I think Beth was wrong about Marge not knowing. I was pretty sure she knew *something*. Maybe not who, maybe not when and where, but she must have had strong suspicions. That would explain her frosty attitude toward Stan.

But how did all that fit in with the mysterious 9-1-1 call Trav had mentioned? Or why Marge's death had become a coroner's case?

I guessed I'd have to wait and see.

# 2

I returned to the old place and my old room where I changed into a navy blue nylon warm-up for a tennis match. You didn't think I'd wear white shorts or one of those cute little skirts, did you?

And that got me thinking again about Tezinex. Damn it, I was going to try it. I'd call Donna today and get some samples.

I was halfway into the pants when my cell phone rang. Giselle, calling from the office.

"*Dr. Norrie? I have someone from the sheriff's department on the line. He says he knows you and needs to speak to you.*"

"Who is it?"

"*Deputy Travis Lawton. He was here—*"

"I know him, Giselle. Put him through."

Travis came on the line and we exchanged the obligatory hellos and how-are-yous.

Then he said, "*You know, I wanted to contact you and realized I had no idea where you live. Plus your phone is unlisted. I could have pulled the deputy sheriff thing on the phone company, but figured it'd be easier and quicker to call your office.*"

I had a feeling this had something to do with Marge, but I kept it light.

"I'm speaking to you from my Fortress of Solitude—actually, the old family home." I gave him a quick rundown of the flood and he was properly sympathetic. "What's up?"

"*It's about Marge Harris.*"

Knew it.

"What about her?"

*"Can we meet someplace to talk?"*

I had about thirty minutes before I was due to hook up with the other three women in the doubles group. I'm a sub—I didn't want to commit to playing every Friday morning—and I fill in when one of the four regulars can't make it. This was one of those mornings.

"How about at the tennis center?" I said. "I can be there in about ten minutes."

*"So can I. See you there."*

"What's this about?"

*"A couple of things. One's about Marge, but the other's about you."*

"Oh?"

*"Talk to you at the tennis center."*

If he'd wanted to grab my attention, he'd succeeded. I hung up, pulled on the warm-up jacket, and hurried for my car.

# 3

When I arrived, Travis was already there, his sheriff's department cruiser parked in a corner of the lot. The white bubble dome of the tennis center loomed behind him like a giant turkey breast. He stepped out as I pulled in next to him. We met between the two cars.

He looked good in his starched, pressed uniform. He asked me a few questions about playing tennis, none of which I cared to answer, but did. I wanted to get to the meat.

Finally I said, "What's going on with Marge?"

He rubbed his jaw. "I'm not sure. But I wanted to ask you a sort of medical question."

I figured I could answer a medical question. But a "sort of medical" question?

"Shoot."

"The ME autopsied her and says he found only coffee and banana in her stomach."

"Nothing that might have contained peanuts?"

He shook his head. "Coffee and banana—nothing else."

"That's weird."

"Yeah, I know. So my question is, could the second reaction have been caused by or be a holdover from or somehow be related to the first?"

I'd been asking myself the same question. And now with no evidence that she'd ingested another peanut product, it loomed disturbingly larger.

"It's unlikely, but not impossible."

He made a face. "That's not what I was looking for. I could

use a clear yes or no."

"There aren't any absolutes in medicine, Trav. A body can react the same way nine-hundred-ninety-nine times in a row, and then do something different on the thousandth. Every doctor has seen it happen. You can prescribe, say, amoxicillin for someone who's had it a hundred times in the past fifty years with no problem, and then on the hundred-and-first time he breaks out in a rash. The reason is that somewhere between the hundredth and hundred-and-first exposures his immune system became sensitized to something on the amoxicillin molecule. Why, we can't say. Sometimes stuff just happens."

His frowned deepened. "Then you're telling me she could have had a reaction to coffee or the banana?"

"I'm not saying that at all. I'm saying that it's unlikely—highly unlikely—that Marge would have a second reaction without exposure to peanuts while she was on the dose of prednisone and other meds I'd prescribed for her. But I can't say it's impossible."

He sighed and shook his head. "I wish you could. It would make things a lot easier—for both of us."

A chill ran down my arms.

"Why do you say that?"

"I stopped by the Harris place and talked to Stan about his whereabouts when Marge had her reaction and—"

"New York, right?"

"So he says."

"Why wouldn't you believe him?"

"I just like to check all the facts."

"There's an evasive answer if I've ever heard one."

"It's a coroner's case and we're keeping certain things close to the vest for now."

"Like the 9-1-1 call?"

His eyes widened. "How do you know about that?"

"You told me. Yesterday, in the ER."

"Damn, I guess I did. Look, don't mention that to anyone, okay?"

"Never mind the call, you've hinted twice now that I'm somehow involved. What's that all about?"

"You're not officially involved, but as I was talking to Stan yesterday he kept mentioning you, how he'd thought all along that you sent Marge home too early. How he'd begged you to keep her another day but you ignored him, and on and on like that."

"He never begged me!"

Trav shrugged. "I can only tell you what he said. Sounded like he was working himself up to calling a lawyer."

My stomach plummeted. Another malpractice suit? Another person accusing me of negligence?

My dismay must have shown. Trav reached out and touched my upper arm.

"Hey, don't take it so hard. He's just blowing smoke. He'll—"

His police radio squawked. He stepped over to the idling car and grabbed the handset. I heard some garbled noise about a car fire. He turned to me and waved.

"Gotta run. Talk to you later. And don't worry. This'll all work out."

Then he was in the cruiser and roaring out of the parking lot.

Some of his last words came back to me. *He's just blowing smoke...*

An odd turn of phrase. Blowing off steam, okay... but smoke?

# 4

Well, after that, playing tennis was the last thing I felt like doing. My racquet became a hundred-pound weight as I carried it inside.

I found Jessica Welch standing in the small foyer beyond the glass door. She's about my age, but that's where the resemblance ends. She's slim and blonde and the third wife of Harry Welch, a vascular surgeon at least a quarter century older. She's not a stereotypical dumb blonde. She's bright with a streak of dark humor. I don't know what she sees in Harry… beyond financial security, that is.

"Norrie! I didn't know you were coming."

"Hi, Jessie. Carol called me yesterday and said she'd hurt her foot. So here I am."

"Great." She looked past my shoulder at the parking lot. "Who was that hunk I saw you talking to?"

Hunk… how odd to hear someone refer to Travis Lawton as a hunk. But that was what he'd become.

"Just an old friend from high school."

"Yeah?" Something in her tone said she didn't quite believe me. "None of my old friends from high school look like that." She leaned closer. "Don't you just *love* guys in uniform. I don't know why, but they do something to me."

"So, why don't you buy Harry a cop uniform?"

Her eyes widened as she grabbed my arm. "You know something? That's a *great* idea!"

I'd been kidding. Now I had visions of Jessie pretending to be a speeder… and Harry in his uniform pretending to pull her over... and Jessie doing whatever necessary to avoid being ticketed...

Some visions I can do very well without, thank you.

"Anyway," Jessie said, "Penny couldn't make it, so guess who's taking her place."

"Who?"

She pointed past me. "Look."

I turned and felt my heart do a little flip-flop when I saw Allie "Barbie" Lerner coming through the door.

"Allie!" Jessica cried. "Isn't this funny? Carol hurt her foot and look who's taking her place. How about that? It's Lebanon Family Practice Day!"

Allie smiled past me at Jessie. "Yes, how about that? Isn't that serendipity?"

I didn't think so, and I'm sure she didn't either. Maybe she meant synchronicity, but I doubted she'd ever heard the word. Sometimes it's hard to tell what Barbie means.

Holding the smile, she turned to me. "Hello, Norrie. How are you?"

"Fine, Allie. How about you?"

Her voice took on a touch of frost. "As well as can be expected."

Great. Ken must have called her right after yesterday's meeting and told her that Sam was bankrupting the group through astronomic pay raises and I was helping him.

"Well, you look great," I said, trying to start a thaw.

I wasn't lying. Allie had a long torso and long tan legs—a body made for tennis.

She nodded as if this were a given. "And you look... healthy."

I've tried to like Allie, really I have—even tried to stop thinking of her as Barbie—but it's hard.

No, it's impossible.

And for all I know, maybe it's equally impossible for her to warm up to me.

We don't run in the same circles: She has her doctors' wives circle and I don't have any circle to speak of outside Mum and Timmy. The only time we're in the same room is when the Glazers, the Lerners, and little old me go out to dinner as a group. If I had a husband—a doctor's husband... sounds kind of weird, doesn't it?—I suppose he'd be expected to come along too. The Glazers and Lerners have been doing this for years as a way to keep something personal in their partnership—adding a dimension to their relationship that went beyond the office.

Gee, I wonder whose idea that was. Let me guess...

But even at these dinners Allie tries to go one up on everybody, even on Sofia, who's very real and seems thoroughly unimpressed that her husband has an MD after his name. Allie is a prime example of the keep-up-with-the-Ozes type of doctor's wife.

Janie Ryan, faked and baked though she might be, is ten times more real than Allie Lerner.

No, make that *Barbie* Lerner.

Any cold, hardshell plastic blonde married to a Ken—even if the real Ken and Barbie have broken up—is a *Barbie*.

Barbie forever.

But what model? How about Doctor-Wife Barbie?

You can't tell I'm stressed, can you? I hide it so well.

Before I could say something I'd regret, Hillary Moore, our fourth, arrived.

I like Hillary. She's older—maybe fifty—but she's half Italian like me and married to Jeff Moore the dermatologist. She has short, sandy hair and a tight, trim body. I was the heaviest one here, but what else was new?

Jessie had the bright idea of teaming the two subs together. I knew her reasoning: Allie was an unknown quantity and Hillary was the best of their regular foursome. She's got twenty years on all of us yet she seems to know where your shot is going to land before you hit it and she's there waiting for it.

Need I say we got killed?

I like tennis, and I'm not a bad player. I love to hustle and can move a lot faster than people expect. But even with Hillary as my partner we'd have lost.

I freely admit that my play today was malodorous to the max. Tennis is a game that lives or dies on your level of concentration. If you focus on the ball, never letting your eyes leave it till it hits your racket, you can play a decent game even without a ton of athletic skill. But lose that concentration and you're dead, even if you have the skills of the Williams sisters.

My concentration level was somewhere south of zero. Too many other things on my mind, plus I'd started watching Hillary—trying to anticipate her next move—instead of the ball. Poison.

On our side of the net, Tennis Player Barbie was no help. She doesn't move. Hit the ball to her and she returns it pretty well, but no way is she going to risk a scuff on those lovely Nikes by scrambling for a passing shot.

Jessie hustles more than Barbie, but not by many orders of magnitude.

Which left the scrambling to Hillary and me.

When it was over I was drenched inside my warm-up and Hillary was panting. She shook my hand over the net and said, *sotto voce*, "At least *we* got a workout."

"I hardly ever get to play these days," Barbie was saying to Jessie. "A little more practice and a more even match-up and I could really give you a game."

I had this sudden, wonderful vision of my racquet around her neck.

She turned to Hillary. "But no matter what, there was no way I could win today."

"Oh?" Hillary said with a quick glance at me. "Why is that?"

"My advisor told me."

"Your financial advisor?"

Barbie laughed. "Oh, no. That's Ken's department. My *psychic* advisor."

I noticed Hillary making a heroic effort to keep a straight face. Her husband, after all, depended on referrals from primary care docs like Ken.

"And… and what did he predict?"

Spiritualist Barbie said, "He told me that Friday would not be a good-luck day for me. And you know what else I learned?" She put her arm around Jessie's shoulders. "Rocha is Jessie's advisor too. Isn't it ironic?"

Ironic? Not even close. She must have listened to Alanis too often.

"How about that?" Hillary said. She'd won the battle for the straight face.

Barbie stretched. "Ooh, I'm so out of shape, I *know* I'm going to regret this. I'll probably have to take a power nap later. Exercise makes me so tiresome by late afternoon."

I was familiar with Malaprop Barbie, so I was cool. But even Jessie blinked. And poor Hillary almost lost it. I saw her turn away and bite down on her index finger—just like my father used to do—and I loved her for it.

When Socialite Barbie began talking about going out to lunch, I took that as my cue to beg off because of impending office hours.

I reached the parking lot and just about ran for my car.

# 5

Showered and back in my pantsuit, I arrived at the office just before one and caught Sam as he finished morning hours. He looked a little better today—maybe because he knew he had the rest of the day off.

Yesterday I'd told him the news about Marge, but now I filled him in on the details—her treatment and what happened to her. I needed some reassurance.

"That's a real puzzler," he said.

"Do you think I should have kept her another night?"

"Of course."

"Oh." My heart plummeted. "But—"

Sam held up his hand. "But I'm speaking from the perspective of a Monday morning quarterback. I know she had a second anaphylactic reaction and I know that the best place to have one is in a hospital. So, yes, keeping her another night would have saved her life."

"But the prednisone—"

"The proper question to ask is, given the information available on Wednesday morning, would I have kept her. My answer to that is a resounding no."

I released a breath I hadn't realized I'd been holding. "You just made my day."

He smiled. "Don't beat yourself up for not being able to predict the future, Norrie. We have to correlate available data with experience and make the best decision we can."

"Tell that to Stan Harris."

I heard Ken's voice say, "What about Stan Harris?"

I turned and found him standing in the doorway. Oh, hell.

I cleared my throat. "A cop I know says he was making litigious noises about Marge's death."

Ken's mouth tightened into a thin line as he closed his eyes for a few seconds. Then he opened them and looked at Sam.

"You know what this is going to do to her malpractice premium? Two suits in one year? It'll go through the roof!"

Hey! I wanted to shout. You can talk to me. I'm only a couple of feet away.

Instead I kept my voice steady and said, "There is no suit, just talk. You can't blame him for being upset over his wife's death."

"Blame," Ken said, focusing on me now. "That's the whole problem. When something bad happens, people want to blame someone. All you need is Stark the Shark to get wind of it and he'll be in Harris's ear promising a big payoff." He shook his head. "You're off to a great start, aren't you."

And then he walked out—no good-bye to either Sam or me. Just gone.

"Thanks for the support and sympathy," I said to the empty doorway.

"He's just upset," Sam said.

"*He*'s upset, *I'm* upset, Stan Harris is upset, Theodore Phelan is upset. What's happening here? This isn't how it's supposed to be."

I felt a lump grow in my throat. I didn't go through all those years of training to upset people. I was here to ease upset and pain and malaise. But it wasn't working out that way. At least it didn't seem to be.

Sam rose and shrugged into a tweed sport coat. "What did I tell you about beating up on yourself. Look at these troubles in a wider view. As for Marge Harris in particular, I don't believe— to use a lawyerly phrase—that you deviated from the accepted standards of medical care."

"Since when does that matter?"

He sighed. "Yes, well, there's always that to contend with."

# 6

With Sam and Ken had gone, and the office closed down for lunch hour, I had the place to myself: Alone with my troubles.

*...didn't deviate from the accepted standards of medical care...* if that was supposed to make me feel better, it failed. Miserably.

The big problem was the helplessness I felt. Lots of us go into medicine because we're problem solvers. I'm no exception. I'm pretty good at solving other people's problems but here I was with a set of my own and nothing I could do about them. I wasn't allowed to go to the source of one of them—Ted Phelan. My lawyer—who hadn't been assigned yet—was supposed to do all the talking for me. That's why they call them mouthpieces, I guess.

Instead of calling Ted Phelan, I called the Cobdica rep instead. Donna was delighted to hear that I wanted to try Tezinex and said she'd be over after hours with samples and "supplies." When I asked her what that meant, she said only, "You'll see."

Work turned out to be a tonic this time around. The late session on Friday is always hectic. I'm the only doctor there, so I have to take all the calls. That worked to my advantage today. The pace helped me put my grief and worries and anger aside. As I got into the rhythm of diagnosis, treatment, and maintenance evaluation, they faded away.

Until Connie, the part-timer who works Giselle's job on Friday's late session, called back that a "policeman" was here and wanted to speak to me. When I learned it was Travis I told her to send him back.

What bad news was he bringing this time? Wasn't once a day enough?

"Got a minute?" he said as he stepped into my office.

Jessie's hunk comment came back to me as I appreciated the way his shoulders filled his uniform shirt.

"Just barely." That came out with an unintended edge. "Don't take that wrong: I'm the only one here, and sometimes it gets crazy."

He smiled. "I'm about to make it crazier."

Just what I needed.

"How?"

His smile faded. "By asking you a very weird question. As you know, we found no peanut or peanut product in Marge's stomach. So... what I want to know is..." He paused as if unsure of how I was going to take it, then said, "Is it possible that someone could have forced a peanut into Marge's mouth to cause the reaction, then removed it?"

I could only stare at him. Where on Earth had he come up with that idea?

Trav looked embarrassed. "Warned you. But it's not as crazy as it sounds. I did some research. Do you know there's a whole bunch of websites devoted to peanut allergy? I spent some time on *peanutallergy-dot-com*—I'm not kidding—and—"

"I believe you. There's a dot-com or dot-org for everything."

"Anyway, I learned that with highly allergic people all it takes is the tiniest bit of peanut to set them off."

I nodded. "Right. Some people are so sensitive to a certain substance—an antibiotic, bee venom, whatever—that just a few molecules can trigger a fatal reaction."

"So the answer is yes."

"A very definite yes. But putting a peanut in Marge's mouth would be... I mean, you're talking murder."

His expression was grave. "I know."

Murder by peanut? He didn't look drunk or drugged. But this was so far out there... like something I'd expect my Uncle Timmy to come up with.

I said, "Okay, let's just say someone did force a peanut into her mouth. Don't you think there'd be signs of a struggle? She wouldn't just sit there and let someone do that. She'd fight them off—I mean, it's only a peanut to us, but it's a life-or-death matter for someone like Marge. She'd kick and claw and—did the ME find signs of a struggle?"

I'd seen Marge in the altogether after she'd died and hadn't noticed any bruises. But then, I hadn't been looking for any. I'd been more interested in restarting her heart.

Trav shook his head. "Not a one—no bruises, no ligature marks, no skin under the fingernails."

"Besides, who would want to murder Marge Harris? And why?"

He shrugged. "Those are questions I have to answer."

"Wait-wait-wait," I said. "Aren't you getting ahead of yourself? Don't you first have to have evidence of foul play?"

"Yeah."

"And do you?"

His expression was glum. "No."

"Then where did this idea come from?"

"From the 9-1-1 call."

"What was it?"

"I shouldn't be discussing this with you. We're still in the very early stages."

"Of *what*?"

"The investigation of Marge Harris's death."

His evasiveness was maddening.

I glanced at my watch. I could feel the patients stacking up in the waiting room.

"I've got to get back to work, but let me say this: You came to me with a question and I answered it. You dangle these awful possibilities in front of me, then snatch them away without an explanation. This should be a two-way street, Trav. Marge was not just my patient, she was an old friend. I think I deserve to know what's going on. And as for keeping secrets, you wouldn't believe what I know about certain people in this town. But you'll never hear about it from me." I waggled my fingers at him. "Come on. Give."

He sighed. "Here's what we assume: It appears Marge had a breakfast of coffee and a banana—her husband says she was always on one kind of diet or another—and then started her Thursday morning routine of paying the week's bills. Around 8:30 or a little before, she began having the reaction.

"How do you know?"

"Because her 9-1-1 call came in at 8:32. First aid and police units responded immediately but, as you know, they were too late."

Too late... if only...

"Okay. But where'd you get this crazy idea about someone forcing a peanut into her?"

"Not so crazy if you'd heard the 9-1-1 tape."

I waited for him to go on, but he didn't.

"Well? Aren't you going to tell me?"

"I'd rather you heard it yourself."

"Come on—"

"No, really. You need to hear her voice. It sounded really strange. Like she was being strangled."

I could have told him then and there what had caused that: Laryngeal edema was shutting down her airway. But I held back. If I told him now I might not get to hear that tape. And I wanted to hear what had made Trav start thinking about murder.

"I don't get it. First I'm not supposed to know what's on the tape, now I'm supposed to listen to it?"

"Why not? I'm thinking I can bring you in as a medical consultant. Hincher will go for that. I'll just tell him I want your expert opinion."

"Don't you have a crime-scene team for that sort of stuff?"

His smile was sour. "I wish. We're a rural county. We can call in a team from the state when we need to, but—"

"Why haven't you?"

"Because the ME hasn't found any signs of foul play. As of now, it's death by allergy."

"And the sheriff won't object?"

"Well, not only are you a doctor, you were Marge's personal physician, and maybe you'll hear something in her voice that we don't." He nodded. "Yeah. That'll fly."

I had a sudden suspicion that Trav wasn't involving me simply to answer a few questions and offer my insight on a 9-1-1 tape. That was part of it, I'm sure, but I had this niggling sense that he was using Marge as way to connect to me.

Or was that simply wishful thinking?

Could Travis Lawton be experiencing the same growing attraction I was feeling toward him?

I decided to test the waters.

"Okay. I'll be your medical consultant. But what's in it for me?"

A hurt look passed across his face. "I don't know if there's anything in the budget to pay you a fee, but—"

"Fee, schmee. You already owe me a lunch. This is going to ratchet that up to a dinner."

His eyes lit. "You are *on*."

"And I want to collect tonight—at Antoine's, right after I hear this tape."

"Deal. Just say when and I'll pick you up at your mom's place."

I told him to pick me up here at the office instead.

After he left I stood there a moment longer. As much as I was flattered by the attention, I had to ask myself if I wanted to get involved with a man with whom I had a history. Not that we had a romantic history—at least not on his part—but we couldn't help but have preconceived notions about each other. And whatever we'd had in common back then was long gone. We were two different people now, separated by a gulf of culture and experience.

Have you noticed how sometimes I overthink things?

# 7

I'd called and told Mum I wouldn't be home for dinner. She had a slew of questions but I dodged them by saying I had to get back to my patients. I finished with my last patient just as Donna showed up. We spoke after I closed us off in my consultation room. I didn't need the staff to know I was taking a diet pill.

"Okay, here's the deal," she said as she placed a bunch of blister-pack samples on the desk. "One pill under the tongue every morning followed by watching a two-minute online video."

"Sublingual?"

She nodded. "As you know, you get the best and quickest absorption that way. We want to get it into your bloodstream ASAP. But the video is a must."

"Really?" Sounded like a bore. "Some sort of motivational spiel?"

"It's simply a pep talk that lays out dietary suggestions for the day. I've read through the clinical trial summaries and there's no question we got significantly better results with the videos on board. The control group that didn't have the video option lagged behind in total weight loss."

"Okay. If you say so."

She placed a three-by-five card on the desk. "That's the website URL and the password to get you in. And one more thing." She reached down into her sample case and came up with two boxes. "Tezinex brand goodies."

I hadn't expected this. "What?"

"We'll be marketing high-protein power bars and shake mix to go with the program. People can use any brand they prefer, but these are nutritionally balanced to keep your cells from going into starvation mode while providing you with few enough calories to guarantee you're burning off your fat."

I shrugged. "I'll try them."

Why not?

"But I really want you to come to my dinner Monday night. Really. You'll be glad you did."

She'd called it "*my*" dinner. After she'd made a special trip to bring me all these samples, I found it hard to say no.

"Okay. Add me to the list."

"Great!" she said with a bright smile. "Doctor Lerner's coming so the two of you can drive in together."

Oh, no. That was not going to happen. Half an hour cooped up with Ken and no escape? No thank you.

She left me her card and wrote her personal cell number on the back. "Call me with any questions or any problems."

Donna and the office staff were gone home by the time Trav pulled up. The sight of his police cruiser startled me, but then I realized I should have expected it. He was here, after all, on official business.

He got out and held the door for me, chauffeur style.

"Madam, your carriage awaits."

"Thank you, Jeeves."

I was trying to keep this light. I was about to hear Marge's last words and wasn't sure I could handle it.

I'd never been in a police car—or maybe I should say a deputy sheriff's car. The first thing I noticed was the short-barreled shotgun fixed upright in a rack between the driver and passenger seat backs. When I dragged my gaze away from that I noticed all the rest of the equipment. It looked like someone had robbed a Best Buy.

As Trav slipped behind the wheel I waved my hands around. "What is all this... *stuff*?"

He started pointing to things. "Well, that's the radio, here's the GPS, this is the onboard computer—"

"Where you play *Grand Theft Auto*, right?"

A tolerant smile: "Only on Tuesdays. No, we use it to run plates and licenses of people we pull over." He pointed to a contraption suspended by the rearview mirror. "And this video camera records the stop. That way no one can accuse us of getting rough with them or performing an illegal search when we didn't."

"Like you see on *Cops*?"

"Yeah. Like you see on *Cops*. "

"Can we get involved in a high-speed chase on our way to the station? Please?"

He put the car into gear. "I'll see what I can do."

As we pulled out of the office lot I put on a deep, official-sounding tone. "Any breaks in the case, detective?"

"Detective? I wish. That would mean a nice raise. But we don't have detectives in the Sheriff's Department."

"Why not?"

"The County Prosecutor's office has the homicide unit."

He drove us onto Route 70 and headed toward the sinking sun. A flood of memories drenched me when we exited into Carmel a few miles later. I never come this way... never see this part of the town where I grew up.

People hear Carmel and automatically think of the California Carmel. The Maryland Carmel shares only a name with its West Coast cousin. It's the county seat—which explains the sheriff's office here—and slightly larger than Lebanon, but other than that the two towns are virtually indistinguishable.

To an outsider, that is. To me there's a world of difference: Carmel was home.

Like Lebanon, Carmel straddles the interstate with its fast food joints and gas stations clustered near the overpass. But unlike Lebanon it has a true center of town, a real Main Street that's home to the sheriff's office, the courthouse, the county jail, and the county administration buildings.

I came to Carmel these days via the backroads, to the old homestead and back. No other reason to visit. I hadn't maintained any of the paltry number of friendships I'd had in high school—my high-school years were, in fact, ones I'd rather forget. So, no nostalgic magnet to draw me back.

But now that I was here…

"Jesus, Trav. What's happened? Where's Ciesla's Dress Shop? And Drysdale's Hardware? And the Book Nook?"

Carmel wasn't what it used to be, and it had never been much. Not that I'd expected the town to put itself into suspended animation once I'd left, but these places had been Main Street landmarks.

"All gone."

"You mean they moved?"

"No. Gone—as in closed up, dead, out of business. Couldn't keep up with Amazon and the Walmart."

We'd passed the huge superstore on our way in.

I pointed to a familiar storefront. "Look. Is that Phil's? It's still in business?"

"Yeah, but Phil isn't. Died a few years ago. His brother runs it now."

Phil's ice cream shop had been the place where all the cool kids from school used to hang. Which had sort of left Trav and me out. Not that they would keep you out, but if you did happen to wander in, they'd look on you as an intruder. You know, like What's someone like *you* doing in *our* place. And a gal my size back then didn't like to be seen in an ice cream shop anyway. I could almost hear people thinking, *The last thing that one needs is a sundae.*

But every so often I'd sneak in and treat myself to a cone of Phil's chocolate peanut butter swirl. Homemade ice cream—Walmart could never offer that.

Trav pulled into the lot by the sheriff's office, parked in a patrol-car-only spot, and led me inside. He gave a few waves, a "Hi" here and there as we traveled a hallway, and then he ushered me into a small, brightly lit room furnished with a scarred wooden table and two chairs. What looked like an old-time portable radio sat on the table.

"This is usually a sweat—I mean an interrogation room," Trav said, pulling out a chair and holding it for me.

I sat. "Where you give suspects the third degree?"

"Yeah. The other name is the 'sweat room.' I knew you were coming so I hid the rubber hoses and phone books."

"Phone books?"

"Sure." He was moving to the chair on the far side of the table. "You can bat someone around, even knock them out with the Baltimore yellow pages and hardly leave a mark."

I stared at him. What kind of world did Trav live in?

He held up his hands. "Not that I've ever done such a thing, or seen it. I've just heard about it."

The half-smile playing around his lips left me unsure as to what he was kidding about: The phone books, or his never having used one.

"Of course."

I looked around at the walls and wondered how much pain and frightened sweat they'd witnessed, how many brutal, sordid stories they'd heard. I suddenly wished we were somewhere else.

"Okay," Trav said, pulling a thumb drive from his breast pocket. "I dubbed this off the master recording and it's a nice clear copy. You'll hear everything there is to hear."

He inserted the drive into the radio—which I realized then was also some sort of mp3 player—and pressed a button on its top. I heard a few clicks, and then a woman's voice.

# 8

"*E*mergency services. *How may I help you?*"
 I heard a cough, then a gasping, rasping, distorted voice that sounded only vaguely female.

"*Help! Please... help!*"

"*Yes, ma'am. Where are you?*"

"*Help! I... can't... breathe! He's... trying to... kill me!*"

A chill rippled over my skin. Marge's voice, barely recognizable. It sounded as if she was being garroted.

"*Who is, ma'am?*"

"*Please! Oh, God! He's... killing me!*"

And then a clatter as the phone dropped. The operator went on talking, her voice louder, her words quicker, her tone more urgent.

"*Ma'am, I have your address from the phone number. I'm sending assistance right now. Hang on, ma'am. Help is on the way.*"

But behind the operator's voice I could hear tortured gasping and wheezing, and then that stopped. But that wasn't the end. I heard thumps and crashes as Marge's body thrashed on the floor in its air-starved death throes. And then everything stopped.

The sudden silence was worse, because I knew she'd never regained consciousness.

Oh, Marge... dear God, Marge...

I'd just heard the end of her life.

# 9

Trav hit the stop button and we sat in silence—out of respect and shock.

I'd wanted to hear this... now I wished I hadn't.

The room suddenly felt hot and small and stuffy, and I realized my skin was sheathed in a cold sweat. I pulled a tissue from my bag and blotted my face.

"Well," Trav said. "What do you think?"

Think? I was thinking it would be awful enough listening to that happening to a stranger... but this had been Marge... my Marge.

I finally found my voice. "That was... wrenching."

He nodded. "I've listened to it a good three dozen times in the past two days, and it still gets to me." He looked at me. "Still think my question this afternoon was crazy?"

I shook my head. "No."

"Doesn't it sound as if someone's strangling her? Yet there's not a mark on her. How do you strangle someone without leaving a mark?"

"From the inside."

Now it was his turn to look at me as I'd been smoking something.

"What? How?"

"In these fatal reactions, the inside of your larynx"—I touched my throat—"that's your voice box here, the Adam's apple on a guy. It's the gateway to your lungs. But in an anaphylactic reaction its lining swells, narrowing, sometimes even sealing the opening."

"The ME said it was 'death by asphyxiation.' So I guess

you're saying she was choked to death by her own body."

"Right."

I tried to imagine how Marge must have felt during her last moments…

I couldn't. I wasn't up to it.

"All caused by an allergic reaction?"

I nodded. "Right."

"Then where's the peanut?"

"Better question: Where was her EpiPen?"

"You mean the emergency adrenaline injection?"

I nodded. "I prescribed one for her when she left the hospital. It could have—*should* have saved her life."

"We found it. In the master bathroom. That brings up another question: She had to know she was having a reaction. Why didn't she just inject herself instead of wasting time calling 9-1-1?"

"Where's the master bath?"

"Upstairs."

"And where was Marge found?"

"Downstairs in a little room she used as her office."

"There's your answer. A severe reaction like Marge's drops the blood pressure so low you can't even stand; climbing stairs would be impossible. Making that call was her only option, and probably took every bit of will and strength she had."

"Killed by a peanut." He shook his head. "I can't wrap my brain around that. I can see how a bee sting could kill you—after all, it's a poison, right? But how does a person develop a fatal allergy to peanuts? They're everywhere."

I paused, gathering my thoughts and trying to convert them into layman's terms.

"It boils down to a misfire of the immune system. Some even say it's the result of a bored immune system."

He frowned. "Bored? How does your immune system get bored?"

"It doesn't really. I was anthropomorphizing a chemical process that no one fully understands."

I saw his eyes cloud at "anthropomorphizing" and realized it was an unfamiliar term, but I didn't want to bruise his ego by explaining.

"Let's get down to basics," I said quickly. "What do you know about the human immune system?"

Trav shrugged. "It protects you from infection."

"Right. And in the old days, before indoor plumbing, it was going full blast twenty-four/seven. Pathogenic bacteria and viruses were rampant, on every surface, in every bite you ate. Plus everyone played host to a variety of intestinal parasites like tapeworms, hookworms, and round worms."

He made a face. "How did we survive?"

"A lot of us didn't. But the ones who did wound up with immune systems that were locked and loaded against a vast array of infections. A better armed system than we modern-day Americans have. Stick one of us in Elizabethan England and within twenty-four hours we'd be so sick we'd wish we could die. Montezuma's revenge would be a walk in the park compared to what you'd catch there."

"Yeah, I've always wondered why Mexicans can drink all the water they want and not get sick."

"Because they've been exposed since birth to the bacteria that causes *turista*. They're immune."

"So what's this got to do with peanuts?"

"Everything. Immune globulin E—IgE for short—is a protein the body produces to fight infections, particularly parasitic infections like intestinal worms and protozoans. In the good old days everybody carried one sort of worm or another, and so IgE had its hands full. But these days, at least here in the US, intestinal parasites are the exception, so there's lots less call for that type of IgE. Some theorize that because of this modern lack of activity, IgE is reacting to proteins that are not a threat."

"Like the proteins in a peanut?"

"Exactly."

"So that's what you meant by 'bored.'"

"Right. Another example is a study that found that kids in daycare had a significantly lower incidence of asthma—another IgE-mediated reaction—than kids who stayed home with Mommy. The daycare kids were exposed to lots more infections, which kept their immune systems busy. The sheltered-at-home kids weren't, leaving their immune systems free to start reacting against innocent inhalants."

I searched for an analogy...

"Imagine a computerized antiaircraft artillery system. Every time it's alerted, it responds with projectiles tailor-made to shoot down the invading planes. It stores images of those planes and keeps the special ammo handy for the next time it sees one. This is pretty much how the body fights viruses, and why you get chickenpox or measles only once: Your body has seen those viruses before and is ready for them."

Trav was nodding. "Got it."

"But if the system isn't kept busy, it's likely to start identifying neutrals or even friendlies as foes. Pollen isn't a threat to the human body, and I'll bet there wasn't a single cavemen with hay fever—their immune systems were too busy with tapeworms and lice and ticks, and so on. You don't have to go back even that far: There are *no* recorded cases of hay fever before 1800. But nowadays something like fifteen percent of the population suffers from it."

"All because pollen is being entered into the databanks as an enemy."

I nodded. He had it.

"Same with the peanut protein that triggers reactions in people like Marge. It's a nutrient that will help feed the body, but it's been tagged as an enemy and so the body attacks it with everything it has."

Trav was shaking his head. "Scary. But people don't die from hay fever. Or do they?"

"No, but that's a local reaction. Bee-sting and peanut reactions are often systemic—anywhere from hives to vomiting and diarrhea to, well, death."

Like poor Marge...

He slapped the tabletop and pointed to me. "See? I did the right thing bringing you in on this. You've earned that dinner."

Dinner... the last thing I wanted to do right now was eat.

"The dinner was kind of a joke. I won't hold you to it."

"No way. I always pay my debts, and this is one I *want* to pay."

That made me feel good enough to smile.

"Well, since you put it that way..."

"I mean it. But back to Marge: She's having this reaction and she calls emergency services. All well and good. But then she tells the operator 'He's trying to kill me!' Who's 'he'?"

"Isn't the husband always the prime suspect?"

"Damn right. But Stan Harris says he was at a meeting in New York."

"Is that confirmed?"

"Not yet. I've been trying to get in touch with the other people he said were there but they aren't returning my calls."

"Even if he was in New York, that doesn't mean he couldn't have had something to do with it."

"You mean he might have, say, hired someone to force a peanut into Marge's mouth?"

"He wouldn't have had to. He could have taken something she liked to eat and laced it with peanuts."

"How do you lace coffee and a banana with peanuts?"

"I haven't the faintest. Inject the banana with a smidgen of peanut butter maybe?"

He leaned back, frowning. "Hadn't thought of that. The ME was specifically on the lookout for a peanut-containing product. He could have missed a tiny bit of peanut butter." His frown deepened. "But then how would she have known it was Stan?"

Talking about possible ways my old friend could have been murdered was making the walls close in.

"Could we continue this somewhere else?"

Trav's thick eyebrows shot up. "Hmm? Oh sure. Why don't we go to Antoine's and finish up there?"

Antoine's Steakhouse was Lebanon's only decent restaurant. But I'd had steak last night and, even if I hadn't, I couldn't face a big hunk of red meat right now.

"How about a raincheck? I'm not very hungry."

His face fell. "Oh. Want me to take you home?"

I wanted that even less than a steak.

"No. But I'll bet *you're* hungry."

"Starved."

An idea hit. "Is the Gold Star still around?"

"Sure is."

"Then let's go there."

# 10

The Gold Star was probably one of the first eateries in Carson County. An institution. A Carmel landmark. I'd have been shocked if Trav had told me it had closed.

A wave of nostalgia hit me as we pulled up in front of it. Same shiny aluminum siding, nicked and dented by years of exposure to clumsy people and the elements, same yellow neon shooting star atop the roof. I remembered Sunday morning breakfasts here with Sean. I was fourteen and he was in college at the time. He was a day-hopper, commuting to Loyola in Baltimore. He would have loved to have lived there but our folks could barely afford the tuition; the room and board fee for on-campus living was out of reach.

Mum and Dad always went to nine o'clock mass at St. Catherine's. As soon as Sean got his driver's license he started sleeping in and going to one of the later masses. That seemed like a good idea to me, so I began sleeping later too and hitching a ride with him.

But not to mass. That very first Sunday I learned an awful truth: Sean didn't go to mass.

He swung by the church, dropped me off by the side entrance, and said, "I'll pick you up later after it's over."

I was shocked, stunned, aghast.

"You're not coming in?"

"No. And don't even *think* about telling Mum."

That might seem silly—a college boy afraid to let his folks know he'd fallen away from the church—but you had to know our folks, especially Mum. Much of our family life revolved around the church and the Pope. The Holy Father's every utterance was law. If Sean went public with his mass-less life, he'd never know a moment's peace in our home.

"But Sean—"

He put the car in gear. "Oh, and make sure to hold onto a copy of the bulletin."

He roared off leaving me standing there, baffled and afraid. Not for myself, for Sean. In those days—maybe it's still so, but I wouldn't know—deliberately missing Sunday mass was a mortal sin. Sean was risking eternal damnation. Unless he confessed and did penance, he'd never get to heaven, never see God. What if he got himself killed in a car crash while he was cutting out on mass...?

I went inside and prayed for my brother. When I came out he was waiting.

"You bring the bulletin?" he said as I got in.

I nodded and showed it to him.

Like just about every other Catholic church, St. Catherine's gave out a folded sheet on Sundays listing upcoming events, announcements, a list of the week's masses and liturgies. On the back page local merchants and the lawyers and accountants in the parish would buy space for tiny ads. Sean apparently considered arriving home with a bulletin in his hand as silent evidence of where he'd been.

"Great. Who said it?"

"Father Cancella."

He smiled. "This is gonna work out great"—then he gave me a hard look—"*if* you keep your mouth shut."

"You're going to go to hell, Sean!"

He sighed. "Yeah, most likely. Assuming there is such a place."

The note of resignation in his voice twisted something inside me. Not until years later did I discover the reason behind his tone.

This went on for about a month. I kept his secret, though I wondered if that might be a sin in itself. And throughout that month I watched for signs of God's displeasure with Sean—bad luck, illness, even a rash—but everything remained fine with him. I, the mass goer, on the other hand, was packing on the pounds while he stayed slim and trim.

So one Sunday morning I mustered up the courage to tell Sean that I was skipping too. He didn't like the idea, but I didn't give him much choice. So he had me run inside, grab a bulletin, and find out which priest was saying mass.

Then we hit the road.

We ended up at the Gold Star where he went every Sunday and killed the forty-or-so minutes of the mass drinking coffee and smoking cigarettes and talking to some guy I'd never seen before. His name was Gary and he was pretty cool. And I felt pretty cool too—a real rebel, skipping mass and hanging out with these two older guys. I wasn't Mommy and Daddy's little girl anymore, at least not completely. I'd taken the first step toward being myself and it felt *wonderful*.

But none of that kept me from going to confession every so often to cleanse my soiled soul.

# 11

I was glad to see that the Gold Star Diner looked pretty much the same inside as well. I knew it must have been refurbished in all the years I'd been gone, but they hadn't changed the retro look: still the Formica-topped, chrome-edged tables, the garish red vinyl on the seats.

As we entered, Trav nodded to a swarthy man with a thick Saddam-style mustache and pointed toward the left. The man nodded back and we headed down the aisle.

"Kind of deserted," I said, looking around at the sparsely populated booths. The counter was empty.

"Wait till the movies start getting out."

Trav led me to an isolated booth at the rear. A middle-aged beehived waitress straight out of central casting approached and gave Trav a motherly smile. Her name tag read *Carlene*.

"Well, well. Howdy, stranger. Ain't seen you around for a while. I—" She squinted at the Band-Aid and surrounding bruise on Trav's forehead. "What happened?"

Trav shrugged and smiled. "All in the line of duty. Been working undercover for the CIA. Very hush-hush. If I told you about it I'd have to kill you."

She laughed and handed us menus. "What can I get you folks?"

"The usual," Trav said without opening his menu.

I glanced through mine but couldn't find what I was look-ing for.

"Would it be possible to get some scrambled eggs?"

"We stop serving breakfast at eleven, hon."

"Hey, Carlene," Trav said. "You're not exactly overwhelmed with customers at the moment. Use your charm to convince Sammy to crack a few eggs for the lady here."

Carlene patted him on the shoulder. "Only for you, deputy. Only for you."

She took our drink orders—coffee for Trav, a Diet Sprite for me—and bustled off.

As soon as Carlene was gone Travis leaned across the table and spoke in a low voice. "Another thing: What if Marge only *thought* Stan had poisoned her?"

He wasn't going to let go of this. Like a dog with a bone, he was going to gnaw it down to the marrow.

"That's a possibility."

He shook his head. "Yeah, but why would she think that?"

And suddenly I found myself faced with an ethical dilemma. Or maybe not. I knew things about the Harris marriage, but I'd learned them indirectly. She hadn't confided in me, but I'd observed unmistakable signs of marital stress. Was that privileged?

And how far did privilege go when the patient had died under suspicious circumstances?

Then I heard her strangled voice.

*He's... killing me!*

That did it. If I could help in any way, then I should do so.

"I think their marriage was in trouble."

Trav stiffened and leaned forward. "Yeah? What do you know?"

"I don't *know* anything per se, but I saw them interacting in the hospital, and Marge was definitely unhappy with Stan."

"Unhappy how?"

"Angry... hostile... frosty."

"And Stan?"

"Very solicitous."

He leaned back. "Uh-oh."

"What?"

"He got caught at something. And ninety-nine times out of a hundred that something—"

He cut off as the waitress brought our drinks.

Carlene winked at me. "I had to twist Sammy's arm and bend him over the grill, but your scrambled eggs are on the way."

"Thanks," I said, and winked back. "You're good. You're very good."

Her face lit up. She didn't have to ask what I was talking about. She recognized a former waitress when she saw one.

"I've had enough practice," she said with a smile. "Your food'll be out in a few secs."

I enjoy watching a good waiter or waitress plying their trade: Working the crowd, playing to the various personalities. It's a challenge, it can be fun, and it definitely pays off in bigger tips.

"Where were we?" Trav said when we were alone again.

"Something about ninety-nine times out of a hundred—"

"Oh, yeah. When you see a huffy wife and a guy falling all over her to make her happy, it means he's in the doghouse, and ninety-nine times out of a hundred he's there because of another woman."

How does he know that? I wondered. Personal experience? Was his marriage kaput because he'd been fooling around?

Not my business.

But Marge was.

"Beth Henderson told me Stan's been fooling around."

He leaned forward. "How would she know?"

"Saw him pulling out of the Starlight with another woman in the front seat."

"She recognize her?"

"No—at least she says not."

Trav gave a low whistle. "I think it's time to check on the Harris's insurance policies."

"Do that. But also check Marge's pantry and her pocketbook for anything that might contain even a hint of peanut."

"But even if we find something, so what? It's not what's in her pantry that counts, it's what's in her stomach."

He was right. But I had my reasons for wanting evidence of a second exposure to peanuts.

"Okay, let's think about her stomach: Nothing obviously peanut there, we're told. But what about something not so obvious? She could have been sucking on a piece of, say, hard candy that contained a bit of peanut extract in the mix. The dissolved candy would hit her stomach as a small amount of liquid, mixed with saliva. It could go completely unnoticed."

"Never thought about that." He smiled and nodded. "Now I'll tell you what you told Carlene: You're good. You're very good."

"Not as good as I need to be. I don't know much about forensics beyond what I glean from *CSI*, but it seems to me there must be some sort of chemical test that can detect the presence of a peanut product or byproduct in her stomach contents."

"Good idea. I'll ask the ME. If there's no trace of peanut, and no recent big insurance policy with Stan as beneficiary, that pretty much takes him off the hook."

And could put me on it.

No peanut trace would open the door to linking the second reaction to the first. *Post hoc, ergo propter hoc.* But I still didn't see how that was possible, given the meds she'd been taking.

"You should still search her house," I said. "And I'll come along to help—to add a medical point of view."

I hoped he wouldn't ask me to elaborate on that. I'd be hard pressed to explain what a medical point of view would add to his search. But I knew what it could add to mine.

"You'd do that?" Trav said.

"Of course. Marge was a patient of mine. I want to know what happened."

That was the absolute truth. I couldn't pass up any chance, no matter how slim, to get to the bottom of this. I owed it to Marge. Maybe Stan Harris's litigious mutterings were a factor too, but I needed to know for my own peace of mind.

"When can you do it?" he said.

The sooner the better.

I was covering the practice this weekend. "I'm in the office all morning… how about we meet at 3:00?"

"Fine. I'll pick you up and we'll go over in the unit—you know, to keep it official."

I nodded. Official would be good. Knowing that Stan Harris thought I'd released Marge too soon, I wasn't looking forward to facing him. But if I came along as a sort of medical consultant, it might be bearable.

# 12

The food came. Carlene served me my eggs and Trav his "usual." I gawked at his double-bacon cheeseburger with fried onion rings and a huge side of cheese fries.

"I'll keep your pie warming until you're finished," she said.

"Vanilla like always?"

He nodded. "Do I ever have anything else?"

"Vanilla what?" I asked.

"Ice cream," Carlene said over her shoulder was she moved away. "How else can you have pie à la mode?"

"Yes," I said softly. "How else?"

I tried to concentrate on my eggs but my gaze was drawn back again and again to Trav's plate. On any other day that double-bacon cheeseburger would have looked irresistible. But not today.

The cheese fries, on the other hand, were a different story. Carbohydrate hell, yes, but I could have stuck my face right into the center of that gooey pile.

I took a bite of my eggs.

Yum-yum-yum, I told myself. Not too wet, not too dry, just the way you like them, Norrie.

But all the while I was wondering what they'd taste like mixed with cheese fries.

"You know, Trav," I said as he ladled catsup onto his burger, "I may not be your doctor—"

"You looked at my stitches, didn't you."

"True, but that doesn't exactly establish a doctor-patient relationship. So let me speak as an old friend who happens to be a doctor."

He took a big bite and spoke around it. "You're going to tell me what's wrong with this meal, right?"

"As a matter of fact, yes. I hate to be a buttinski, but—"

"Seeing as it's your butt, go ahead. Butt in all you want."

That brought me up short. What was he saying?

"I'm not sure how to take that."

His smile showed a hint of uncertainty. "If that was out of line, I'm sorry. I just meant that you… you've got a nice butt, that's all."

I felt heat in my face. Oh, damn, was I blushing? And was this Travis Lawton talking about my butt?

Always quick with the witty retort, I said, "I guess you must be more impressed by quantity than quality." I smiled and pointed to his plate. "To which your 'usual' bears ample witness."

Trav only shook his head. "You were always too hard on yourself, Norrie. Much too hard."

I didn't want to go there, so I said, "And on the subject of your meal, it's got to be a couple of thousand calories, maybe more. Almost all of them from saturated fat."

Another bite. "And?"

"And it probably shouldn't be eaten without a defibrillator handy."

He laughed. "I know what you're saying, but it doesn't seem to matter. I get an annual check-up and my cholesterol comes in around one-eighty every time—no matter what I eat."

"Really? You're lucky."

"I suppose so. Especially because no matter how much I eat I don't gain weight."

"That's wonderful," I said and ate another forkful of scrambled eggs.

He was trying to make me hate him. That was it. I mean, what other reason could there be for saying such a thing? No question about it: He wanted me to hate him.

"Just like old times," he said, breaking the silence.

"What do you mean?"

"You and me, sitting in the Star, talking."

"Until you hooked up with Diana."

He glanced away. "Yeah, well, that didn't work out real well."

"Can I ask what happened?"

He shrugged. "Bunch of stuff. It built up until we came to the point where we couldn't stand being in the same room with each other."

"Sorry to hear that."

"And I was sorry to hear about your dad. I would've made it to the wake but Dee and I were on the ropes then and, well... I'm sorry."

"It's okay. I was in such a state of shock at the time I couldn't tell who was there and who wasn't."

Neither of us spoke for a few heartbeats, then...

"Funny thing is," he said with a faltering smile, "we get along much better since we split."

"I hear that happens a lot."

I wanted to bite my tongue. You are *so* lame, I told myself.

# 13

The talk drifted to people we knew in school, with me asking *Whatever happened to...?* and Trav filling in the blanks as he finished every last crumb on his plate, then started in on his apple pie à la mode.

I didn't fight him for the bill—he'd had all the fun, after all.

As we headed out I noticed couples and groups starting to stream in. Looked like the movies were getting out.

He dropped me off at the office. "Three tomorrow, right?"

"On the dot."

He took my hand and gave it a gentle squeeze. "Thanks, Norrie. I appreciate this."

He walked me to my car and didn't head back to his until I was rolling out of the lot. And all the way home my fingers tingled where he'd touched them.

Back home, Mum wanted to know where I'd been. I told the truth: dinner at the Gold Star with an old friend, but no details.

I would have loved to turn on my computer and surf medical sites for articles on anaphylactic reactions, but the old house was Internet free. Probably would have had a hard time concentrating anyway.

Travis Lawton said I had a nice butt.

Did he mean it?

Yes, I believe he did.

Cool.

# 14

Tomorrow was my Saturday in the office so I left Mum watching a *Quincy, ME* rerun on TVLand and hit the hay. I don't know how it is with other professions, but it's hard to watch a medical drama when you're a doctor. Every minor error is distracting. And *House...* don't get me started on *House.*

I dozed off pretty quickly, but sometime during the wee hours...

*Norrie?*

A dream of a strange voice calling my name...

*Norrie!*

No. Not a dream. I was awake—or at least thought I was. I opened my eyes—

And gasped at the glowing mist—I'd seen it last night too—hovering beside my bed. I shot up to a sitting position.

"Wha—?"

*Shhhh! You'll wake your mother.*

The voice wasn't coming from the mist. In fact, it wasn't coming from anywhere. It was inside my head.

"No, wait. This can't—"

I hadn't been drinking, so I couldn't blame it on that.

*Don't you recognize your Babbo?*

Oh, no. Oh, no. We weren't going there. The clock read 3:14. The whole house was asleep—including me. This was a dream and the only way I was going to get out of it was to wake up.

I pinched the flesh under my upper arm. It hurt like hell, but the mist remained.

*Norrie, it's me. Please don't run from me.*

"Dad?" I whispered. "This can't—"

"*Please?*"

Wait-wait-wait. I couldn't imagine anyone who'd want to gaslight me like this—and even if I could, this was a pretty damn elaborate gaslighting. Plus the voice wasn't at all like my father's. He'd been born in Calabria and always spoke with a slight Italian accent. So it had to be a dream.

I decided to go along with it.

"There's no such thing as ghosts."

A mirthless laugh. "*Didn't I tell you that all the time?*"

Oh, God, he had.

"But you don't sound like you."

*How can I sound like me? I haven't got a voice.*

"Well, if you haven't got a voice, how can I hear you?"

*I'm speaking into your head. I got no body, Norrie. No voice box. Sound is a vibration in the air, right? So how can I vibrate air if I got no throat?*

He was right—a hundred percent right.

He added, *With all your medical school, you should know that.*

I did know it, I just wasn't thinking straight.

"But you don't sound like you. Where's your accent?"

*What I'm doing is thinking of what I want to tell you and you're hearing what I'm thinking in your head. Do thoughts have accents?*

Did they? Probably not. But…

"How the hell should I know? This is all new to me."

*Me too.*

"How come you don't look like you?"

*You mean, like my body looked?*

"Yeah."

*My body's gone.*

Okay, he had a point.

*What clothes did you bury me in?*

"Your fire department uniform. Don't you know?"

*I wasn't there. I been here… in the house. You expect me to be wearing my uniform? That's gone too. It's very hard for me to appear at all. I don't look like I used to.*

I didn't know what to expect. What a weird dream. Or could it be some kind of trick?

I stood up and reached out to the glowing mist. My hand went into it and through it. It felt... *cold.*

My knees got a little weak and I plopped back down on the bed.

"This is crazy."

*You should be on my side. I never believed in ghosts and now... now I am one.*

I closed my eyes. Either I'd had some sort of psychotic break, or the ghost of my father was hovering in my room.

*Norrie, I don't have much time.*

"How can you not have time?"

*I can drum up the strength to be seen and heard for only a little while at a time.*

"What do you mean?"

*It's hard.*

"Wh-wh-why aren't you in heaven?"

That just popped out. I don't even believe in heaven.

*I don't know. Ever since I died, I been here in the house.*

"And you've never tried to talk to Mum?"

*Of course I've tried. But she never hears me. Timmy neither. Like I'm not there. But you...*

"I can hear you fine."

*You think it's because we're blood?*

"Blood?"

*Yeah. You and me... we share blood. You mother and me, we don't.*

I saw what he was getting at: Only I could see him because I was his only direct relative—no parents, no siblings around, just me.

"But you mean you've been floating around the house since you died?" I'd been finishing med school then. "That's like six years, Dad."

*It's been that long? At first I didn't know where I was. Then I'd start seeing blurs, and hearing people talk. When I realized I was still in the house, I thought I wasn't dead. But then no one can see or hear me. I scream, I shout, I try to throw things off tables, but no good. Nothing.*

I couldn't help thinking of *The Sixth Sense*... all those ghosts around but only the little kid could see them.

*I keep trying but there's nobody around to tell me what to do. A TV or a car, they come with a manual that tells you how it works. But me? A ghost? Nothing. Not a clue. So I try different things. I've been trying what you see here for a long time but you're the first to see me.*

"Are there other ghosts around? Can you see any?"

*No. Just me. I don't even see you. You're just a glowing blob to me, just like I am to you, but I know you're my little girl.*

Weirder and weirder.

"You know, they say ghosts stay behind because they've got unfinished business. Have you got some unfinished business?"

A long pause, then, *Maybe.* The voice suddenly sounded faint.

"Like what?"

*I'm running out of energy now.* The mist was definitely fading. *I'll come back when I can.*

"Dad, wait!"

*Too weak. Love you, Norrie.*

It trailed off to nothing like a volume switch being dialed down.

"Dad? Dad?"

I sat on the edge of the bed looking around my empty room, wondering what had just happened here. Despite all my mother's tales of ghosts as I was growing up, I never bought into them. They sort of went the same way as Santa Claus and the Tooth Fairy.

But now... I'm not a gullible person, but that had been pretty damn convincing.

I still could be dreaming, though.

As a test, I got up and walked out to the kitchen to where my mother kept a note pad for her shopping lists. I took the pencil and wrote *Norrie was here*, then returned to my room.

I don't know how, but I eventually got back to sleep. At least I think I did. I do know it took an awfully long time.

# SATURDAY

# 1

Next morning I hit the snooze alarm half a dozen times before dragging myself from under the covers. Not until I was standing under the shower did I remember that incredible—in the truest sense of the word—dream about my father's ghost.

As soon as I was dry, I wrapped the towel around me and hurried to the kitchen. I beelined for Mom's pad but found it blank.

I leaned against the counter and stared at the empty pad, not sure if I was relieved or disappointed. Ghosts weren't real. Nothing more than wishful thinking. I'd have to revise everything I believe about science and reality to accept a ghost.

And yet... it had been wonderful to talk to my father again. I still missed him.

Like I said... wishful thinking.

I jumped as my mother walked in. "What was that you wrote on my pad?"

I stiffened. "What? When? Where?"

"You scribbled something. I put it over there."

I darted over to the opposite counter where she'd pointed. A page from her pad lay there...

*Norrie was here*

# 2

I somehow managed to take my first Tezinex and watch the online video. I was so distracted, I barely remember what it said... something about having a power bar for breakfast and remembering to have a bar or one of the shakes during the day, even if I wasn't hungry, to keep up my energy. A lot of positive statements like: *You're not going to be as hungry today and you're going to eat less than usual.* Also a pep talk about changing eating habits and avoiding snacks, blah-blah-blah. Like I didn't know.

That note... *my* note... kept running through my head. It meant I hadn't been dreaming. Well, at least not when I'd written it. But what about before that? Had I really been talking to the ghost of my father?

I couldn't think about this now. I had to tuck it away in a mental corner, drive to the hospital, and be a family doctor. I ate a Tezinex bar on the way. Not bad tasting—pretty good, in fact. As I started rounds on the group's patients, I was especially interested in seeing Amelia Henderson. Or rather her daughter.

Unfortunately Beth hadn't arrived yet. I'd been hoping to squeeze a little more Stan Harris juice out of her.

Amelia was sitting bedside as usual, but her oxygen line was looped behind her headboard. She'd been successfully weaned.

"Can I go home today?" she said with a pleading tone.

Her latest X-ray showed moderate improvement. So did her numbers: Her white count was down and she hadn't spiked a fever in thirty-six hours. I listened to her lungs through the open back of her gown and heard only the faintest rales in her left lower lobe.

"*Please*, can I go home?"

I hesitated. The infection was on the run, the lady was eating and drinking, her confusion had cleared, and yet...

I couldn't help thinking about Marge, who hadn't survived twenty-four hours after I'd discharged her.

I said, "One more day on the IVs, Amelia. As soon as I see you up and about on your own, I'll send you packing. For starters, I'm going to have one of the nurses walk you up and down the hall today. We'll see how you do with that before we let you up on your own."

Her face fell.

I rubbed her shoulder. "You're almost there, Amelia. Monday morning for sure."

Then to the office. We schedule only one doctor on Saturday mornings, and Ken and I rotate. This was my turn.

The first thing I did was look at the appointment sheet. I keep telling myself not to do that. Most days it's not a problem, but every so often I spot the name of a weirdo or a Patient From Hell and it casts a pall over the coming session.

Perhaps Patient From Hell is too strong. Then again, sometimes it isn't.

We doctors are—surprise—human. Some of us are nice people, some of us are bastards. The same is true for patients. Some are sweethearts, some are nasty, bitter, disagreeable s-o-b's. Many in the latter category are that way due to physical illness or mood disorder, but some were simply born with a permanent chip on the shoulder and dealing with them is more than a chore, it's a penance.

As a rule, any patient who comes to a doctor for treatment is... treated. We put aside our personal feelings and give them our best. But sometimes enough is enough. If a patient is noncompliant or repeatedly abusive or disruptive, we have the option of discharging them from the practice. We give them thirty days to find another doctor, telling them that we'll treat them for emergencies during that period, but after that it's *sayonara*, baby.

I haven't yet had to resort to that, but Sam and Ken have. They say it's unpleasant, but sometimes it's the best for all concerned, especially the staff, who usually bear the brunt of the abuse.

With that glass-half-full thought in mind, I started on the morning's patients.

# 3

By 12:30 I'd dealt with everyone on the appointment sheet. I was surprised to realize I wasn't hungry. Tezinex seemed to be working. I used the skim milk we always keep in the break room fridge to mix myself a shake anyway, just to stay with the program.

Finally I stepped out of the office. The last thing I did before leaving was sign out to Sam. Though he'd opted out of Saturday office hours, he stayed in the weekend call rotation, and this was his weekend in the barrel.

Free at last. The rest of the weekend was mine, mine, mine.

Well, not really. I'd promised to meet with Trav, which meant I wouldn't be able get my nails done today, so I canceled the appointment and moved it to Thursday. Then I called Trav and told him to meet me at Holly Ridge instead of Mum's. I had to check up on my place and maybe pick up a few odds and ends I'd forgotten.

As I parked outside my building, Janie pulled in next to me in her sleek, silver Mazda RX8 coupe. I looked at my watch: almost 2:30.

"Don't tell me you're just getting in."

"Nah." She flashed me a crooked smile. "Been out doing a little shopping. What's shakin'?"

Just my love handles, I thought.

Janie, of course, doesn't have love handles. Doesn't even have mildly infatuated handles. She stood there handle-less in a short sweater top that stopped two millimeters below her bra, and low-rider jeans with a waistband that started two millimeters above her pubic bone. Her dark hair was pulled back in a scrunchy. No lipstick or mascara—but the day was still young.

"Not much," I said.

"That's not what I hear." She popped her trunk lid.

"Oh? What's that mean?"

She lifted out a bag of groceries and was trying get a grip on a second. I grabbed it for her.

"Thanks." She gave me that smile again as she slammed the lid. "I heard that a certain eligible young lady doctor was seen out and about last night with a member of Carson County's finest."

I almost dropped the bag. "I don't believe this. I stop by the Star to have a bite to eat with an old high-school friend and people are talking about it?"

"Believe it. Lebanon's a small town."

"We were in Carmel!"

"Same difference, 'specially when you're seen leanin' close with a hottie like Travis Lawton."

We'd been leaning close because we didn't want anyone to overhear, but Trav... a hottie?

I mulled that as we carried the bags into our building.

"So?" Her brown eyes fixed on me from under her bangs. "What's he like in the sack?"

This was typical Janie: No subject is too intimate. She talks about sex like I might talk about the weather.

"I wouldn't know."

"Oh, come on. You mean you two aren't getting it on?"

"No." I laughed. "Tuesday was the first time I've seen him in a dozen years."

That smile again. "And your point is?"

I wondered who'd been whispering in her ear. Could have been anyone, even Carlene the waitress. I wasn't keen on my relationships, platonic or otherwise, being discussed in the laundromat or over coffee and Danish. *We saw the doctor and the deputy together—they must be an item*—can quickly become, *We don't see the doctor and the deputy together anymore—they must have broken up. Poor doctor Norrie.*

I had to nip this in the bud.

"We're just friends, Janie."

She rolled her eyes. "Hmmm… where have I heard that before?"

"It's true. We were friends all through high school." Well, most of it, anyway.

Her brows shot up. "Friends? How do you stay 'friends' with a guy who looks like that?"

"Trust me, he didn't look like that in high school."

"Late bloomer, huh?"

"You got it."

She laughed. "Sounds like you two have a lot of time to make up for." She'd fished out her key and was unlocking her door. "Either get it on or stock up on batteries for your vibrator."

"I don't *have* a vibrator, Janie."

"Wanna borrow mine?"

I had to laugh as we both made faces and did the teenage, "Eeeeuuuwww!" in unison. This girl was too much.

"Come on, will you?" I said. "He's just asking me about the medical aspects of a case he's working on. Really."

"Yeah? You mean like *CSI* stuff?"

"Not quite."

"Why? Been a murder or somethin'?"

That was uncomfortably close to the truth—the *possible* truth. So far, Trav's suspicions of foul play were just that: suspicions.

I said nothing as I followed her inside and deposited the grocery bag on the kitchen counter. Her apartment was laid out in the mirror image of mine, with the bedrooms on the left side of the hallway. It was also a mess. Smelled of tobacco smoke. Clothing, some of it male, lay strewn about on the furniture and the floor. I itched to tidy up.

"Just medical stuff," I told her.

As I was looking for a way to change the subject, it occurred to me that if Janie was tuned in to the local gossip, she might know about Trav's marriage, especially since she thought he was such a hottie.

Trav the hottie… I still couldn't grasp that. Maybe it was the uniform.

She started unpacking. "You want a beer or somethin'?"

"I'll take a rain check," I said, then sidled into my subject. "You know, Trav and I never got around to our personal lives last night and—"

"Yeah, right."

"No, it's true. I left town right after high school and come back a dozen years later to find out he has a child and an ex-wife. I don't know him well enough anymore to ask him the details. You know anything?"

She looked at me. "I guess you *are* just friends after all." Her eyes narrowed. "Oh, I get it: You're looking to make a move and—"

"Would you stop that? I'm not looking to do anything. I'm just curious, okay?"

Janie shrugged and lit a cigarette. "Okay, okay. I don't know much, but what I heard was that he and his wife Diane—"

"Diana. Diana Robinson when I knew her."

"Whatever. She got knocked up and so they got married and had the kid. Way I hear it, this Diana went blimpo during the pregnancy and stayed that way for years and years afterward. All of a sudden she starts losing weight and takin' care of herself. You can guess what that means, right?"

"Not another guy?"

"Better believe it. And would you believe her hairdresser? Shit, mine would rather get it on with the deputy than me, if you know what I mean."

"Poor Trav."

"Yeah, well, he found out and that was it."

"And I suppose he's been having a grand old time with the unattached female population ever since."

I immediately wished I could take that back. It sounded as if—

"Ahh-ha!" Janie grinned and pointed her cigarette at me. "You *do* have a thing for Deputy Dawg."

Yes, that was exactly what it had sounded like.

"I don't." At least I didn't think I did. "Don't go looking for things that aren't there. I knew him as a kid and I'm just curious as to what kind of man he's become."

"Suuuure you are."

Time for another try at shifting the subject. I glanced at the end of the counter and did a double take.

"Is that a chess set?"

"No, it's a blender." She laughed. "Told you I played."

"Yes, I remember, but I thought…"

"I was putting you on?"

"That did cross my mind."

"Hey, just because I look like a bimbo—Christ, I don't just look like a bimbo, I *am* a bimbo—that doesn't mean I'm a *stupid* bimbo."

"You're not a bimbo."

"I'm a stripper who likes to party and have sex. What else would you call me?"

Her candor threw me. How often do you meet someone who isn't kidding herself?

"Well, I'd call you a most unusual chess master."

She beamed at me. "You know something, Doc? I like you. You're okay. In fact, you're kinda cool."

Now it was my turn to laugh. "You're talking to one of the uncoolest people on the planet."

"No, you're probably the *squarest* person on the planet, but that doesn't mean you can't be cool." She stubbed out her cigarette. "So, want a game some time? I'll whip your ass."

I'd played some chess in high school and college, but I was rusty. Still, it might be fun to get back into it.

"You name the time and place, sweetie," I said in my best tough-girl voice, "and we'll see whose ass gets whipped."

Then we laughed. I do like her.

# 4

I could almost feel Janie's eyes on my back as I stood outside. Her condo overlooked the parking lot and I felt sure she was watching to see who picked me up.

True to his word, Travis showed at three sharp, dressed in full uniform and driving a sheriff's department cruiser. Like last night, he opened the front passenger door for me. As I slid into the seat I glanced up at Janie's windows. Though not closed, her blinds were down and I couldn't see inside. Just for the hell of it I waved toward the windows.

"What was that for?" Trav asked.

"What?"

"The wave."

"Just a nosy neighbor. Do you know that people are talking about us being out last night?"

He smiled and nodded as we pulled out and headed for the highlands and Well-to-do-ville.

"Yeah. It's been mentioned twice to me already. We're an item."

"Crazy."

"What's so crazy about it?"

I realized he might have taken that the wrong way.

"Well, I mean, all we did was stop for a bite to eat. Kind of crazy to make something out of that."

"Yeah, I suppose. Who's the neighbor?"

"You wouldn't know her."

"Try me. You'd be surprised who I know."

"Janie Ryan."

He laughed. "Janie Ryan? You know how she earns her bucks, don't you?"

"I believe she's an ecdysiast."

"A what?"

"A stripper."

"Right. You're living next to Poochie Sutton."

I wondered how Trav knew her—wondered how *well* he knew her. Had they had a fling? I wondered if I could catch him.

"How many times have you seen her show?"

"None."

Okay, he avoided that one.

Then he added, "How about you?"

"Never." I grinned. "She's not my type."

"That's a relief."

"Then how do you know her?"

He shrugged. "Everybody knows Janie. She's like a local legend. Works out now and then at my gym. You wouldn't believe what she wears."

"You mean *doesn't* wear. I've seen."

"Then you know why she's a living legend."

"Enough about legends," I said. "What are we hoping to accomplish this afternoon?"

I was a little hazy on that, and Trav didn't seem too sure either.

"We'll be looking for a peanut source, of course, but I also want to get an overall sense of Harris and the house and…" He shrugged. "And whatever."

"Please don't tell me you're going to put on a deerstalker hat and go around with a magnifying glass."

He laughed. "Not likely. This will all be assigned to one of the county detectives come Monday, and—"

"Why don't they have one on it now?"

"First off, they say they're shorthanded, and second, Hincher isn't convinced there's even been a crime."

"That's the way to commit the perfect crime—make it look like an accident."

"The thing is, when Monday comes I'd like to be able to hand over more than just that 9-1-1 recording."

"You mentioned something yesterday about wanting to be a detective, didn't you?"

"I'd *love* to be a detective. That would mean transferring to the County Prosecutor's office, which wouldn't be a bad thing."

I was beginning to get the picture now. Trav wanted to move up and figured the suspicious circumstances around Marge's death could be a way to demonstrate his investigative mettle.

Nothing wrong with ambition. In fact, give me a choice between a complacent guy who's happy just where he is and a guy looking to better himself, and I'll take the latter any day.

As for my part, I was glad to help Trav. Especially if it meant nailing Marge's killer—*if* she'd been killed.

Up on the Hill now, the huge Castanon house was visible on the crest. Home to the area's major used-car dealer. I could see the central, castle-like turret and sloping lawn.

Trav must have followed my gaze.

"All it needs is a moat, right?" he said, pointing. "Who'd ever think you could make that much money selling cars."

"A lot more than I'll ever make."

He looked surprised. "You're kidding, right?"

"Not at all."

"But you're a doctor."

"Maybe some subspecialist could afford that, but not me."

Trav shook his head. "Man, you save lives and he sells cars. What's wrong with this picture?"

I shrugged. I was sure Bert Castanon worked hard, just as I was sure he'd suffered through his share of lean years along the way. I don't begrudge anyone an honest-earned dollar. I avoid the envy trap. Give it an opening and it will eat you alive.

Trav turned onto Lantern Lane. He pulled into the driveway of number 1242 and stopped beside an old green Ford Taurus parked by the side-entry garage.

"Looks like he may have company," I said.

"I told him I'd be over sometime today. Didn't say when because I wasn't sure."

I took in the exterior: a good-size two-story colonial, maybe three-thousand square feet, brick front, beige vinyl siding on the sides and most likely the rear as well; a neatly trimmed lawn, rhodos planted against the foundation and surrounded by beds of freshly planted petunias. Someone—Marge, I assumed—had put a lot of care into this yard.

I had a sudden thought.

"Does Harris know about the recording?"

He shifted into PARK and we sat there with the engine idling. "He shouldn't. Only a few in the department know, and nobody outside."

"You hope."

He sighed. "Yeah. I hope. Lots of loose lips around here."

"No kidding. But, if he hasn't heard, he won't know he's a suspect."

"Right. And what convinces me of that is how he agreed to let me come and look around without a search warrant. No way he'd allow that if he knew about the call."

Something in what Trav said struck a sour note.

"You said he agreed to let *you* look around. What about me?"

He turned off the engine. "He doesn't know you're coming."

"Oh, that's wonderful. Just wonderful. He blames me for his wife's death and you're going to just spring me on him? He'll throw a fit."

I was pretty damn annoyed and racing toward outright anger.

Trav patted my arm and opened his door. "Don't worry. I'll take care of him. You're a very necessary part of this."

"One more thing," I said. "Does Harris know about Marge's stomach contents—that no peanut was found?"

"No. Even fewer people know about that."

Well, I thought as Trav got out and put on his tan Stetson, that at least was something. The lack of a peanut product in his wife's stomach would make me look all the more culpable in Harris's eyes.

My own stomach tightened as I stepped out and slammed my door. I felt like Daniel heading for the lion's den. This could turn into one ugly scene.

# 5

Stanley Harris looked a little confused when he opened his front door.

"Yes?"

"Deputy Lawton again, sir," Trav said, touching the brim of his hat. "I talked to you yesterday about inspecting the house for peanut products."

"Oh, yes. But I don't think—" And then he spotted me. "What's *she* doing here?"

Travis cleared his throat. "Doctor Marconi is helping the Sheriff's Department and—"

"I don't want her in my house."

I was noticing something a little off center about Harris, the slightest slurring of his speech. Drinking? Or tranquilized?

"Sir—"

"She killed my wife."

So far he hadn't spoken to me, and I'd been content to let Trav do the talking. But I wasn't letting that pass.

"Mr. Harris, you have no idea how sorry I am about Marge."

"Not as sorry as you're going to be!"

"You may not know this, but she was more than a patient to me. I knew her back when she lived in Carmel and she meant a lot to me. But I followed standard medical procedure and—"

The corner of his mouth lifted in a snarl. "A lot of goddamn good it did her. I told you to keep her another night but you wouldn't listen. If you had she'd still be alive, wouldn't she. *Wouldn't she!*" He shouted the last two words.

I kept my voice calm and low. "Yes, Mr. Harris, she probably would be. And if there'd been a medical reason to keep her I would have, but—"

"But now she's dead because you *didn't!*"

"Yes. And you can't know how many times since the moment I started trying to resuscitate her in the emergency room that I've wished I had."

He blinked at me. I think that might have taken him by surprise.

Trav jumped in. "Mr. Harris, you don't have to let Doctor Marconi in, but since this is a coroner's case and since your wife did die of a medical condition, we feel everyone's interests will be best served by having a professional who knew her medical background along while we look for possible causes."

"I *know* the cause," he said without energy. "She died of an inadequately treated allergic condition."

I bit my tongue. Trav and I waited in silence.

I was trying to get a clear read on Harris. Was he genuinely angry with me, or simply laying the groundwork for a lawsuit? Was he really sad about Marge's death, or merely playing it up? I sensed some sort of conflict within him but couldn't fathom what it might be.

Finally he let out a long sigh that seemed to deflate him, leaving him looking old and defeated.

"Well, whatever. This isn't a good time anyway. If you really think it's necessary, we'll have to resched—"

"Wait," Trav said, holding up a hand. "What's that?"

I cocked my head and listened. Somewhere in the house a woman was sobbing.

# 6

The three of us stood silent, listening.

"Is someone hurt?" Trav asked.

"What?" Harris looked confused, then flustered. "Oh, that's just Alison."

"The cleaning girl?" I said. I got a look from Trav as if to say, *How on Earth do you know the Harrises' cleaning girl?* So I added, "She saved Marge the first time, on Tuesday, by using her EpiPen."

"The poor girl is really torn up by all this," Harris said. "She usually comes Tuesdays and Fridays but she never showed yesterday—not that I even noticed—but then she shows up this morning thinking it's Friday."

He turned and walked back into the house. He didn't invite us in, but he didn't shut the door. Trav and I looked at each other, then he shrugged and stepped over the threshold. He removed his Stetson and motioned me to follow.

I stayed close behind as we followed Harris into a marble-floored foyer. Straight ahead a stairway ran up to the second floor. The living room lay to the right, a small office to the left. Harris was moving along a short hallway to the left of the stairs. We followed, passing a busy array of photos on the walls leading to the kitchen.

The kitchen was spacious with a center island. To the right was a dining room, to the left a family room with a big flatscreen TV on the wall.

A young woman with short, bleached hair sat at a round table in the breakfast nook, her head down, propped in her hands.

Alison.

When she saw Trav and me she shot to her feet with a startled look and quickly dabbed her eyes.

"I'm sorry. I—"

"This is Alison Crowley," Harris said to Trav. "She takes care of the house for Marge."

Alison looked up at me with narrowed, red-rimmed eyes. "You're the doctor from the hospital, aren't you?"

Was that a note of hostility in her tone?

"Yes," Harris snapped. "The one who let Marge go too early."

That explained the hostility—Harris had been filling her head with his accusations.

When I refused to respond, Alison looked from me to Trav. "Why—?"

Trav said, "We're searching for a peanut product that may have sneaked under Mrs. Harris's radar."

"If only I'd been here like last time," Alison said. "I could have saved her, you know. But now she's gone." She sobbed. "She was a good person. She didn't deserve to die."

"You probably should go, Alison," Harris told her. "You're too upset to get anything done today. We can put off any cleaning till next week."

She looked at him with tear-filled eyes, then grabbed her bag and brushed past us. I turned to watch her go. She paused outside the little office off the foyer, looked through the double doors, then back at Harris.

"At least let me clean up her office. It's such a mess and she always kept it so neat."

"Leave it for now," Harris said.

"Yeah, but if she ever saw..." Her voice choked off.

"Just go home and get some rest."

Her gaze drifted to me. Our eyes met and held for a second. She glared at me, then shook her head.

"The place feels so empty," she whispered.

She left without closing the front door behind her. Didn't anyone shut doors around here?

I turned back to find Harris staring at us with a suspicious look.

"How usual is it for the police to search the home of some-one who died of *medical neglect*?"

Again I said nothing. My tongue was becoming studded with bite marks.

"I wouldn't know about that, sir," Trav said. "What I do know is that your wife's death was unattended so that makes it a coroner's case and this is his idea."

Uh-oh. Not true. The coroner had no idea I was here. I hoped Trav's words wouldn't turn around and bite him.

Harris studied us for a few heartbeats, then heaved another sigh.

"All right. As long as you're here, you might as well get on with it. The sooner we get this over with, the better, I suppose."

We were in.

"But I'll warn you," he added. "You're wasting your time. Marge and I were *very* careful about the ingredients of anything edible we brought into this house."

Again I sensed conflict in Harris. His attitude puzzled me. So matter of fact. The cleaning girl seemed far more upset about his wife's death than he. Of course, if he'd killed her, that would explain it. But you'd think he'd at least try to fake a little more grief.

But then, if he *was* guilty, why was he letting us search?

Then I thought I might have the answer. Stanley Harris was no dummy. Refusing us and demanding a search war-rant wouldn't look good—it would attract attention by blowing something minor into something major. The other reason might be arrogance: He was so confident he'd covered all his tracks that he didn't care who poked around.

Well, he'd let a wolf into his house: me. I was going to poke like no one had ever poked.

The question was, where to start?

# 7

I turned to Trav. "Where was the"—I caught myself. I'd almost said *body*. "Where was Marge found?"

I knew the answer but didn't want to let on that he and I had been discussing this.

Harris opened his mouth to answer but Trav beat him to it. "In the study."

"Then let's start there."

Harris said, "I thought you were going to search for peanut products. That would be the kitchen and pantry."

Did he *not* want us exploring the office?

"These reactions can strike like lightning," I told him. "If the office is where she was found, then it's likely that's where it hit her. And if so, that's where we should look first."

Trav led the way. As we passed near the front door—I couldn't help it—I reached out and closed it. Harris brought up the rear.

The office was a stuffy little box with a pair of windows in the left wall and shelves across the rear. A desk, a high-backed swivel chair, a computer, a printer, and a three-drawer filing cabinet pretty much filled the rest of the space.

What a mess. Papers were strewn about the desktop and the floor—no doubt the result of the EMTs trying to save Marge's life. I fought an urge to straighten up. If this turned out to be a crime scene, I should leave it all as is.

Trav pointed to the space beside the desk. "This is where they started resuscitation." He turned to Harris. "Was it your wife's office?"

"We both used it."

Trav nodded. "Any idea what she might have been doing when... when it happened?"

"I can tell you exactly what she was doing: paying bills. Every Thursday morning she'd sit down here and pay the week's bills."

"Did she do it through the computer?" I asked.

Harris shook his head but didn't look at me. He answered grudgingly. "No, I wanted her to, told her it would be much quicker and easier for her, but she was set in her ways. She'd always written the checks by hand and saw no reason to change."

"Computerphobe?"

"No. She loved chat groups and online shopping."

The chair had been pushed into the right rear corner. I stepped around the desk and rolled it back into position before the kneehole. Then I sat in it.

"What the hell do you think you're doing?"

"I just want to see where she was before it happened. If she ate something, the culprit should be somewhere nearby."

"The culprit is sitting in her chair!" Harris said.

He turned and walked out.

Suddenly the office seemed brighter. Stanley Harris was the sort who could light up a room by leaving it.

"Sorry," Trav said. "Maybe this wasn't such a good idea."

"No, it's a very good idea. And since we may never get this chance again, let's make the most of it. Why don't you start on the pantry while I check out this place?"

"Sounds like a plan," he said, and moved off.

# 8

Sitting here in a dead friend's chair made me feel like some sort of ghoul. But this was where Marge had been struck down, where she died. I had to stick with it. I put aside the uneasiness and started with the desktop.

The computer monitor took up a good amount of space, but the most striking feature was the array of pigs lining the perimeter—plush, plastic, papier-mâché, Beanie Baby, you name it. If it went "oink," it was represented.

A checkbook, a pen, and half a dozen bills lay scattered across the remaining area. To the right I noticed an amber plastic pharmacy bottle labeled *Cimetidine 150 mg,* and a blister-pack of Benadryl capsules with a few missing. My discharge instructions had included regular doses of each until she saw me again.

Neither cimetidine nor Benadryl contain peanut protein.

I checked the three drawers to the right of the kneehole, hoping to find some sort of goody she might have stashed away for a snack, but came up empty. Nothing but office supplies.

I pushed the chair back and dropped onto my hands and knees inside the kneehole on the chance she'd dropped whatever she might have been eating. I found a wastebasket and the computer's dark, silent tower.

The basket held possibilities. Hoping for a candy wrapper I pulled it out and searched through discarded flyers that accompany most bills. The only other things I found were patient information printouts from Gold's pharmacy about cimetidine and prednisone.

I rose and gave the shelves behind the desk a thorough going over, removing all the books, manuals, and office supplies—and pigs—from each section to make sure I didn't miss anything. The shelves weren't exactly jam packed, so it didn't take long.

Again, nothing.

I did a slow turn. The only place left was the three-drawer filing cabinet in the corner next to the door. I stepped around the desk and checked to see if it was locked.

Yes. Damn.

But I remembered seeing a couple of keys in the desk. I went back to the top drawer and found them. The lock popped with the second key I tried.

Now the big question: Did I dare?

Poking through a locked file cabinet was way overstepping my bounds. But *why* was it locked? No children around. Who were they barring from their files? Alison?

On the other hand, it might be simple anal-retentiveness.

I tried to talk myself out of it. I failed. What if one of the drawers hid a jar of Skippy Super Chunk?

But before I did anything I wanted to locate Stanley Harris.

# 9

I walked into the kitchen and saw Trav in the pantry, studying what looked like a box of pancake mix. Beyond him, in the family room, Harris sat slumped in a chair before the TV, abusing the remote.

"Any luck?" I said.

"I'm going cross-eyed reading these labels."

"Told you from the start," Harris said without looking up. "You're wasting your time."

"Can I borrow your flashlight?" I said to Trav.

He gave me a questioning look as he unhooked it from his belt. I had Harris's attention too.

"I want to check the floor under the desk," I explained, loud enough for Harris to hear. "Just in case she dropped something. You know, my hard candy theory."

He nodded. "Good luck."

I took a quick look at Harris before returning to the office. He was back to staring at the screen, flipping through the channels at a rate too fast for anything to register.

I headed straight for the filing cabinet, went down on one knee, grabbed the handle of the bottom drawer, and hesitated. Harris could walk in on me at any time. Trav didn't know what I was up to, so he couldn't run interference or give me warning. And if Harris did find me pawing through his papers, what would I say?

My palms were moist and I felt shaky inside. I'm a straightforward person in a straightforward profession. I'm not cut out for this type of thing, and I'm sure as hell not experienced in it.

But I had to know.

So I yanked back on the handle and slid the drawer open. Inside sat a row of hanging folders. Each of their multicolored tabs contained a neat little typed label.

Yeah, some definite anal retention going on here. I liked it.

I started at the rear and worked my way forward, peeking into and between each of the folders.

No luck in the bottom drawer so I eased it shut and paused, listening.

I could still hear the TV, but nothing from Trav or Harris. Good. Most likely neither had moved from where I'd left them.

I opened the middle drawer: same contents, same story. Nothing edible.

Another pause, another listen. Nothing seemed to have changed. I moved on to the top. No sign of any edibles there either, but I did come across a pair of neighboring folders, one labeled *POLICIES—Marge*, the other, *POLICIES—Stan*.

I couldn't resist. But as I opened the *Marge* file and started sorting through it, I caught a shadow of movement in the doorway and froze. Someone was standing there, watching me.

Oh, God. Busted.

I turned my head and went weak-kneed with relief: Trav.

He stared at me, eyes wide, a baffled expression.

"What—?"

I shook my head and put a finger to my lips, then waved him away.

He gave me one last puzzled look, then headed back toward the kitchen.

I was breathing quickly, almost panting as I flipping through the policies, doing a quick survey of their provisions. Marge had three term policies on her life—two for $500,000 and one for $200,000.

I felt my jaw clench. Stanley Harris was heading for a million-plus windfall, all of it tax free.

Someone might call that motive.

# 10

I wanted to search a little further but couldn't stand the tension any longer. I eased the drawer closed, relocked the cabinet, returned the keys to the desk. Again I noticed Marge's cimetidine bottle and Benadryl package, and that raised a question.

Where was her prednisone? I'd seen the P-I sheet from the pharmacy in the wastebasket, but where were the pills? I'd prescribed three doses a day until her follow-up visit.

I shuffled through the bills on the desktop, but no prednisone. Maybe Harris knew.

Trav looked relieved to see me when I stepped into the kitchen. I gave him a quick, reassuring smile, then moved to the edge of the family room where Harris still mindlessly surfed the channels.

"Where did Marge keep her meds?"

Harris glared up at me. "I thought you were supposed to be looking for peanuts."

"We are, but a medication I prescribed as post-hospital treatment seems to be missing."

He jerked his thumb toward the kitchen. "Marge kept her vitamins and such in the cabinet above the dishwasher. If it's anywhere, it's there."

I went to the cabinet and found an array of plastic bottles—multivitamins, calcium, evening primrose capsules, an omega-3 supplement, and a white paper bag from Gold's pharmacy.

I pulled that out and found it stapled closed. The still-attached receipt read:

*Margery Harris*

*Prednisone 10 mg.*

Why hadn't she opened it?

"Mr. Harris," I said, carrying it to the counter. "Can you think of any reason why Marge wouldn't take a prescribed medication?"

His head swiveled toward me. "What are you talking about?"

I held up the bag. "This is what I prescribed for her when she left the hospital. She had it filled but never took any."

"Don't be ridiculous," he snapped, rising from his chair and approaching. "She was religious about taking pills."

"Not these." I jiggled it. "They've been untouched since they left the pharmacy."

He snatched the bag from my fingers. "Impossible."

But as he examined it his expression slipped from annoyance into bafflement. He ripped the bag open and pulled out an amber vial with a white safety cap. He shook it, rattling the pills inside.

"I... I don't understand."

"Neither do I." I extended my hand. "May I see?"

He handed it over and I examined the label. It listed her name, my name, the drug name and dosage, and the instructions: *Three (3) tablets three (3) times a day for three days, then as directed.*

Exactly as I'd prescribed.

I looked up at Harris. "I saw the two other meds I recommended on her desk. She'd been taking those. Why didn't she take these? They would have saved her life."

"So *that's* it!" Harris said, his snarl back. "This is some sort of trick. This whole little venture is just a smoke screen so you could plant these pills and get yourself off the hook."

Trav said, "You're way out of line, sir."

I felt myself reddening—not just with embarrassment, anger bubbled as well. Nobody accuses me of something like that.

"You know, Mr. Harris, you can talk like a fool if you want, but don't make *me* sound like one. The when and where of that prescription can be checked with a simple phone call to Gold's. Bad enough you slander my integrity and this police officer's, but then you accuse me of being an idiot as well!"

Maybe the word "slander" made a splash in his suit-happy

mind. Whatever it was, he backed off.

"All right, all right. I'm upset, okay? My wife died a couple of days ago, remember?"

I remembered. Damn right I remembered. And if this vicious little man was upset now it was probably because he saw the huge malpractice suit he'd been fantasizing about—maybe he figured he could add it to his insurance payout and retire to Tahiti—turn to smoke and begin blowing away.

And that was when it hit me: Marge's death wasn't due to being discharged too early, it was due to ignoring my advice.

But why would she do that?

A sudden thought: Could Harris have hidden the prednisone from Marge?

And then I remembered the patient information sheet in her office. I groaned.

"What's wrong?" Trav said.

Instead of answering him, I turned to Harris. "Marge was trying to lose weight, wasn't she? That was why she was eating that diet bar that caused the first reaction."

He nodded. "She was trying very hard to drop a few pounds but wasn't having much luck."

Yeah, and I could guess *why* she was trying so hard: She knew her husband was fooling around and she wanted to return to a slimmer, *younger* figure.

I said, "Wait a second."

I hurried back to the office, snatched the prednisone information sheet from the wastebasket, and returned to the kitchen, reading along the way. I shook my head as I ran down the list of what it called "the most commonly encountered side effects."

*Sodium retention*
*Increased appetite*
*Increased fat deposits*
*Increased acid in your stomach*
*Increased sweating, especially at night*
*Increased hair growth*
*Acne on the face, back, and chest*
*Bone and muscle problems*
*Growth problems in children*

*Increased sugar in the blood*
*Increased sensitivity to the sun*
*Delayed wound healing*
*Decreased ability to fight infection*
*Thrush (Candida) growth in the mouth*
I handed the sheet to Harris and pointed to the list.

"Here. Imagine you're a woman desperate to lose weight and you read the first three side effects."

He stared at it a moment, then looked up at me.

"Why would anyone prescribe something with such horrible side effects?"

I met his gaze. "To keep someone from having another severe allergic reaction."

He looked away.

"But what galls me," I added, "is that it's half-assed information. It's like putting a warning sticker on a car saying this piece of equipment will kill fifty-thousand people a year, pollute the atmosphere, and help thin the ozone layer. If I may paraphrase you: 'Who'd buy something with such horrible side effects?'"

"It's not the same."

"It's all true, isn't it?"

"Yes, but—"

"Right. It *is* all true. *But...* the sticker makes it sound as if a single car will do all that. What it doesn't say is that it takes millions upon millions of cars years and years to generate those effects. Just as the prednisone P-I sheet doesn't say that the listed side effects come from long-term use. Marge would have suffered none of them during the two-week course I'd planned for her."

Harris dropped the sheet on the counter. He turned and walked to the sliding glass doors that led to a rear deck; he stood there staring out at his backyard, saying nothing.

Trav picked up the sheet.

"My God," he said after a few seconds. "She didn't take her pills because she was afraid of gaining weight?"

"That's my sense of it," I said.

"You don't know that," Harris said to his backyard, then turned to face me. "Maybe you didn't impress on her how important it was to take those pills."

"You were right there when I wrote the prescription. You heard me tell her that they'd keep any residual effects under control and to be sure to take them as directed and not miss any doses until she saw me on Friday."

He shook his head. "I don't remember any such thing."

I wanted to ask him if he remembered ever hearing the term "lying bastard," but bit it back. It would accomplish nothing.

But what *he* had accomplished was the hardening of my resolve to prove him guilty of causing Marge's death.

*Please! Oh, God! He's... killing me!*

Marge might have been an unwitting accomplice by not taking her meds, but that 9-1-1 call said she knew something we didn't. And I was more determined than ever to find out just what.

Harris smirked. "And how do we know Marge even *looked* at that printout?"

"I think we're getting sidetracked here," Trav said.

His voice sounded strained. His fists were knotted as if he wanted to punch someone. I could guess who that someone was. His reaction warmed me.

I looked at Harris. "You said Marge liked to go online, right? Let's try a little experiment."

I turned and walked back toward the office, crooking a finger over my shoulder. I hoped I looked more confident than I felt, because if I was wrong, this could backfire big-time.

# 11

As we stepped into the office I gestured toward the desk chair. "Have a seat, Mr. Harris."

He didn't move. "What's this all about?"

"Just humor me."

"Yeah," Trav said from behind him. I detected an edge on his voice. "Humor her."

Harris shrugged and moved toward the chair. "I don't know what you hope to accomplish by—"

"Before you sit down, please put your hand on top of the monitor."

He gave me a strange look but complied. "Now what?"

"Feel any heat?"

He shook his head. "No."

"Good. Then I think we can agree that the computer has not been on recently. Right?"

Another shrug. "I suppose so."

Well-well-well. We agreed on something. How about that?

"Now, have a seat and boot up the computer if you will."

As he did so, I slipped around behind him and waited for the screen to come to life. When it did it showed a typical Windows desktop with the Chrome browser's familiar icon front and center.

The wallpaper behind the icon tugged at my heart: a photo of a grinning eight- or nine-year-old boy on skis. His face bore a distinct resemblance to Marge's.

I was pretty sure it was their dead son, but I asked anyway. "Who's that?"

"Tommy."

He stared at the screen for a few heartbeats. When he spoke again his voice had lost its edge.

"It's been five—no, six years. We were never the same after we lost him. It changed everything. Might have been different if he'd had an illness like cancer or leukemia or something and we could have seen it coming. But who could see something like a drunk running your son down with a truck and leaving him in the street like roadkill? Took me a long time, but I managed to get back to normal. But Marge… a part of Marge died along with Tommy."

For a moment the only sound in the little office was the whir of the computer's cooling fan. And for a moment Stanley Harris seemed almost human.

But with a shake of his head he returned to form.

"What am I doing here anyway? What's this supposed to prove?"

I spoke past the lingering lump in my throat. "Let's bring up Chrome."

Harris clicked on the icon and Chrome opened onto a Google screen.

"Now, click on that little arrow to the right of the address box." I touched the screen. "Right… there."

Another click and a history window dropped from the box listing all the Internet sites the browser had recently visited. I did a quick scan of the contents, praying I wouldn't be left hanging. It wasn't looking good, and then, halfway down—

"There. Look. '*Google search: prednisone.*' That clinches it."

"Clinches what?" Harris said.

"That she did read the P-I sheet and didn't like what she saw, so she went on the Internet to double check it."

Harris slammed his hand on the desktop. "All right. That does it. I've had enough. I want you two out of here. Now!"

"I'll be only too happy to comply," I said.

I slipped past Trav and headed for the front door.

Behind me I heard him say, "Thank you for your cooperation, Mr. Harris," and then he followed me out.

# 12

"Can you believe that guy?" Trav said as we pulled out of the driveway. "What a rotten son of a bitch."

"You won't hear any argument from me. Can you imagine him having an affair? With whom? She's probably inflatable."

Trav laughed. "Whoa! That's cold!"

"He's just been added to my list of most unfavored people."

"Mine too."

I looked up and saw a woman standing by the curb, waving. She wore a blue blouse and baggy jeans. Beth Henderson. Seen in this light, she didn't look quite so spinsterish. But she needed an extreme makeover in the clothing department.

"Wonder what she wants," Trav said.

He pulled over and leaned out the window. "Can I help you, Miss Henderson?"

"Well, yes. Is something wrong again at the Harrises'?"

"Why do you ask?"

She got that haughty look. "Well, I see a police car at a house where a woman just died and I have to wonder. Has Stanley had an accident as well?"

"Everything is fine, Miss Henderson."

"Then why—?"

"I'm sorry," Trav said. "I have to get back to the office right away."

I leaned forward and said, "I missed you at the hospital this morning."

She looked embarrassed. "I overslept. Thank you, by the way, for taking such good care of Mom." She squinted at me.

"May I ask why *you* were at the Harris house? Is there a medical problem?"

Trav said, "Thank you for keeping an eye on things."

She huffed. "I know people think I'm nosy, but I'm not. I'm simply a concerned citizen."

"And we could use more like you." As he pulled away he raised the window and, as soon as it closed, added, "Not." He smiled at me. "A piece of work, isn't she."

"Every town's got one. I guess she's ours."

Trav took a breath. "Okay, besides learning that Stan Harris is an s-o-b, what exactly did we accomplish in there?"

"I don't know about accomplish, but we certainly *know* more than we did. We know that Marge was not taking her prescription."

"Yeah, I've been thinking about that. If anything, it takes some of the heat off Harris. Someone could make a case that since Marge didn't take her predisone—"

I couldn't help it: "Pred-*ni*-sone. It's got an 'n' in there."

"All right, prednisone. My point is, she wasn't taking it, and so someone could say that Tuesday's allergic reaction wasn't completely cured and came back on Thursday. And since she'd left herself unprotected, it killed her. That sort of lets you *and* Harris off the hook."

I hadn't looked at it that way. I'd been too relieved that I hadn't been responsible.

Well, partially relieved.

Maybe I was legally off the hook, but a residue of guilt clung in a small cold clump to the back of my neck. Should I have anticipated the pharmacy's P-I sheet and clarified it in advance? But how could I have known it would be so misleading?

Poor Marge… she'd known only part of the story. And just like anything else, that can be worse than knowing none of it.

But she could have called me, damn it. She knew I'm always available to answer questions, especially from her. She should have asked before deciding on her own to ignore medical advice.

I said, "It doesn't let him off completely. There's still that recording."

"Yeah." Trav shook his head. "That damn call."

I figured now was the time to drop my bomb. "Take the tape, and add the one-point-two million bucks he'll be receiving in death benefits, and what have you got?"

The car swerved a bit as Trav reacted. "One-point-two—how do you know that?"

"Saw the policies in the filing cabinet."

"Oh, Christ. I wanted to talk to you about that. You could have landed me in *big* trouble if he'd caught you."

That startled me. "You? How so? You didn't—"

"I brought you to his house, and my line about you working with the coroner and the sheriff's office wasn't exactly true. I could have been on my way to the unemployment office."

I mentally kicked myself. What a dummy. The possibility had never crossed my mind. I'd thought I was putting only myself in jeopardy.

"Sorry," I said. "I saw the opportunity and…"

I let it end there. I felt bad. I'm compulsively careful in my medicine, but I can be impulsive elsewhere.

His smile was thin. "No harm done this time, but next time you feel like playing Nancy Drew, promise to let me know."

That stung.

"Nancy Drew? Thanks a lot."

"All right then, Jessica Simpson."

"*What?*"

He reddened. "I meant that lady from *Murder She Wrote*. Jessica something or other."

I couldn't think of her last name either.

"The Angela Lansbury character?"

"Yeah. Her. Promise, okay?"

Neither comparison was without a barb. Nancy Drew was a kid and Jessica Whatever an old lady—but I guess I deserved it. Some of it, anyway.

"Promise. But the end result is that we know about the insurance. That's motive, isn't it?"

He shook his head. "Officially we do *not* know about the insurance. You made a *very* illegal search. That said, did you notice if any of the policies were brand new?"

"No. They were all dated five or ten years ago."

"Damn."

"But if he'd bought a new one, he might not have got around to filing it."

Trav bopped the steering wheel with his fist. "Nothing in this is straightforward. We've got a guy who lost his wife two days ago but doesn't look all that unhappy."

"If they weren't getting along—and from what I saw, they weren't—and if he'd rather be out catting around instead of married, and if he was a cold-hearted creep—"

"That's not an *if* in his case."

"—then he might see Marge's death as some sort of gift: No messy, expensive divorce, and he keeps all their assets, plus he gets an extra million-two in his pocket."

"So you're saying, given all those ifs, what's not to like?"

"Right."

We cruised down the hill in silence.

Then I said, "Sure would help if we knew where he was Thursday morning. Still no corroboration on his alibi?"

Trav laughed. "'Corroboration?' My, my, you do pick up the lingo fast."

"Hey, I watch *Law & Order*. And as for corroboration, I take it you don't have any."

"You take right. The only phone numbers we have are businesses and we haven't been able to track them to any homes. Follow-up will most likely have to wait till Monday."

"Well, I guess there's no rush. He doesn't know he's in your sights, so I can't see him taking off before he gets his insurance money. And that's going to take a while."

I remembered how long it was before my mother received Dad's death benefit check. And when it came she hadn't wanted to accept it—something about it being blood money or haunted or some sort of Irish voodoo—but I'd insisted. I'd taken the check and deposited it in her account myself. She'd needed it.

"I suppose," Trav said. He didn't sound happy.

I felt bad for him. I knew he wanted to hand the county detectives something more than the 9-1-1 tape, but we'd hit a wall. All we knew was that Marge hadn't taken her medication, which only enhanced the possibility that her death might not have been the result of foul play.

We did know about the insurance...

"At least the detectives ought to find Harris's million-plus bonanza interesting."

"I can't tell them."

"Why not?"

"Because I'm not supposed to know about the Harrises' insurance, and I don't want to compromise anything." He sighed. "And as information goes, it's not that valuable anyway."

"Sure it is."

"The first thing they do in a suspicious death is find out who has the most to gain. In other words, follow the money. So the first thing they look into is insurance."

"Oh."

"Yeah. Oh."

I wasn't about to give up. Stanley Harris had accused me of letting Marge down... of *negligence*. If he'd said it out of grief, okay. People need to place blame when they've lost someone dear. But if Harris was grieving he was doing a bang-up job of hiding it. It seemed obvious to me that avarice not grief was fueling his accusations.

If so, he'd made a big mistake. I was determined to make him regret using me as his whipping girl.

# 13

"What's the next step?" I said after a while.

Trav shrugged. "Don't know. I don't see any place else to go. I'd say we've gotten all we're going to get out of Harris, wouldn't you?"

I nodded. "I think that's a pretty safe bet."

"Then where else do we look? I'm open to ideas."

I didn't have any.

Silence as Trav turned onto 206.

Finally he said, "If only I knew where he was—or wasn't—when Marge was dying. If he wasn't in New York Thursday morning, I'd have some leverage on him. But like I said, we won't be able to nail that down till Monday."

And on Monday the case would be out of Trav's hands.

"Let me play devil's advocate," I said. "What if you got a call right now from your office and they told you that Stanley Harris's presence at that meeting in New York had been confirmed? Would that let him off the hook in your mind? Or would you still think he was guilty?"

"Still guilty, but that would really put me in a box. Tying him to Marge's death would be almost impossible then."

"Why? There's still that recording."

"Yeah. But Marge says '*He's* killing me.' She doesn't say *Stan* is killing me, or *my husband's* killing me. If she'd mentioned him by name, that would be different."

"So maybe it wasn't Harris."

"Who else, then? Harris is the only one with one-point-two-million reasons to want Marge dead."

"Okay," I said, "but if he was out of town, how did he kill her?"

"Maybe by leaving a tiny bit of peanut protein in something he knew she'd eat."

"But how could he know what she'd eat?"

He gave me an exasperated look. "What's with the third degree?"

"Devil's advocate, remember? Just to be sure that we're not going off half-cocked. Pointing at the wrong man would be worse than pointing at no man, right?"

He nodded. "Right."

"Okay, so the question on the table is: Assuming Harris dosed something with some sort of peanut product, and assuming he wasn't going to be there to put it on her plate, how could he know what Marge would eat?"

"Maybe she always ate the same thing every morning. I know I do."

"Really? What?"

"I have my Mr. Coffee set on a timer so it's all perked when I get to the kitchen—gotta have that first cup before anything else. Then I have a bowl of cereal and—"

"What cereal?"

A sheepish smile. "Trix."

I had to laugh. "*Trix*? Ever have a silly rabbit try to steal them?"

"Hey, I like Trix. Liked them since I was a kid."

"I would have figured you more the Wheaties type. You know, 'Breakfast of Champions' and all that."

"I like them too. Can't think of too many things I don't like to eat."

I knew the feeling.

"Okay, let's forget about *your* routines and get back to Marge's. Let's assume she ate the same thing every morning. Harris would know that, of course."

"Of course."

"And she had coffee and banana in her stomach, right?"

"Right."

"So... what if he doctored the coffee... or the banana?"

"How do you doctor a banana?"

I thought about that a moment. "You could inject it with peanut oil."

"How would you know which banana she'd pick?"

"You inject every banana in the fruit bowl. Or you inject just one and take all the rest, leaving her only one choice."

He gave me an appraising look. "You're scary, you know that?"

I thought about that, about what I'd just said, and kind of scared myself.

"I don't mean to sound cold-blooded. I'm just looking for answers… trying to think like a murderer."

"And doing an awfully good job. Too good." He smiled. "Remind me not to let you get too mad at me, okay?"

I returned the smile. "Remind yourself. Tie a string around your finger."

Another silent moment as Trav guided us back toward my condo.

"So it seems to me," I said, "that unless the ME can find some sort of test for peanut protein to use on Marge's stomach contents, Harris is going to walk away a rich widower."

Trav's expression was grim. "So it seems."

As he turned into the Holly Ridge parking lot I got to thinking about the empty evening ahead of me. I was tempted to bring up the dinner he'd promised, but held back. I wanted him to take the lead.

He pulled up by the curb in front of the entrance to my building and turned to me.

"Thanks a million, Norrie. I really appreciate your taking the time to help me on this, even though I wasted it."

"It wasn't wasted."

"Well, it all seems to add up to a big So What?"

From his end, maybe that was true. I waited for him to say something else but he didn't. So I gave him an opening.

"Well, what next?"

"Next?" He glanced at his watch. "The next thing for me is to go back to the department and sign out, then go home for a quick shower. Got to look good for my big date tonight."

My heart didn't actually sink, but it tripped over a beat.

"Oh?"

"Yep. Dinner and a movie with my number-one girl."

I wasn't sure I wanted to hear the rest, but I had to ask.

"And who might that be?"

"Maddy."

"Maddy who?"

"Maddy Lawton. My little girl."

I felt a welcome bubble of relief rise from my stomach through my chest.

"Oh, yes. I remember you mentioning her. How old is she?"

He grinned. "Ten going on forty. You know the type. Between her and her mother and me, she's the most mature. This is my night to take her out. She gets to choose the restaurant and the movie."

"That's great that you stay so close. It must mean so much to her."

"I hope so. I know it means everything to me." He looked at me. "And you mean something too, Norrie. I'm glad that car thief took a swing at me, otherwise I wouldn't have been in the ER the other day."

He took my face between his hands and kissed me on the lips, sending a tingle down to my toes.

When our lips parted I felt a little breathless.

"You know," I managed to say, "we've known each other for, what, twenty years, that's the first time you've kissed me."

He smiled. "Unlucky me. I hope it won't be the last."

I left that hanging. I still remembered the kiss I never got after the Sadie Hawkins dance. I wondered if he knew how I'd felt about him back then? Did that make him think I'd be a push-over now?

Overthinking again.

"See you Monday," I said as I made my exit.

He frowned. "Mon—?"

I pointed to his bandage. "The sutures, remember?"

He grinned. "Oh, yeah. Monday it is. And I still owe you that dinner."

"I remember. I've never been one to forget a free meal."

He laughed and waved as he drove off. I headed toward my building envying a ten-year-old.

# 14

Back in my place, I got Spotify to play me some Nora Jones as I checked out the damage again. The bathroom ceiling would have to be patched or replaced. And the hallway rug for sure. I emptied out the linen closet and moved the towels and such to the spare bedroom that acted as a study. The floor there was dry, at least. I didn't want rot setting in. I dried the shelves and threw all the ruined boxes of tissue and rolls of toilet paper into a plastic garbage bag.

I'd called a cleanup-restoration service and put them in touch with my adjustor from the insurance company. They said they'd take care of everything—remove the damaged rug and even fix the ceiling. I'd have to arrange for new hall carpet, though.

In my study I sorted through the latest crop of journals, most of them freebies supported by advertising. I tossed *Physician's Money Digest* into the circular file without opening it. I had no extra money. I kept the latest issues of *Family Practice News* and *American Family Physician*. They often carried a couple of articles germane to my practice. I kept *Consultant* too. I liked to test myself with its monthly "Photoclinic." I usually do pretty well.

Next stop was the kitchen. Normally I'd be famished by now but I wasn't a bit hungry. Hooray for Tezinex. I ate another power bar. After that I was ready to call it quits. I gathered up my garbage bag and headed out to the dumpster.

Outside, the moon had just peeked over the eastern horizon. I stood in the dark by the dumpster and found Venus hanging in the west. Astronomy had been another of my geeky high-school hobbies. I could still name all the constellations. I—

Something rustled in the bushes behind me. I jump-turned and scanned the foliage. A raccoon, maybe, waiting to get at the garbage. I listened but the sound wasn't repeated.

I lifted the top and threw in my garbage, then checked the sky again. Mars should be—

Another rustle, louder this time. I turned and made out a man-shaped figure in the shadows, moonlight gleaming off a cap and a shoulder...

Someone was staring at me from not ten feet away.

Moonlight glinted off something long and metallic in his hand...

A knife?

Suddenly he leaped toward me. I let out a scream and ran—not the loping style of running I do every morning, this was a mad headlong dash at full speed toward my building's lighted entrance. I heard footsteps pounding on the grass behind me. Knowing it would slow me down, I didn't look back. I let panic push me to a speed I never thought myself capable of.

I pulled out my key card and had it ready when I hit the lit-up entryway. I swiped it and pulled open the door. As I slipped inside I turned and yanked it closed with every ounce of strength I had and—

No one was there.

I stood gasping and sweating, my heart an angry fist pounding against the inside of my ribs.

I hadn't imagined it. Someone had been out there, and he'd come after me. I knew it.

I ran up to my apartment, double-locked the door behind me, and went to call Trav. He'd left me his home phone number... where had I put it? I found it in my wallet and dialed. After four rings his answering machine picked up. I hung up without leaving a message and dialed 9-1-1. I couldn't help thinking of Marge punching in those same three digits two days ago.

An operator came on and I started babbling...

# 15

The police had come and gone without finding anyone lurking about. I was no help as far as a useful description. I'd seen part of a shadow, nothing more.

To their credit the two officers hadn't treated me like a nutcase. And I wasn't. I'd heard as well as seen. All I could guess was that the lurker had turned away when I reached the lighted area.

They promised to run a patrol car through the parking area regularly to discourage any outsiders with theft or worse on their mind.

They wrote out their report, offered all sorts of assurances, and left me.

The first thing I did was hop in the car and head home. As I drove, my thoughts zoomed every which way: Marge… Travis… his date with Maddy… Stanley Harris… peanuts… malpractice… Eddie the Shark Stark…

But they kept returning to tonight's incident: Was I a random target, or had someone been watching me? Was it a coincidence that hours after I'd been poking through Stan Harris's house someone tried to assault me? Had he realized I'd invaded his filing cabinet and feared I'd seen something incriminating?

Stan Harris stalking me with a knife seemed way over the top, but if he'd killed Marge, was it so farfetched to think he might kill again to protect himself?

Questions… questions… and no answers.

And behind them all, the memory of Marge's pale, slack, staring face. And her last words.

*He's killing me!*

Who, Marge?

The "he" had to be Stan.

But why—*why* did she think someone was killing her?

She'd realized something at that moment... something she never had time to tell.

But *how* had she known? Had she tasted something? I stiffened behind the steering wheel. Taste!

That was it!

I looked at the dashboard clock: *11:13*. No way Trav would still be out with a ten-year-old—*if* he'd been out with a ten-year-old. I grabbed my cell, scrolled through RECENT CALLS and thumbed his number.

Trav picked up on the second ring. "Lawton."

He must have thought I was someone from the department.

"Trav, it's Norrie."

"*Norrie! Anything wrong?*"

"Look, I'm sorry to call you at this hour but—"

"*Forget it. I wasn't sleeping anyway.*"

"That's a relief. I hope I didn't wake Maddy."

"*There's no phone in the other bedroom. What's up?*"

I told him what had happened.

"*Jesus! Why didn't you call me?*"

"I did but you weren't in."

"*I'll give you my cell number. Jesus, are you okay there alone? Want me to—never mind.*"

"Never mind what?"

"*I was going to offer to come over but I can't with Maddy here.*"

"That's okay. I'm on my way to my mum's"

I told him my suspicion that Stan Harris might have been the one who'd chased me.

He said, "*I can't see him doing something like that. He's no dummy, and that would be very dumb. Probably some drug-starved mook looking for someone to rip off. I doubt he'll be back.*"

"I hope you're right." I felt better just talking to him. "But that's not why I called. I've been thinking about Marge."

"*Me too.*"

"I think I know why she thought someone was killing her."

*"I'm listening."*

"She'd detected a peanut flavor and knew instantly that she was in big trouble."

*"Okay, but that doesn't mean someone was trying to kill her."*

"It does if the peanut flavor was where it shouldn't or couldn't be naturally."

I stopped and let him take the next mental step.

*"Like in a banana, for instance?"*

"Exactly. Can't you picture Stanley Harris drawing peanut oil into a syringe, then injecting it into a banana?"

*"I can picture him doing just about anything. But where'd he get the syringe? You can't simply walk into a drugstore and buy one. And where'd he dispose of it?"*

"I can't answer that, but—oh jeez, wait..."

*"What?"*

"The reaction." I slammed my palm against the steering wheel. "It just occurred to me. The reaction would have been immediate. By the time Marge recognized the peanut flavor, the symptoms would have been escalating. If the reaction occurred in the study—and no one seems to dispute that—then where are the coffee cup and the banana skin? They weren't in the office when I was there. You were at the house right after the EMTs arrived. Do you remember seeing them?"

*"No, but things were in such an uproar, I could have missed them."*

"Well, if they were there, they aren't now. Which means someone moved them."

I gasped as an awful scenario flashed through my mind.

*"What?"* Trav said.

"I just had a picture of Stanley Harris standing in the kitchen listening to Marge's strangled cries as her throat closed, waiting until she stopped, then going in and removing the cup and the remains of the banana."

I shivered.

*"And then what?"* he said.

"And then taking the banana along as he left before the EMTs arrived."

Another pause. *"You really think Harris is that cold-blooded?"*

"I don't know. Maybe."

Another shiver. I didn't want to think anybody I'd been in the same room with could be that cold-blooded.

"*Yeah, but that scenario leaves him without an alibi.*"

"Not if he has people to cover for him."

"*Yeah, well… I can see people covering for something like an affair or a night out with the boys, but with a dead wife involved…*"

I sighed. "You've got a point."

"*Let me play devil's advocate this time. You've been dealing with an awful lot of ifs. Let me give you one: What if we search the house and find the banana skin in the garbage and there's no needle hole in it? What then?*"

I thought about that. Good question. And a good idea: Look at the flip side.

"Okay, if the banana's innocent, and the reaction occurred in her office…"

"*And don't automatically assume that Harris is involved. Just come up with some innocent way Marge could have gotten some peanut into her system. Once we've got that, we can figure out whether or not it was the result of foul play.*"

"Tough one. It looked to me like she was taking her diet pretty seriously—I couldn't find a single edible in that office."

"*Could there be another way?*"

I couldn't imagine one. I closed my eyes and pictured Marge's desk… the bills… the envelopes, some sealed, some not… the—

Envelopes! I felt a rush of adrenaline.

"Oh, my God!"

"*What? Tell me.*"

"She was paying bills… she was part way through the stack when the reaction hit."

"*How do you know?*"

"Because I remember some of the envelopes were sealed. And to seal them she had to—"

"*Lick them!*" he cried. "*Goddamn! She had to lick the flaps! Just like in* Seinfeld*!*"

"*Seinfeld*? What are you talking about? This isn't funny."

"*The* Seinfeld *episode where George's fiancée dies after licking the envelopes for their wedding invitations. You must have seen it.*"

"No, sorry. Never."

*"Come on! Everybody's seen it."*

"Well, then, meet Ms. Everybody-Minus-One." I'd never gotten into *Seinfeld* first run—too young. I'll catch the occasional rerun nowadays, but fatal envelopes didn't ring a bell. "But the envelopes weren't poisoned, were they?"

*"No, just an accident. It doesn't matter."*

"But it does. If someone watched that episode and got the idea of spreading just a tiny bit of peanut oil on the glue strip—"

*"There you go again. Looking for murder. In the show it was cheap glue that happened to be toxic. This could be similar: What if the envelope company used a glue that just happened to include some sort of peanut-related product?"*

"But it's obvious from the call that Marge recognized a peanut taste and knew that Stan had set her up."

*"She suspected. She couldn't know."*

"But it's perfect!" I said. "Harris knows his wife does bills every Thursday, so on Wednesday morning he smears a little peanut oil on the glue strip of one of the envelopes, then takes off for New York. He's out of state when his wife has the reaction."

*"But he couldn't know she'd die."*

"No, but if she does, he collects a million or two. If she doesn't, he gets to sue me. It's win-win."

During the ensuing silence I could hear Trav breathing on the other end of the line. Finally...

*"I've got to get hold of those envelopes. An unfortunate ingredient in the glue lets Harris off the hook. But a smear of peanut oil..."*

"Yeah. Then he's cooked. But how do we get them?"

*"We?"*

"Yes, we. You can't let Nancy Drew figure this out for you, then leave her out of the kill."

*"I'm not going to kill him."*

"Just a figure of speech. But Trav, I'm serious. I want to be there when you go back."

I wanted to watch Stan Harris's expression, wanted to look into his eyes as the deputy sheriff asked him for the envelopes.

# 16

Mum was nowhere in sight when I got home. No surprise there. She tended to be early-to-bed type and Saturday was just another night to her.

So much had happened today that not until I was through the door and on my way to my bedroom did I realize that I might have to face my father—or his revenant or whatever—again tonight. Despite everything, I still didn't believe in ghosts. I couldn't. It wasn't in me... yet.

I stopped before the landscape, canted as usual. I'd always found it a bit annoying but tonight it was definitely on my nerves. If I was going to be living here for a few days, I couldn't leave it like that. So I straightened it. It still didn't look right. So I tried again. Still not right.

I'd be up all night if I kept this up. I forced myself to head for the shower.

When I finally got under the covers, sleep seemed far away. The residual adrenaline from the attack by the dumpster plus the anticipation of an apparition kept my brain humming.

And slowly, something began to glow in the air near my bed.

*Norrie,* said that flat voice between my ears. *It's me. I'm back.*

"Hello... Dad."

God, it felt weird whispering that.

*Sorry about leaving so suddenly last night. I couldn't hold on any longer.*

"I understand."

I didn't really. My mind kept balking at the possibility that I was talking to my father's ghost, but I was. I *was*!

*I used up lots of energy last night.*

"I hope it was worth it."

*You're worth everything to me, Norrie.*

I think I might have choked up at that. Not might have—definitely.

*You asked me what was holding me here.*

"I told you I'd heard it's usually some unfinished business."

*Yeah, and I've been thinking about that all day.*

"By the way, where do you go during the day?"

*I'm here, but it's like I'm asleep. I can't see anything in all that light. But about unfinished business...*

"Right. Have you got any?"

*I think so. It might be forgiveness.*

What? I was instantly incensed.

"Someone has to forgive you? That's ridiculous. You don't need forgiveness for anything. You were—"

*No, Norrie. Me forgive. I'm the one to forgive.*

"Who?"

*You know who.*

And suddenly I thought I did. But I wanted to hear it from him.

"I'm afraid I don't."

*Yes, you do.*

"No. Stop playing games and tell me."

Actually I was playing a game: I wanted him to say the name.

*All right.* Can a ghost sigh? Because I swear I heard him sigh. *Corrado.*

Corrado... Uncle Corry... my godfather and his old best friend who disappeared.

"That's the first time I've heard you say his name since I was thirteen."

*Well, maybe being dead gives you a little... perspective. Maybe I'm here until I forgive Corrado.*

His best friend from the old country... Dad called him his *fratellino*—his little brother. He and Corrado Piperno had been inseparable. They both came over from Italy as kids and formed the unbreakable bond of two immigrants making their way together in a new land.

And then one night when I was around twelve or thirteen, Corrado sneaked out of his house, leaving his wife and daughter alone, and was never seen again.

"Well, do you?"

*Forgive him? Not yet.*

"Dad, it's been—"

*He left Marie and his little Angelina. No note, no nothin'! He's scum!*

Dad wasn't saying it, but his *fratellino* had left him without a word too.

I remembered the commotion in the house, the police talking to Dad, me listening at the top of the stairs as they asked him if Corrado had been involved with the mob—he was Italian, after all, so of course he was, right? When my father shot that down they asked about another woman. I can still hear Dad saying no-no-no over and over.

"Why don't you try to work on forgiving him, Dad?"

*How do I work on forgiving scum?*

"Because if you can find it in your heart to forgive him, maybe you can move on."

*To where?*

"To... I don't know... heaven?"

*Forgiveness comes from you heart. I've got no forgiveness for him there. I can't fake that.*

"You don't have to fake it. You can—"

*What if it's something else, Norrie?*

"Like what?"

*I have no idea but I could be stuck here until I can figure that out.*

"Stuck here forever?"

*I'm losing strength now,* he said, the voice fading with the glow in the room.

"Dad, wait. Please."

But he was gone and I was alone.

# SUNDAY

# 1

Idid manage to doze after a while, but my internal clock had me awake at sunrise.

I still had a warm residual glow from talking to my father, though I was sad he was still carrying a grudge against Corrado. For once I was glad to be back at the old place instead of the condo—especially after last night's attack. I would have been afraid to go out for a jog back there. But nobody knew I was in Carmel.

I got up and dressed. Once outside, I tried to forget last night's fear and enjoy the scenery. The breeze blew cool but promised to warm as the day grew, and the trees were showing off their new leaves. I love May.

And I love to be out early on a Sunday. It's as if I have the world to myself. No commuters heading for Baltimore, no school bus fumes, no traffic rumble from the interstate. It's even too early for church bells.

And I was anticipating the coming day: Trav and I were going to nail Stanley Harris for Marge's death.

Not that I truly believed that. The real, legally correct nailing would take longer. Much longer. But I knew that later today, when I saw his reaction to Trav's request for the envelopes, I'd know. I had faith that the detectives in the county homicide unit could piece together a case against him from that point, after which a jury would have its turn with him.

But today, in my head, he'd been declared guilty. And sentenced to hang.

This morning's jog wasn't an easy one. Lack of sleep made

the air feel thick as Jell-O. Still I kept forcing my way forward, hoping for a shot of those elusive endorphins.

It never came. But I did get a call from Travis.

"*Good morning,*" he said. "*I trust the rest of your night was uneventful.*"

"Blessedly so." No way was I mentioning dear dead Daddy's ghost to anyone—*anyone.* "So what's up?"

"*Well, I've got good news and I've got bad, depending on how you look at it.*"

Uh-oh.

"Give me the good news first."

"*It's all one. I called the department this morning to check my messages. One of our clerks had managed to find the home number of one of Harris's alibis and she left me the number. I called as soon as the clock hit nine, and the guy confirms that on Thursday morning he was in a meeting in Manhattan with Stanley Harris.*"

"You think he was telling the truth?"

"*Yeah, I do.*"

I chewed on that.

"This complicates things, doesn't it."

"*Well, it does help Harris.*"

"But it doesn't get him completely off. We've already figured out how he could have coated the glue strips on the envelopes before leaving."

"*Yeah, but we've yet to establish that the envelopes are the culprit.*"

"Oh, right. I've been so sure they're to blame that it's become a *fait accompli.*"

"*Hmmm?*"

The culture gap again.

"I've been thinking of it as a done deal. But it's not, is it."

"*No.*"

"We've got to get those envelopes, don't we."

"*We do.*"

"When do you want to go see Harris?"

"*Well, I'm taking Maddy out to breakfast—probably a late one since she's still asleep—and then I've got to get her back home so she can study for a geography test tomorrow. How about twelve thirty or so? Pick you up?*"

"You don't have to. I can meet you there."

"*I want to. And besides, I think it's better if we arrive in an official unit.*"

"Don't you ever get a day off?"

"*I'm supposed to be off today, but this is important, and tomorrow will be too late—I'll be out of it.*"

"You really want this, don't you."

"*Yeah, I guess I do.*"

So did I. Very much.

"Then we'll just have to find a way to get it. I'll be waiting outside my mom's place. You know the address?"

He remembered from when we were kids.

# 2

Back home I took my daily Tezinex and munched a power bar as I watched another video on my laptop. Then into the shower. My body was already dry and I was into my robe when Mum knocked on the door.

"I'm going to church with Timmy. Want us to drive you?"

I stepped out and kept drying my hair. "No. I'll catch a later mass." Not. "What's up?"

"I checked with Sean and he'll be coming to dinner. Isn't that wonderful?"

"Super."

"You'll be here, of course."

"Of course. Do I ever miss Sunday dinner?"

Am I ever *allowed* to miss?

"Well, there was that time just this past February when—"

"I was a thousand miles away, Mum. At the internal medicine update. Remember?"

*I* remembered. The fact that I'd chosen a course in Miami during the dead of winter hadn't been a coincidence. Heavenly warmth. I'd come back refreshed. Wiser too.

"I know that, but still... we missed you."

Guilt springs eternal.

"But you survived, right?"

"Of course, dear."

"Tell me... is, um, Kevin coming?"

"Doesn't he always?"

He does. You rarely see Sean without Kevin.

"Want me to whip up an appy while you're out?"

"That won't be necessary, dear, but thank you. Timmy and I will stop at the store after mass. We'll keep it simple so that Sean can get back to the city."

"Oh, right. Wouldn't want Sean staying out too late."

Big brother was coming.

Yippee.

Not that I've anything in the slightest against Sean. I love him. He's a great guy. He can't help that he's the first-born son of an Irish mother, and therefore right up there with the saints.

Saint Sean... who turns water into wine and then walks on it... whose presence demotes the faithful daughter to scullery maid: "Norrie, hang up Sean's coat"... "Norrie, fetch Sean a beer..."

To Sean's credit he'll always insist on hanging up his own coat and fetching his own beer.

As I said, it's not his fault. Except maybe that he doesn't visit as often as he could. If he were more of a regular, maybe his visits wouldn't be state occasions.

But Sean has perfectly understandable reasons for maintaining a certain distance, and I sympathize with them.

Still, it rankles a bit.

Timmy honked out front and she hurried out to join him, leaving me alone in the living room... with the damn crooked landscape. I straightened it half a dozen times this way and that but it never looked right. I was getting ready to put a match to it.

# 3

By twelve thirty I was in the passenger seat of a sheriff's department patrol cruiser. I'd left Mum a note saying I'd be back in time for dinner. Trav looked spiffy in his pressed uniform and his polished leather belt.

I wasn't quite so spiffy in my jeans and a red Henley shirt, but damned if I was going to dress up for Stanley Harris.

"We have to phrase this just right when we ask him," I said as we turned onto Lantern Lane and headed for the Harris house.

"Meaning?"

"We can't let him know he's under suspicion. We can't even let him know we suspect foul play. We have to ask for those envelopes in the most innocuous way we can think of."

Trav frowned. "Well, I wasn't about to go up to him and say, 'We think someone smeared peanut oil on one of the flaps and we want to check it out.' But I don't know… what's the best way to put it?"

"Just say it occurred to you that since it seems highly unlikely that Marge ingested a peanut-containing food, perhaps it got into her system from a non-food source—like the glue on an envelope."

"If he tampered with those envelopes, he's going to know he's a suspect."

"Not if you talk fast, saying you think it's possible one of the envelope companies used a peanut-derived compound in its glue."

"'Peanut-derived,'" he said, nodding. "Got to remember that.

But even then, why should he give them to us? If I was him, I sure as hell wouldn't."

"But we'll see his face when you ask for them. His refusal will tell us something too, right? What grieving husband wouldn't want to pin down the cause of his wife's death? Unless, of course, *he* was the cause."

We pulled into Harris's driveway and stopped. Trav turned to me; he looked uncomfortable.

"You know, Norrie, the more I think about it, the more I think maybe it might be better if you stay in the car."

Demons would be ice fishing on Lake Hell before I'd agree to that, but I wanted to hear his reasoning.

"Oh, really? And why is that?"

"Don't get all huffy now."

"I'm not huffy."

"I hear huffiness in your voice, but just let me say that I thought your being a doctor and all could, you know, lend some credibility to this peanut-protein-in-the-glue thing."

"And now?"

"Now I don't want to listen to Harris going off on you again about letting Marge out of the hospital too early. He's got no right."

"Maybe he has."

He blinked. "What?"

"Well, if I'd kept her until Thursday morning, he wouldn't have been able to use his New York trip as a cover, and Marge would still be alive."

"That's the—"

"Stupidest thing you ever heard? Yeah, I agree. I guess I've been thinking about this too much. And that's not good when you're Irish—even half Irish. I mean, we can always find ways to blame ourselves."

"So you agree with me that—"

"No, I don't. Why else am I along? Just for a Sunday afternoon car ride to the Hill? I don't think so."

"Okay, okay. But just let me do the talking, all right?"

I've never been one for letting someone else do all the talking, but I could see his point here. He didn't want to make waves.

Fair enough. But that did not mean I would go gently into silence. Not without a few parting shots.

"Can I nod my head when the situation warrants it?"

"Norrie…"

"I have this little lever in the middle of my back. If you push it up and down my lips move. That way I can say anything you want."

He sighed. "You're not making this easy."

"Only kidding. I'm cool. My lips are sealed."

He looked at me with a relieved expression. "Then you're not upset? You understand?"

"Perfectly."

"Great," he said with a smile. "Let's go get this turkey."

As he opened his door, I couldn't resist: "Where's my leash? You don't want to let me out of the car without it, do you?"

He rolled his eyes. "Jesus…"

I gave him a smile to let him know I was through, then joined him on the other side of the car. He adjusted his Stetson, then cocked his head toward the front door.

"Let's roll."

He led. I followed a subservient two steps behind.

# 4

Stanley Harris did not try to hide his displeasure at seeing us on his doorstep again. He threw me a quick glare then concentrated on Trav.

"I thought I made it clear yesterday that you two were no longer welcome here."

"You may change your mind when you hear what I have to say."

"I doubt that, but go ahead."

"Well, sir, since we couldn't find any peanut-containing food in the house, I got to thinking that maybe it came from a non-food source. Doctor Marconi came up with the idea that maybe there was a peanut-derived substance in the glue on one of the envelopes that came with the bills Mrs. Harris was paying."

I took passing note of the credit Trav gave me for coming up with the idea, but I was more interested in Harris's reaction.

If he was guilty, he hid it well. Bluster is a great camouflage.

"That's ridiculous! Peanut protein in glue? You've been watching too much *Seinfeld*."

So… Stan had seen that episode too. It might have inspired him.

"I know it sounds farfetched, sir, but it could help the coroner close the case."

He stood staring at us, silent, his expression guarded. I wished I could read minds. What would it be like to be a fly on the wall of that nasty little brain?

"That's an interesting theory," he said at last, "but I'm afraid you're too late."

"How do you mean, sir?"

"I mailed the finished envelopes yesterday."

To Trav's credit he didn't throw his hat on the ground and stomp on it, saying Shit!-Shit!-Shit!

I did, however, notice him swallow hard before replying.

"That's unfortunate, sir. They might have answered a lot of questions about what happened to your wife."

Harris turned his stony gaze on me. "I have no questions. I *know* who's at fault."

I wanted to say, *Give it a rest!* but I'd promised Trav to keep mum.

I'd watched Harris closely through all this. The evidence against him was lost in the US mail, out of reach, yet I detected no relief or triumph.

Trav looked at me. The disappointment in his eyes tugged at my heart. Harris had won.

Or maybe not. Not yet, at least.

I broke my promise and said, "Where did you mail them, Mister Harris?"

He pointed to his mailbox at the curb. "I put them out for pickup."

I felt my thoughts kick into high gear. This was Sunday... no mail today. If he'd put the letters out after the mail truck had made its Saturday pass, they'd still be in the box.

"Can we check your mailbox?" I said. "It's possible you missed the pickup."

"I doubt it," he replied. "But go ahead. Knock yourselves out."

Trav started toward the street but I jumped ahead of him.

"I'll check it,"

I didn't want to be left standing alone with Stanley Harris. Not just because of his attitude or because he gave me the creeps.

I crossed the lawn to the box and pulled open the little hinged door. I didn't hold much hope of finding anything, but as the door swung down I spotted a stack of four envelopes.

Please let it be outgoing mail, I prayed. *Please.*

I pulled them out and immediately checked the return address stickers: *Margery Harris... 1242 Lantern Lane...*

I suppressed an urge to do a victory dance and simply held up the stack.

"They're still here!" I hoped it didn't sound like a cheer.

The sudden light in Trav's eyes sent a tingle of delight through me. He was still in the game.

He immediately turned to Harris and said something I did not hear. I hurried back across the lawn and reached them in time to catch the reply.

"Oh, I don't think I can let you do that. I've got bills and checks in those envelopes. I can't let you simply walk off with them."

Oh, he was a cool one, this guy.

I said, "What if you remove the contents and just give us the envelopes?"

He opened his mouth to reply, then closed it.

Gotcha.

"How about it?" Trav prompted.

Harris thought about it for a moment, then shrugged. "I guess I could do that."

I was stunned. I'd been sure he'd refuse. He *had* to refuse…

That is, if he was guilty.

But if he wasn't, it wouldn't matter to him.

Unless…

Unless he'd taken the precaution of substituting fresh envelopes for the doctored ones. He could have burned the originals or torn them up and flushed them into the sewer system.

I wouldn't put it past him. He seemed sneaky enough.

I glanced at the faces of the envelopes. Three were of the pre-printed reply variety, but the fourth was handwritten. The script looked neat and vaguely feminine. Marge? Or Harris imitating her hand?

Harris started to nod. "Yes. Let's do that."

I handed him the stack and we followed him inside to the office. He sat at the desk and pulled a letter opener from the top drawer. He carefully slit the top of each, pulled out the check and the return portion of the bill, then laid them aside.

"There," he said, holding up the empties but keeping them out of Trav's reach. "You can have these on one condition."

"What would that be, sir?"

"If you do find something, I want to know immediately—I want to know the guilty company and I want the fatal envelope returned to me."

Trav said, "I don't know when I'd be able to get the envelope itself back to you, but I've got no problem with letting you know the rest."

"But the envelope will be kept safe?"

"As part of a coroner's case, of course."

Harris mulled this a moment, then thrust the envelopes toward Trav.

"Very well," he said with a tight smile. "See what you can find."

I'd watched his eyes the whole time and was unsettled by what I'd seen.

# 5

I turned to Trav as soon as we'd slammed the patrol cruiser's doors shut.

"He didn't do it."

Trav stopped in mid-reach for his keys.

"What?"

"Harris didn't kill Marge."

"You of all people—how can you say that when we haven't tested the envelopes yet?"

"If we find anything, it won't be Harris's doing."

"You don't know that."

"Yeah, I do. Did he look the least bit guilty? Did you see *any* trace of fear or uncertainty in him today?"

"Well, no, but he could be a stone cold psycho."

"Even a psycho wouldn't hand us the evidence that could hang him."

"You mean you think he pulled a switch on us?"

"I did at first, but then I saw something in his eyes I've seen before."

"What? When?"

"He showed up at the ER when I admitted Marge to the hospital. As the possibility arose that the diet power bar she'd eaten might have caused the reaction, he became excited and started lawsuit talk."

Trav's mouth twisted. "Yeah. He's big on that."

"Well, I saw that same look when he handed over those envelopes. Not guilt, not worry, not even a smug I'm-one-step-ahead-of-you-dummies look. I saw dollar signs."

"You mean—?"

"Yeah. He's hoping, he's *praying* we'll find peanut protein on one of these envelopes."

Trav leaned back in his seat, staring through the windshield. His voice was barely above a whisper when he spoke.

"He's looking to sue."

"Right. The company that sent the bill, the company that made the envelope—wrongful death suits that will net him big bucks. I may not know crime but I know people, and I know a murderer would be thinking about saving his skin, not cashing in."

I winced at the unintentional rhyme. I sounded like I was rapping.

"Shit," Trav said. Then he pulled himself together and straightened in his seat. "Seems like a waste of time to check those envelopes then."

Not to me. I still needed to know what kicked off Marge's second anaphylactic reaction.

"Well, finding peanut protein in one of the glue strips would close the coroner's file. You'll have solved the case."

His smile was wan. "Yeah, there's that, I suppose. Still…"

I knew what he was thinking: He'd rather bring in a human culprit than an envelope.

He started the car. As he pulled out of the driveway I held one of the envelopes to my nose and sniffed along the flap seam.

"What are you up to?"

"Call it preliminary testing."

I meant that as a joke. It stopped being funny when I sniffed the L.L.Bean envelope.

"Oh my God!"

"What?"

"This envelope! It smells like—here!" I shoved it under his nose. "What's that smell like to you?"

He shook his head. "Can't go by me. I've got a rotten sniffer."

"Well, I've got a good one, and mine's yelling, 'Peanut!' loud and clear."

"You're sure?"

"Absolutely. And it's too strong to be just an ingredient in the glue. This flap has been dosed with peanut oil."

"What the f—" He caught himself. "What the hell is going on here?"

I gave that a moment of thought.

"Well, as I see it, we have two options: Either Stanley Harris is the stupidest murderer on Earth—and he's not stupid—or he doesn't have a clue about what's on this envelope."

Trav's eyes were wide. "Somebody else?"

"Has to be."

"But who?"

Random thoughts swirled through my brain. Suddenly two of them bumped and clicked.

I slapped Trav on the arm. "Turn around."

"Why? If you're thinking of going back to Harris—?"

"No way. I'm thinking of going a little farther down the street. To talk to one of his neighbors."

Trav looked at me as if I'd just told him I was a space alien.

"But—"

"Just humor me while I check with Miss Neighborhood Watch to try to confirm a crazy hunch."

# 6

Beth Henderson answered the door. Her hands shot to her mouth when she recognized me.

"Oh, no! What's happened? Is Mom—?"

"She's fine. This is about something else."

"Oh, thank God! I mean, her doctor and a deputy... for a minute I thought..."

"So sorry. She's fine, really. I'm sending her home tomorrow as planned. May we come in?"

"Yes, of course." She backed up and we stepped into the living room. She turned to Trav. "I suppose then that this is in response to my call."

Trav frowned. "What call? I haven't—"

"It was only a few minutes ago. I guess you'll get the message when you check in."

"What was it about?"

Her tone chilled. "Stanley Harris's paramour."

I said, "The one you told me you saw him with coming out of the Starlight Motel?"

She nodded. "Yes. He should be tarred and feathered!"

I couldn't have agreed more but kept that to myself.

"What about this woman?" Trav said. "As I understand, you didn't recognize her."

Beth hesitated, then sighed. "But I did. It was the cleaning girl."

After running into Alison at the Harris place yesterday, I'd begun to wonder if they might be involved. Now I knew.

"You're sure?" Trav said.

Beth nodded.

"Why didn't you tell us this earlier?"

Beth looked away. "I didn't want to get involved." She looked at me and shrugged. "I know it's a terrible cliché, but I didn't. People already think I'm a terrible busybody. But now with everything that's happened, I think someone should know."

My thoughts were racing in all different directions.

"When was the last time you saw Alison at the Harrises'?"

"Yesterday. I saw her leave shortly after you two arrived."

"And the time before that?"

"Wednesday morning."

"Wait a minute," Trav said. "We were told her cleaning day was Tuesday. That's how she was there to save Marge the first time."

Beth's expression turned to granite. "Yes, she was there as usual on Tuesday morning. But she was also there Tuesday night."

I said, "Night? While Marge was in the hospital?"

The bastard.

Beth nodded. "Poor Marge! What a terrible thing to happen to such a good woman."

"We'll all miss her," Trav said, "but what about Tuesday night?"

"Stanley drove up with the girl in his car. It was dark then and he probably thought he was sneaking her in."

"But you caught him in the act."

She looked uncomfortable. "Well, I just happened to look out the window at the moment she got out of the car. The two of them hurried inside but not before I spotted her short, brassy, bottle-blonde hair."

Yeah, that would be Alison.

"Did you see her leave?"

She nodded. "Stanley Harris drove her home early the next morning."

# 7

"Alison," Trav muttered as we returned to the cruiser. I nodded. "Alison Crowley: cleaning girl, paramour." His eyebrows lifted. "And maybe murderer?"

"Yes. Maybe."

I felt lax, enervated, mentally fogged. As if someone had pulled my plug. This turned everything around. I'd sighted in on Stanley Harris, focusing on him to the exclusion of all other possibilities.

With my scientific training, I should have known better. After overseeing clinical trials of a number of new drugs during my residency, I should have *damn* well known better.

I'd broken the first rule of the scientific method: I'd closed my mind. I'd started with a preconceived notion and let it preclude other possibilities.

"This needs some thought," Trav said, "and I don't think well on an empty stomach. You hungry?"

I shook my head. "No. Big breakfast." The Tezinex and the protein shake at noon were holding me. But I was low on caffeine. "I'll have a cup of coffee though."

We used the drive-thru at Burger King near the Safeway. I didn't feel like running into patients inside. I was angry with myself and not in the mood to make nice-nice.

BK coffee isn't great but it's better than none. Trav bought a Whopper and fries. Plus a Kids Meal with a Coke.

"You must have skipped breakfast."

"Not really. Had a Tremendous Twelve when I took Maddy to Perkins. But it was early."

Tremendous Twelve… I'd seen that on the Perkins menu. It needed almost twelve lines to list the items.

"But the Kids Meal is just to get the toy for Maddy." He held up a clear envelope containing a little plastic figurine that looked like a cross between a turtle and a duck. "It's a character from the Disney flick we saw last night."

"So you're just going to throw out the Kids Meal?"

"Hell no. That would be a waste. You want it?"

"No, thanks," I said, hoping I didn't sound too sloppy. The aroma was making me salivate. "A Tremendous Twelve, a Whopper, fries, and a Kids Meal. And you don't gain weight?"

"Not an ounce."

I eyed his pistol in its leather holster. A couple of quick moves and I could have it out…

No jury in the world would convict me.

He parked us in a remote corner of the parking lot and chowed down.

"So let me ask you," he said between bites. "If Stan didn't dose the glue strips, that leaves Alison. But if it's Alison, why did she save Marge's life the first time around?"

I added a packet of Splenda to my coffee—I keep a supply in my bag.

"That's the part that doesn't fit. If she'd wanted Marge out of the picture, she could have simply turned her back and waited for her to choke to death. Yet she saved her. Would she set her up for a second reaction? Doesn't make sense."

I took a sip. Yuck. I groaned.

"The coffee's that bad?"

"The way I've approached this—it's all wrong."

Trav shrugged. "Happens all the time. It's not like it's a science."

"But it is. It's very much like a science."

"Science is a bunch of facts—"

"No-no-no." This pervasive misconception was one of my pet peeves. "It's anything *but* a bunch of facts. Everybody thinks science is carved in stone, but it's really an ongoing *process*. You start with an observation: Let's say, for instance, you've noticed that plants tend to grow better in the sun than in the shade. So you come up with a hypothesis: plants need light to grow. You test that hypothesis by taking a field of a hundred plants and leaving fifty in the sun and depriving the remaining fifty of all light. If the second fifty die, you've bolstered your hypothesis; so you keep repeating the experiment and refining as you go. After enough successful experiments, you can form a *theory*, which is a set of related hypotheses generally accepted as true."

"Like the theory of evolution."

"Yes!" He's got it. By George, he's got it. "Evolution is a perfect example of science as a process. Although nobody with half a brain denies evolution itself, the how and why of it are still up for grabs. Theories abound. For a long time it was generally agreed that the earliest ancestors of humans arose in East Africa five million years ago. But then a skull was discovered farther west that was dated as *seven* million years old. What did scientists do? They didn't say, 'That has to be wrong because it's written here that the first hominids appeared five million years ago, not seven.' Instead they said, 'Hmmm, what's going on here? Maybe we were wrong. Let's look into this. If the data check out, we'll have to revise the theory.' So you see, science isn't knowledge, it's a process of *uncovering* knowledge, and it's constantly revising itself."

Trav nodded. "Like a crime investigation."

"Exactly. Einstein said we should look for what is, not what we think should be. I broke that rule by committing the scientific cardinal sin of prejudice. I prejudged Stanley Harris. I tried and convicted him, *then* went looking for evidence. Yes, he had motive and opportunity, but I never asked the next question. In science you always ask the next question, and in this case it was, Did anyone *else* have motive and opportunity? I'd been told that he was a having an affair. But did I consider the possibility that the Other Woman might have a motive for wanting Marge out of the way? No. I never gave that a thought because it led me *away* from Harris and I was interested in only what led *to* him."

"He could have put her up to it."

I shook my head. "If so, he never would have let us take the envelopes. No, Stanley Harris hasn't a clue."

Trav extended the French fries container past the upright

shotgun between us, offering. I was about to wave him off, but changed my mind.

"All right. Just one."

I took three. I refrained from cramming them into my mouth and forced myself to nibble.

God, were they good.

Trav had finished the Whopper and now held the Kids Meal burger poised before his mouth.

"I still don't see why Alison would save Marge one day and kill her the next."

"Neither do I. But let's just say she saw Marge as a roadblock on the path to wedded bliss with Stanley Harris." I shuddered—*there* was a thought to kill my appetite for more fries. "When did she poison the envelope?

"Tuesday night or Wednesday morning." He bunched up the wrapper. He'd finished the smaller burger in three bites. "We know she was there: We have a witness."

"Yes we do. Thank God for nosy spinsters."

For a few seconds we sat in silence, staring out the windshield.

Then Trav said, "Alison... she would have been way down on my list."

"Why?"

"Remember when we went into Harris's house yesterday?" Trav said. "She was crying. She looked sad. I mean, really sad."

I remembered. I could picture her teary, red-rimmed eyes.

"More than sad. She looked devastated."

"Think she was acting?"

"Anything's possible. But if that was acting, she deserves an Oscar."

Trav sighed. "I don't get it. I just don't get it."

"Neither do I. But I remember something else from yesterday."

"What?"

"As Alison was leaving, she wanted to straighten up the office."

He nodded. "Right, right. She said something about how it was a mess and Marge kept it so neat. But you know, she could have been more interested in the envelopes than the mess."

"Exactly."

"Still… why did Marge say, '*He*'s trying to kill me'?"

I said, "Because she'd tasted peanut on the envelope, knew someone had put it there, and could think of only one person who'd do something like that."

"It all fits, doesn't it."

"Seems to."

Though I was pretty sure it was Alison, I was doing my best to keep an open mind.

I said, "Let's look at what we have: One of the envelopes smells like peanuts; Alison knew from first-hand experience that Marge had a life-threatening allergy to peanuts; Alison had opportunity; and Alison has motive."

He nodded. "I agree right down the line. But it's all way circumstantial. We may be able to prove that someone put peanut oil on the glue flap, but proving beyond a reasonable doubt who did it is a whole other story."

"There's got to be a way."

He turned to me. "Okay. Let's try this: Pretend you're Alison. You bought some peanut oil and dabbed it on the glue strip. Now what do you do?"

"I get rid of the peanut oil."

"How?"

"I stick it in somebody else's garbage."

Trav shook his head. "Uh-uh. Too risky. You might be seen. And don't forget, garbage is picked up only once a week. That someone else might go out to their can with more garbage and see the peanut oil."

"You're giving her a lot of credit. Somehow I don't think she's that smart."

"Maybe not so smart, but crafty. She came up with the idea of poisoning the envelope."

"You said it was on *Seinfeld*."

"Well, yeah, but she was smart enough to adapt it. If Harris had put the bills out a little earlier yesterday, the murder weapon would be lost in the US mail now, headed for L.L. Bean. Let's not underestimate her."

Good point.

I closed my eyes and tried to be Alison Crowley. I couldn't. I couldn't imagine murdering a man's wife, no matter how much I loved him. And if that man were Stanley Harris—I quelled a wave of nausea and skipped over the whys and wherefores to picture myself after the deed. What would I be thinking?

Keeping my eyes closed, I said, "Wait… if I'm Alison, I'm not worried about being caught. I'm not thinking of myself as a suspect or even a possible suspect, because I have no idea that anyone's investigating Marge's death as a possible crime. I might even keep the peanut oil and use it for cooking."

"That's pretty cold. As I remember, her tears looked real."

My eyes snapped open. "Guilt?"

"Could be."

"Well, if she feels guilty, the peanut oil will be a constant reminder of what she did. She'll toss it." I looked at Trav. "Let's find out where she lives."

"Why? We can't go search her place."

"Just get her address and see if you can find out when they pick up garbage in her neighborhood."

He smiled. "Talk about a crafty mind."

# 8

He spent more than a few minutes on the line with the sheriff's department, asking questions, taking notes.

"Guess what?" he said when he finished. "Our little lady has a record."

"Violent?"

He smiled. "Not quite. Shoplifting when she was eighteen. Tried to walk out of Ames wearing two pairs of jeans."

"That's a teenage thing. Doesn't quite qualify her as a hardened criminal."

"Right, but I thought it was interesting." He consulted his notes. "She's a renter at 111 Morgan Lane. And the clerk told me garbage pickup day in her area is Monday."

"Tomorrow."

"Let's go for a ride."

"Anyplace in particular?"

"Nah. I just thought we'd cruise around a little."

"South of the interstate, perhaps?"

He smiled. "Sure. Why not?"

"Okay, but let's take my car. A sheriff's unit might spook her—spook the whole neighborhood."

Trav couldn't leave his cruiser unattended in the Holly Ridge parking lot, so we made a quick trip to Carmel and returned it to the Sheriff's department. There we transferred to his dark-blue Ford 150 pickup.

Didn't I say that Carson County was a pickup kind of place?

I scanned the interior as he started the engine and shifted into reverse—a standard shift. Real men don't do automatic transmissions.

"Pretty clean for a truck."

"I hardly spend any time in it. Mostly drive it to the department and back. It's okay, but what I'd really love is a Chevy SSR. They are *hot*."

I had no idea what a Chevy SSR was, but gathered it was another brand of pickup.

I nodded knowingly. "Aren't they, though."

"Trouble is, they start north of forty grand."

"Ouch. For a pickup?"

"The SSR's not just a pickup, it's a cross between a pickup and a sport coupe. It's unreal."

Men and their surrogate penises.

We took the interstate back to Lebanon, then turned south on 206 toward the lower end of town. From a distance we looked like any other couple out for a Sunday drive.

We passed the packed fairgrounds. The Carson County Fair is always the third week in August, but the land is used for a weekend flea market the rest of the year.

"Look for West Fenton," he said. "It should be—" He made a sharp right turn. "Here she is."

Half a mile along Fenton we found Morgan Lane. The street started between two brick pillars that informed us we were entering Morgan Park, a nest of well-kept trailers.

He slowed slightly as we approached the trailer at number 111. It looked like all the rest. The old green Ford Taurus we'd seen in the Harris driveway was parked in the carport attached to the left side.

"Looks like she's home," Trav said.

A number of the trailers we'd passed had already moved their garbage cans to the curb. Not Alison. Hers was nowhere in sight. She probably kept it behind the trailer.

"Damn," I whispered. I didn't know why I was whispering; she couldn't hear me. "How are we going to check out her garbage?"

"We're not."

I looked at him. "Then why are we here?"

"I mean, as long as it's on her property, we can't. Not without a warrant."

The trailer slid past and I watched it over my shoulder.

"Can't you get one?"

He laughed—bitterly, I thought.

"On a Sunday? In Carson County? On the suspicion that Ms. Alison Crowley's garbage may contain a murder weapon—said weapon being a jar of peanut oil? Not likely."

"So that's it? We just let the department of sanitation haul it off and lose murder evidence forever in the dump?"

"Without a warrant we can't touch her garbage till she puts it out for collection. After that it's fair game."

"Does that mean a stakeout?"

I was kidding. Well, mostly kidding.

Another laugh. "I don't think so. The sanit guys hit the road at six thirty a.m. I'll be back here before them to do my own pickup."

"What if she forgets to put out her garbage?"

He shook his head. "Not if she's guilty, she won't."

"If she's upset, she could be in there now with a twelve-pack of Coors Light. She could pass out and not wake up till the garbage truck has come and gone."

He sagged—fleetingly, infinitesimally—but I caught it before he reclaimed his macho front.

"Then it'll be the detectives' problem."

"What if you just bend the rules a little? You know, sneak back after dark and—"

"No way. Whatever I found would be inadmissible."

"Who's going to know?"

"I'll know. I'm supposed to uphold the law, not break it." He looked at me. "I know that sounds like a line straight out of *Dudley Do-Right*, but I do take this seriously."

A straight arrow... I liked that.

"Sorry. I—"

"And there's another, more practical reason: If I do something like that and it comes out, I'll not only look like a jerk, it could cost me my job. Even if it doesn't, I'll always be the Guy Who Blew the Marge Harris Case."

"Okay. Forget I mentioned it. But I'll never understand the rules of evidence."

"They're pretty clear."

"No, I mean the logic behind them. It's like they exist in an alternate reality. Okay, so you sneak onto Alison's property and go through her trash and find evidence against her. Sure, doing that is against the law, and so you're guilty of trespassing and stealing someone's garbage—no argument. And so they fine or punish you for that. Only fair. But then they say the evidence you found doesn't exist. That's absurd."

"They don't say it doesn't exist. It's just that because of the Fourth Amendment it can't be used in court. Fruit of the poison tree, and all that."

"Why should *anything* be kept from a jury? Where does a court get the right to expect twelve people to come to a fair decision with only part of the story? It's like, say, if I have a sick patient and need a reference immediately. The computers are down and the library's closed, so I break in and copy the pertinent section out of a textbook. But then the hospital tells me I can't use that information to treat my patient because I trespassed to get it."

"It's different..."

"Same logic. So tell me: Am I crazy or is the system wacky?"

He smiled at me. "I'll bet *Dirty Harry* is one of your favorite films."

"Damn betcha," I said, trying to sound tough.

He laughed as we turned off Morgan Lane onto a road that would take us back to 206.

Truth was that I'd started watching it once—only because young Clint Eastwood is so hot—but turned it off halfway through. I don't go for shootings and beatings.

I said, "So when are you planning to come back?"

"I figure if I'm here around five thirty, that ought to give me plenty of time. Of course if, like you said, she doesn't put her garbage out, it won't matter what time I come back."

I patted his arm. "Don't worry. I'm just a pessimist. It's my upbringing. I'm sure she'll put it out."

"Sure? How can you be sure?"

"Just a feeling."

More than a feeling, actually. I *knew* Alison Crowley's garbage can would be curbside before sunup tomorrow.

Because if she didn't put it out, I'd do it for her.

# 9

We didn't talk much on the trip back to my place. My fault. I was suffering an attack of the downs.

I'd started thinking about the banal tawdriness of the Marge-Stan-Alison triangle, and how badly it had ended. That led me to the guilty realization that I'd started treating the whole mess as a big puzzle, another problem to be solved. After all, that's what I do every day with my patients—solve their problems. Or at least try to.

But I'd become so involved in the gamesmanship of fitting the pieces together, of trying to outsmart first Harris, and now Alison, that I'd started losing sight of the human cost. Margery Scarborough Harris was dead. She'd never organize another Children's Concert, never run another fundraiser for the hospital, never... never do *anything* again.

My throat constricted.

"Penny for your thoughts?" Trav said.

I shook myself out of my funk.

"Just thinking about Marge and all she did for everybody." For me.

"Yeah, we're going to miss her."

"How does someone do that?" I said. "How do you decide to kill another person?"

Trav shrugged. "Happens all the time."

"I'm not talking about flying into a rage and picking up a knife or a baseball bat. And I don't mean a revenge killing— the you-raped-my-sister-now-you're-gonna-pay type of thing. I'm talking about deciding to kill someone who's never harmed you, just because they're in the way. How do you *do* that? And how do you live with yourself after?"

"People have been asking that since Cain and Abel."

I tried to picture Alison sitting in her trailer and plotting to kill Marge. Was she that desperate to be with Stan? Okay, she obviously didn't have much going for her—living in a rented trailer, cleaning houses, no prospects, nothing in her future but a lot more of her crummy present. I can see feeling down about it, maybe even a little desperate. But to kill an innocent woman?

I decided then to stay in the game, but not for the game. For Marge. The scales were unbalanced and needed to be leveled. If Trav got the credit, great. If not, that would be too bad. But the real shame would be if Marge's murderer got away with it.

"Here we are," Trav said as he pulled into the curb before Mum's house.

"Yes. Here we are."

I was stalling for time, dithering about whether I should invite him in.

"What've you got cooking the rest of the day?"

He shrugged. "Probably go home, watch some of the O's game, catch up on my Z's—got to be a wide-awake early bird tomorrow if I expect to catch that worm." He hesitated, then added, "Not doing anything for dinner, though. You ready to collect on that meal I owe you?"

This was the other question I'd been debating: Should I invite him to my mother's for Sunday night dinner?

My first impulse was, Why not? Sean always brought Kevin.

But bringing Trav along would put a shock into them—all of them. I've *never* brought anyone home for dinner. Which meant I'd be hearing about it nonstop afterward—Mum pestering me about when Trav and I were going to get engaged, Timmy running Internet background checks on the poor guy.

But that was thinking only of me. What about Trav? Exposed to my whole family at once? And then having to eat my mother's cooking?

No. Couldn't do it to him.

And really, were we at that stage yet?

I didn't think so.

"I'd love to Trav, but I'll have to take a rain check. My mother's got this special family dinner prepared for my brother"—I emphasized *family* and neglected to mention Kevin—"and I can't miss it." And then all of a sudden I heard someone saying, "Why don't you come with me?"

Hey. It was my voice. Where had that come from?

"To your mom's?" he said. "I'd like that—no, I'd love that. I haven't seen her in ages. But it's kind of short notice, don't you think?"

"Always room for one more at her table. But I've got to ask if you've got anything against leg of ram."

"You mean lamb, right?"

"No. I mean ram."

"I don't—"

"Don't ask. I can't explain. But you'll understand if you come."

"Count me in. What time do I show up?"

"Five ought to do it."

"What do I wear?"

I pointed to his uniform. "Something less formal than that. Slacks and a polo shirt should do fine."

He grinned. "Okay! See you then."

He leaned over and kissed me. I kissed him back. We held it for a while, but not long enough for an official accusation of Public Display of Affection. PDAs had been discouraged in high school.

"Thanks for thinking of me."

He waved and drove off.

Time to start making myself presentable for His Majesty's visit.

# 10

On my way to my room I called to Mum in the kitchen and asked if she minded setting an extra place.

"Of course not," she said. "You'll be bringing a friend? Who is she?"

"Not a she, a he."

I heard a loud clatter from the kitchen.

"Mum? Did you just drop the phone?"

More clatter as I heard her stage whisper. "Timmy! Norrie's bringing a beau for dinner!"

"Mum? Mum!"

"Yes, dear?"

"He's not a beau. It's just Trav."

"Travis Lawton? But he's married!"

"Mum, he's been divorced for five years."

"Not in the eyes of the Church!"

"He's just an old friend, Mum. Nothing's going on between us. But if you want me to tell him—"

"It's too late for that now, isn't it. Well, we'll just have to make do."

This had the makings for a tense evening. A disaster even.

# 11

"I was expecting him at five," Mum whispered as Trav rang the front door bell. "He's late."

The wall clock said 5:06.

Tell Mum to meet you at 6:22, and she'll be there at 6:22. She expects the same from everybody else. Well, almost everybody else.

Mum wore her good blue polyester suit. She kept it on after church only for special occasions, the advent of Prince Sean being such.

An odd look crossed Travis's face as I opened the door and ushered him in.

"What's wrong?"

He shook his head, his expression puzzled. "I just had the strangest feeling... like a chill."

My mother always kept the thermostat high. "You getting sick?"

"No-no. It's gone now. But for a second there it went straight to the bone." He smiled. "Hi, Mrs. Fogarty," he said as my mother approached. "Thanks so much for having me."

She shook his proffered hand. "Yes, well, we'll see about that."

I gave her a look.

She understood and added, "We're happy to have you."

He showed her a bottle of wine.

"It's Pinot Noir. The guy down at Corky's said it goes great with lamb."

"Well, thank you, Travis."

"But does it go with ram?" I whispered. "I told you we were having *ram*." Before he could respond, I turned to Mum and said oh so innocently, "Where's Sean?"

I hadn't seen his Saab out front. Hadn't expected to.

"He must be stuck in traffic. You know how it is getting out of the city."

I nodded. "That Sunday rush hour is a killer."

"You have to make allowances, dear. He'll be here any minute, I'm sure."

More like any *hour*. Sean usually arrives after Godot. For him, "on time" is a ritual practiced by the inhabitants of Saturn, not Earth. At least not his Earth.

At the opposite end of the house, Uncle Timmy leaned out of the kitchen archway and waved to Trav.

"Welcome!"

I dragged Trav back through the dining room to the kitchen and introduced him. They shook, then Timmy took the Pinot Noir and set it on the counter.

"We'll be making short work of that." He turned to me. "Your usual, Norrie?"

I'd changed my "usual"—a sea breeze—a few months ago when I realized its carb count, but Timmy never failed to ask.

"Just a glass of red, Tim. How about a nice '84 Haut-Brion, preferably from the southwest corner of the vineyard?"

He laughed. "Coming right up. And you, deputy? What'll it be?"

"A stout if you've got one."

"There's my boy!"

"Love stout."

Timmy's eyes lit. "You don't say?" He winked at me. "I like this fellow already!"

Timmy poured the drinks, handed them out, and toasted us with his own stout.

"Here's to you."

We all clinked glasses.

"Do you know where that comes from?" Timmy said.

"The wine?"

"No, the clinking of glasses."

I didn't. And I didn't have to ask, because I knew he'd tell me.

"It comes from the old days when nobles were always poisoning each other. So to assure themselves that it was safe to drink, each would pour a bit from his cup into the others'. Every time they poured, you'd hear a clink as the rims touched." He again clinked his glass against mine. "The tradition continues."

I hadn't a clue as to whether the story was true or not, but it fit nicely with Timmy's conspiratorial view of the world and its history.

As for me, I was flashing on the poison goblet scene from *The Princess Bride*, a favorite movie from my teen years. I suppose wishing back then for a handsome prince to seek me out and take me away had had something to do with it—okay, a *lot* to do with it—but it was laugh-aloud funny too.

Mum returned from her watchpost at the front door. "Timmy, would you pour me a bit?"

He lifted a small tumbler with a finger of Bushmills swirling in the bottom.

"Got it waiting for you, Kate."

"There's a luv." She claimed her glass, held it up and said, "*Sláinte!*"

"*Sláinte!*" Timmy and I echoed—Trav tried but mangled it— as we all clinked, then drank.

Timmy fixed Trav with a stare. "So, what are your intentions with our Norrie?"

"Unk!"

"Well, with Rocky gone, I feel it's my duty to—"

I turned to Trav—"Do *not* answer"—then back to Timmy. "Can't we just have a nice dinner? Friends and relatives, that sort of thing?"

Timmy shrugged. "I suppose, but I think we should—"

"You're married, aren't you," Mum said.

Oh, hell, here we go.

Trav looked uncomfortable. "I was. We got divorced and—"

"There's no such thing as divorce. The Church says—"

I had to distract her.

"Mmmm, whatever's cooking sure smells good."

No lie. It did.

"Just the roast."

Trav's eyebrows rose. "Leg of...?"

Mum looked at him as if he was daft. "Lamb, of course. What else would you have for a Sunday dinner?"

Trav didn't reply but looked relieved.

What else indeed? After Dad died, Mum didn't even attempt to try making his meatballs. She returned to her own family tradition: Sunday dinner was roast leg of lamb with mint jelly, roasted potatoes, and carrots and peas. As usual, she'd probably started cooking the meat last Tuesday.

"What's different?" I said.

"Oh, I added a touch of garlic. That may be what you're smelling. Sean likes garlic, you know."

My mother... experimenting with food... only Prince Sean could bring about such a miracle.

We wandered into the living room and Travis stopped before the landscape.

"Does that look tilted to you?"

"Does it ever. Driving me crazy."

"Really? Want me to fix it?"

"Sure," I said. "Go ahead."

He adjusted it and stepped back. "There you go. Nice and straight."

"Thanks," I said. But it wasn't straight. Still canted. I said nothing, though.

Mum was back at the front door, staring through the glass.

"Now where is that boy? Traffic must be bad. I hope he's all right."

I noticed a tremor in her fingers. Nervous about Sean, or early Parkinson's?

It's no fun being the doctor in the family.

"Don't worry about him, Mum. They'll be here soon."

She returned to the kitchen, shaking her head. "You know, I don't know why he always brings Kevin along. Just one time I'd like to see him by himself."

"Well," I said carefully, "Kevin is his partner after all."

"I know that, Norrie. But after seeing Kevin all week at work,

you'd think he'd want a rest from him for just a little while. And
with Sean's business being so small, I don't know why he needs
a partner anyway."

Trav's expression was an uncomfortable mix of bafflement
and embarrassment. I glanced at Timmy who gave a helpless
shrug.

Mum doesn't always pay close attention to the details of the
world around her, but she's not stupid.

I'm sure somewhere in her heart she knows her son is gay.

# 12

I didn't find out myself until about five years ago.

Shortly after I arrived in Baltimore to start my residency, Sean invited me to his place downtown in the Mount Vernon section. Kevin was there and I assumed he was just a roommate until I realized they shared a bedroom.

Blew. Me. Away.

Eight years in Greenwich Village and Chelsea had made gays an everyday fact of my life.

But my brother? Sean?

No way.

I hadn't sensed even a hint growing up. Sean was this good-looking guy who cut a swath through all the adoring girls. Quite the ladies' man. But he told me that night at his apartment that the real reason he'd been so determinedly hetero back then was denial. Finally, in college, he'd given in to who he knew he was.

Timmy had figured it out years before I knew, but never spoke of it to Mum. He once confided to me that he felt sorry for Sean. The poor lad is the victim of a plot by the Illuminati wing of the New World Order. For years now they've been poisoning public drinking water with a drug that turns people gay. This is why Timmy drinks only bottled water. The idea is to turn so many Americans gay that we can't reproduce. When our numbers have declined to the point where we can no longer defend ourselves, "they" will move in and take over the country.

Or something like that.

Mum couldn't have escaped the realization that Sean is gay, but I don't think she's allowed her conscious mind to admit it.

After all, Holy Mother Church, despite all her gay priests, considers homosexuality a mortal sin. It's her form of denial: If you don't acknowledge it, you don't have to deal with it; and something you don't have to deal with is functionally nonexistent.

Or am I, as usual, thinking too much?

The truth is that Sean is comfortable with his lifestyle—I know because he and Kevin had me over to their place dozens of times during my residency—but he's not in your face about it. Neither he nor Kevin would light up your gaydar, but spend any time with them and no way you can't know they're a couple.

I guess I shouldn't say no way. Mum found a way.

The fact that Sean always introduces Kevin as his "partner," not his lover, gave Mum an out: Kevin was tagged as a partner in Sean's graphic design firm.

Sean once asked me if he should simply sit her down and flat out tell her. He was out in Baltimore and everywhere else— everywhere but his family home. I was against it, and still am. Mum had decided to ignore the elephant in the room. In her world, Sean and Kevin are friends and partners in a small company, nothing more; and she declares that someday, when he finds the right woman, Sean will marry and settle down and start a family. That's her comfort zone. What would Mum or Sean gain by destroying it?

Sean couldn't think of a thing.

So the show goes on: Mum acting as if she doesn't know, and the rest of us—Sean and Kevin included—acting as if we don't know either.

Actually, it's kind of fun in its own absurd way.

# 13

Sean and Kevin finally arrived at five to six. Big Mum-hug for Sean, little Mum-hug for Kevin, a big Norrie-hug for each, followed by Timmy handshakes. I introduced Trav. Sean remembered him from the old days. Kevin asked him what his intentions were. Ha-ha-ha.

Timmy poured drinks—Harp lager for Sean, Chardonnay for Kevin—and another round for Trav and me.

"Norrie," Sean said, slinging an arm over my shoulder, "I can see why Travis is hanging around you. You look more svelte and more beautiful every time I see you."

Did I happen to mention that I love my brother? Do you see why I can't be jealous or resentful of him, even though he gets the royal treatment and inherited all the good-looks genes?

Sean has the Marconi dark hair and complexion, but the Fogarty blue eyes. He's a striking man—slim, trim, staring forty in the eye but you'd think he was my age.

I really should hate him but I can't.

Perfectly groomed Kevin is younger, more fair, and good-looking as well. Sean tends to be laid back about his clothes, but Kevin is always impeccably in style.

Mum brought out her traditional—and only—hors d'oeuvre: Kraft Easy Cheese swirled onto Ritz crackers.

"There they are!" Kevin cried. He immediately grabbed one and popped it into his mouth, then closed his eyes and moaned. "I've been looking forward to these all day!"

This never fails to amaze me. Here's this gay urban sophisticate, who's probably used to caviar and baked brie, swooning over a cheeselike substance sprayed from an aerosol can onto a cracker. Maybe he's tired of the high-class stuff, maybe there's something campy about it, I don't know. I do know he's not acting. Not the way he scarfs them down every time he's here.

"Nobody else in the *world* serves this," he said, reaching for another.

Well, maybe not in his world.

I watched Travis try one. His face lit with surprise.

"Hey, they're really good!"

Kevin leaned toward me but didn't lower his voice. "This one's a keeper, Norrie!"

Everyone—except Mum—thought this was hilarious and I felt my face redden. Damn, I hate when that happens.

The evening went smoothly as we moved from the appetizers to the main course. We settled around the table and Mum said grace. And then added something:

"Before we start, and while I have the two of you here—" meaning Sean and me—"I want to let you both know that I'm seriously thinking of selling the house." Silence descended on the table. "Timmy is a big help, but it's getting too much for me. They've got some nice condos in Lebanon where everything is taken care of for you. Just giving you fair warning, is all."

Sean and I looked at each other, both in shock. We grew up here. I think we both thought the place would always be here. But Mum wasn't getting any younger.

I forced myself to say, "You do what's best for you, Mum."

Sean echoed that but inside I knew we were both crushed.

She ducked into the kitchen and returned with the meal's centerpiece: roast leg of ram.

And I do mean *ram*. After my mother has her way with a leg of lamb, its very DNA is altered. How can I describe this gustatory experience? How about: the consistency of linoleum but less flavor? That comes close, but not quite it. It's so dry it shreds when you try to carve it.

Growing up, Sean and I had affixed the label "roast beast" to any meat our mother cooked, because no matter what the animal of origin, it all tasted the same by the time she was through with it.

I've tried countless times to convince her that she doesn't have to incinerate meat. It's okay to let it keep some of its juices. And would she consider maybe leaving just a touch of pink?

That always sets her off.

"Pink?" she says, shocked. "Pink means it isn't cooked! You'll be sick! Sick as a dog!"

But hungry people will eat anything, even Mum's ram.

I leaned close to Trav and whispered, "The secret is to keep your palate moist; then you can get it down."

As a kid I'd use milk or Pepsi; as an adult, wine does the trick very nicely. Have enough and you don't notice the toughness and total lack of flavor.

He nodded absently. He'd seemed strangely distracted since his arrival. Thinking about handing over Marge's case to the detectives, maybe?

The good news for me was that I wasn't hungry. Not just because of the ram. I was pretty sure the Tezinex was working.

We all discovered that Pinot Noir went as well with ram as lamb. I would have liked more but was limiting my intake tonight.

Had to stay sharp for the errand I had planned.

# 14

The ram had been followed by ice cream and coffee—I managed to avoid Bailey's in mine. When Mum banished us all from the dining room to the living room, Trav sat down at the piano and started playing. I thought he might do one of the numbers Marge taught us but instead he broke into "That's Amore." I was shocked. That was a song my dad and Uncle Corry used to sing together after they'd had a few.

Sean got up, leaned against the piano, and started to sing. I felt I had no choice but to join him. It was sort of a family song. I noticed Sean grinning and perhaps taking too much pleasure in singing the "Like a gay tarantella" line.

When we finished, everyone applauded, including my mother, grinning with tears in her eyes. Trav had made a breakthrough.

Sean said he had to get back to Balto and I used his and Kevin's departure, followed by Timmy's, as the cue to walk Trav out to his car.

"Whatever prompted you to play 'That's Amore'?"

He shrugged. "It just came to me. I didn't even know I knew the song. It just popped into my head and I started playing."

Weird… did my father have something to do with that?

He slid an arm around my shoulders and pulled me close.

"But it capped off a nice evening. Your family is… unique."

"Well, that's one way to put it."

He leaned closer. "A *great* night, and I don't want it to end yet. How about you?"

How about me? I was feeling pretty amorous myself. If this were outside my condo, I might have invited him up. But I had to get over to Alison's to make sure her garbage can was out at the curb for Trav tomorrow morning.

Even so... I felt myself start to vacillate. Maybe we could sneak back there for a little while, and then—

No. I had to do this. For Trav.

"Neither do I, but I don't think I'm ready for the next step just yet."

"But you think you will be ready someday? Someday soon?"

My mouth felt dry. "Yes... yes, I do."

"Well, then, all right. At least I'll have that to take to bed with me."

# 15

Fifteen minutes after Trav departed, Mum retired to her room, and I sneaked out and headed south toward Lebanon. I found Morgan Lane again and drove past Alison's trailer: No garbage can in sight.

I checked the dashboard clock: 11:40. All her lights were out. I couldn't make out even the pale glow of a TV. Damn, she hadn't put the can out before bed.

If she slept late tomorrow, the garbage truck could come and go with her trash can languishing in the backyard, out of Trav's reach.

I'd come here to prevent that. Now I wasn't so sure.

During the drive over I'd been hoping I'd see the can out at the curb, turn around, and head back home. Since that wasn't the case, I had a big decision to make.

I drove on and stopped at the far end of Morgan Lane to examine my options.

I could still turn around and drive home. Trav knew nothing about my little scheme, so no one would be the wiser.

No one but me.

All right, if I was going to go through with it, what was the best approach?

I realized I hadn't thought this through—after all, I don't normally do this sort of thing. I couldn't simply park in front of her trailer and walk into her backyard. I had to be sneaky.

I've never been good at sneaky.

After looking at the problem from all angles, I could come up with only one way to go about it.

I drove back around to the top of Morgan Place and parked my Jeep near one of the brick pillars. I pulled the flashlight from my glove compartment and walked down toward Alison's. The trailer park lay quiet around me. I'd have preferred more noise. I felt like someone arriving late for church and having to walk down the aisle to an empty seat. Every footstep on the pavement sounded like a gunshot—at least to me.

Most of the trailers were dark—tomorrow was a workday, after all. Fortunately for me, Morgan Lane had no streetlights and the moon wasn't up yet. Still, I felt exposed. The street offered no cover. The faint starshine allowed me to find my way without the flashlight, but it also left me visible to anyone who might glance out a window.

When I reached Alison's I stopped at the property line and listened. Still dark, and no sound from within. The carport lay on the far side. Earlier today, as we drove by, I'd noticed a short gravel driveway leading to it. I wanted to avoid gravel.

After a quick look around to assure myself that no one else was out and about, I tiptoed across the scraggly grass that passed for her lawn and reached the rear of her trailer.

A couple of tall trees overhung her backyard, making it darker here. After my eyes adjusted I spotted the garbage can nestled against the back steps. When I reached it I risked a quick look with my flashlight—on and off in an instant.

I was relieved to see it was vinyl. Better than an aluminum or galvanized metal rattletrap that would wake up the neighborhood when I carried it to the front. A bungee cord held down the cover—an added level of protection against raccoons, no doubt.

I stuffed the flashlight into my pocket, grabbed the handles, lifted—

—and almost fell over because the can was so light. It felt empty.

Not good.

I put it down, unhooked the bungee, and removed the lid. Another quick zap of the flashlight showed some glossy junk-mail fliers and a small flattened cardboard box stuffed in on an angle. Where was her garbage? Had she taken it directly to the dump?

I bit back a curse as I reattached the bungee. Not only was Trav out of luck, but Alison Crowley quite literally was going to get away with murder.

When I had everything back to the way I'd found it, I turned to go. As I moved, my foot struck something, knocking it against the rear steps. It sounded like an empty can—a paint can?—but the noise echoed through the night like a cannon shot.

And then a sudden glow through the window above me—someone had turned on a light. A shock of panic bolted down my spine. I ducked into a crouch and scampered around the corner into the shadows along the side of the trailer. I hugged the wall and waited.

The backyard was abruptly bathed in light. I dared a peek around the corner. I could see the back steps through a narrow gap between the siding and a corner downspout—see without being seen. The light by the rear door was on. The door opened and out stepped Alison, dressed in jeans and a sweater. She must have been sleeping in her clothes.

"Who's there?" she said.

Something glinted in her hand.

I ducked back.

Good God, she had a knife.

# 16

"Who's there?" she repeated.

I held my breath and listened to my heart pound as I mentally kicked myself for being such a jerk. If I got caught trespassing, sneaking around someone's yard in the dead of night, and taken in, I'd be through in Lebanon. Ken would fire me, and I doubted very much Sam would stop him. If places were reversed, I'd want me out too.

I waited. No more calling, but no sound of her going back inside either. I risked another peek.

Alison still stood on the steps, but held the knife—a big kitchen knife—lower. Her posture was more relaxed. The knife had been for protection. Understandable for a woman living alone.

Knife... something about the gleam off the blade reminded me of the figure in the brush last night. Could that have been Alison?

But why?

She couldn't know anyone suspected foul play. So why come after me?

Finally she turned back toward the door. She was about to step inside when something caught her attention. She was looking down.

I made a frantic search of my pockets. Had I dropped my flashlight? No. Here it was.

"Oh, shit," I heard her say in a resigned voice.

She went back inside but didn't close the door.

I debated my next move: Leave now and risk being spotted

walking away, or wait here until things quieted down again. My hindbrain, locked into flight mode, was calling for the first option: *Go now! Now-now-now!* But I held back. Patience. Caution. Impulsiveness had landed me in this pickle; I needed a more deliberate approach to extricate myself.

I held my position. After a minute or so Alison reappeared carrying a bulging, white plastic garbage bag. She opened the can and tossed it in, then refastened the cover. When she reached for the handles, I realized what was coming next and put myself into motion.

Still in a crouch, I turned and padded around to the front yard. I was on my way to the far side of the trailer when I remembered the gravel driveway—the noise would give me away. Another shot of panic hit as I looked around and realized I had no place to hide—no trees, no foundation plantings, nothing except—

The front steps.

They numbered three, wooden, with an open railing up each side. Meager cover...

The sound of Alison coming made the decision for me. I darted to the steps and crouched on their far side, praying I wouldn't be seen.

A few heartbeats later Alison rounded the corner of the trailer lugging the garbage can. She placed it at the edge of the pavement, dusted her hands, and returned to the backyard.

I stayed where I was, waiting, listening, praying she'd go right back to sleep. Despite the cool evening, I was bathed in sweat. I promised myself and the Almighty that if I reached my car without being discovered, I would never, *ever* pull another harebrained stunt like this.

# 17

*N orrie, I am so weak.*

He came to me as soon as I was in bed and didn't have to tell me his condition—the faint voice in my head and the barely visible glow hovering by the bed told the story.

I tried to hide my alarm.

"Does this mean you're going... home?"

*No. It just means I'm weak. I feel drained tonight.*

A thought struck. "Did you have anything to do with Travis playing your old song?"

*I don't know. I wanted you or Sean to play it—*

"You used to sing it with Uncle Corry."

*It had nothing to do with him. With all of you together, I wanted to hear it.*

"And Travis played it. Do you think you influenced him?"

*Not on purpose. Maybe he sensed what I wanted. Maybe he's one of those people who are sensitive to the spirits. Back in the Old Country we had Gypsies who said they could talk to the dead.*

"Well, Trav's no Gypsy."

*I know, but maybe he's sensitive.*

I remembered the sudden chill he'd had on walking into the house. Was that related?

*So weak tonight. It's like I'm a battery and I've got to recharge. It takes energy for me to hear what's going on. Maybe I used it too much listening to you and Sean sing.*

Did Trav's sensitivity have anything to do with that?

*I like that Travis. Bring him back soon. But I need to tell you something. I need your help.*

"What? Anything."

*This unfinished business. I try but I can't forgive Corrado for what he did. Unless maybe...*

"Maybe what?"

*Maybe if I know what happened to him, why he ran off, maybe if I understand that, then I can forgive.*

Made sense to me.

"You want me to see if I can find out?" How was I going to do that? "Didn't the police investi—?"

*The police do nothing. You... I need you to find out. You'll help your Babbo?*

How could I say no?

"Of course. I'll get started right away."

As soon as Marge's murder was settled.

*That's my Norrie.*

His voice faded at the end. So did the glow.

"Dad? Dad?"

Gone again. But at least now we had a plan to get him out of neutral here in this house and on his way to a better place.

Not much of a plan... no plan, really, but at least a direction.

I fell asleep smiling.

# MONDAY

# 1

An all-news station out of Baltimore burst from my clock radio at 5:15 a.m. Trav had said he was setting his alarm for 5:30, so I went him one better. Not that I needed it. I'd awakened spontaneously about an hour before and found myself too wired to go back to sleep.

This, after all, was the day I might help trap a murderer. How many times in my life would I be able to say that?

I hopped out of bed and hit the shower, then dressed for the office in traditional slacks and blazer and shell. I didn't know if I'd have time to return home before hours started, and I didn't want to be late. Mondays are always wild.

I beat Trav to Morgan Park. I was sitting where I'd parked last night and sipping a container of Dunkin' Donuts coffee when he showed up in his official sheriff's department cruiser. I flashed my lights and he pulled beside me.

The almost-full moon and pre-dawn light lit his features as he rolled down his window. His smile was rueful.

"Norrie. Why am I not surprised to find you here?"

"You didn't think I'd miss this, did you?"

His smile faded. "You should have stayed in bed."

"Why do you say that?"

"Because her garbage can's not out."

The words hit like a punch.

"Not out? But—?"

"I drove past last night right after I dropped you off and the can was nowhere in sight. Her lights were out so it was plain she was asleep."

"When was that?"

"Oh, about eleven or so."

I relaxed. He'd been here just before me.

"She might be an early riser."

"Somehow I doubt that."

"Only one way to find out."

I climbed into his cruiser and we drove down to Alison's trailer.

"I'll be damned!" he said in a hushed voice. "There it is."

Surprise, surprise.

"Never give up hope," I said.

He looked at the trailer. "Still no sign of life. When—?"

"Don't worry about it. Maybe she fell asleep on the couch and something woke her during the night." I wasn't about to tell him that I'd been that something. "On her way to the bedroom she probably realized she hadn't put out her garbage, and so..."

Strange how things work out. Because she'd spotted her garbage can when she came to the door, she'd carried it out to the curb for me.

Trav shrugged. "Guess it doesn't matter. The important thing is it's now fair game."

We got out and I stood by as he unhooked the bungee cord and pulled off the lid.

"It's a long shot," he said as he began untwisting the tie, "but we've got to try."

"Do we have to do it out here?"

"Why not?"

"Well, the sun will be up in a few minutes."

He looked around. "Good point. I'm not looking to draw a crowd, and I sure as hell don't want to answer a bunch of questions."

He yanked out the bag and tossed it into the trunk of the cruiser. As he went to replace the top I spotted the fliers and the cardboard box. The way it was angled, something could be under it. I reached in and pulled it up.

A jar of some kind sat in the bottom. I could see only its red plastic top.

"Trav! Look at this!"

I was about to reach in when he grabbed my arm.

"Let me."

I watched as he pulled on a pair of latex gloves.

"Going to operate?"

"Maybe."

He reached in and came up with the jar. I checked the label.

"Peanut butter."

He smiled. "Let's go."

"Where?"

"Don't know yet. I'll take you back to your car and you can follow me."

# 2

He led me back up 206 to the service station cluster near the interstate overpass. We pulled into the Shell and parked under one of its bright overhead lights.

I joined him as he opened the trunk.

"What next?"

He wiggled his gloved fingers. "I operate on Alison's garbage."

"But we've already got the peanut butter jar."

"Yeah." He shook his head. "The murder weapon. Never dreamed I'd say 'peanut butter' and 'murder weapon' in the same breath. But as for the rest of her trash, who knows what else we'll find?"

I looked around. "Isn't there a less public place to do this?"

"I need the light. Besides, this shouldn't take more than a couple of minutes."

"Can I help?"

"I don't have another pair of gloves. Sorry."

"That's okay. I've got some."

"You do?"

"Sure. I always keep a few pairs in my glove compartment. I mean, what if I stop to help at a car accident? I don't want some stranger's blood on my hands."

Trav nodded. He pulled the bag open without removing it from his trunk. I retrieved a pair of gloves and joined him.

We found an array of empty Nacho Doritos bags, Pringles canisters, and fast food containers. Here was someone else who could eat all the wrong things and stay thin as a rail.

"You sure know how to show a gal a good time," I said.

"You mean you're not having fun?"

We pawed through empty cigarette packs, beer cans—I'd been wrong about Coors Light; she drank Bud Light—and dozens of damp used paper towels. Alison didn't seem to be into recycling.

Finally Trav said, "Well, nothing else in here." He shook the bag down, retied it, then picked up the jar. "I wonder why she didn't bag this along with the rest?"

"Could be guilt. Could be she couldn't bear the sight of it so she got it out of the house as soon as she could." I looked closer. "Hey, it's the natural kind, where the oil separates."

We looked at each other. No need to spell it out. We both had the same scenario playing in our heads: Alison buys the peanut butter, siphons off a little of the oil, then brings it to the Harris house where she spreads a tiny bit on one of Marge's envelopes.

He said, "Do you realize how lucky we are she didn't take this stuff to the dump or stick it in a trash can outside someplace like McDonald's?"

"But why would she? As far as she knows, everyone thinks Marge's death is due to a medical mishap—*my* fault. If it's not considered a crime, then no one's looking for a criminal. Why deviate from your routine?"

"Luck or not"—Trav pumped a fist—"we've got her!"

Did we? I wasn't so sure.

But even if we did, somehow it didn't feel like enough.

# 3

The waitress brought our coffees and asked if we were ready to order breakfast. Trav said just coffee would do for now and I went along.

"You're not eating? No Tremendous Twelve with a hind quarter of beef on the side?"

He shook his head. "I'm too wound up to eat."

After Trav had placed the jar of peanut butter in an evidence bag, we'd driven to Perkins for a post mortem.

He looked overwound, like a third-year medical student about to make his first incision through living skin.

"You've got what you wanted, right? You'll be handing those detectives a lot more than just a 9-1-1 tape."

He rubbed a hand over his mouth. "Yeah, but it's all so circumstantial. Peanut oil isn't exactly a deadly weapon—or weapon of any sort."

"It is when you're highly allergic."

"You know what I mean."

I did. Obviously we were suffering from the same malaise.

I sighed. "Right. How many homes in this country *don't* have at least one jar of peanut butter somewhere?"

"She tossed hers in the garbage, but she could easily explain that by saying she tried a new brand and didn't like it."

"So what are you telling me?"

I knew, but I wanted to hear him say it.

"Alison's going to walk, Norrie."

Yeah. She was.

Damn-damn-damn! I couldn't let that happen. Not Marge's

killer. There had to be a way...

An idea had been simmering since we'd retied her garbage bag. I wondered...

"Let me run this past you: What if we can get her to confess?"

"If I may quote Aerosmith: 'Dream on.'"

"Just hear me out. Everybody watches *CSI*, right? But because it's got to squeeze its stories into a set number of minutes, it gives the false impression that DNA matches can be had almost immediately."

Trav snorted. "Takes us weeks."

"Exactly. But I'll bet Alison doesn't know that."

He leaned back, chewing his upper lip. "You think I could snow her?" he said after a moment.

"I think *we* could snow her."

"Oh, now wait a minute—"

I held up my hand. "Having a doctor—*Marge's* doctor—along, using judicious amounts of medical jargon to bolster the evidence against her, might mean the difference between her stonewalling or opening up."

More lip chewing, then a nod. "Okay."

I doubted this would work with an experienced criminal or a sociopath, but I sensed that Alison's tears in the Harris kitchen had been the real thing. If so, then she felt miserable about what she'd done. And maybe deep inside she *wanted* to get caught. All she'd need was a push.

"But we've got to plan this out," I said. "We need props. Do you have Marge's envelopes?"

He shook his head. "They're in an evidence locker back at the department."

"Well, maybe the peanut butter jar will be enough. But we've got to work this out in advance. We've got to have a script in our heads when we go in there."

We began rehearsing...

# 4

We arrived at Alison's trailer a little before seven. Trav knocked three times before he got a response.

A window slid up to our left and a sleep-thick voice said, "Who's there?"

"Carson County Sheriff's Department, ma'am. I'd like to ask you a few questions."

"What about?"

"Might be better if we discuss it inside, ma'am."

A pause, then. "Give me a second."

A couple of minutes later Alison pulled open the door. She wore the same jeans and sweater I'd seen her in last night. She didn't have enough hair to have bed head, but her face was puffy and still creased with pillow lines.

I caught her glaring at me as she let us in. What was that all about?

The place was a mess—clothing and issues of *People* and *Entertainment Weekly* scattered on the worn chairs and couch. She cleaned houses for a living, but I supposed she was like the mechanic whose own car never gets a tune up.

She didn't offer coffee or even a seat. Not that I wanted either. My stomach was wound too tight for even a drop, and the rest of me too tense to sit. Even the clutter failed to bother me. We were taking a big risk. When we finished talking she'd know she was a suspect. And that would change everything.

"What's this all about?" she said, rubbing her hands together Lady Macbeth style.

"We have some questions that we think you can answer."

"Oh? What about?"

"Mrs. Harris's death."

"Like what?" The hand rubbing accelerated.

"We found peanut oil on the glue strip of one of Mrs. Harris's envelopes."

Her hands flew to her mouth. "Oh, no!"

To justify my presence, I said, "And as you know after witnessing what happened to her on Tuesday, even a little peanut protein can be fatal to someone as allergic as Mrs. Harris."

"Ohmigod! Just like on *Seinfeld!*"

Was I the only person in the whole world who hadn't seen that episode?

Trav lowered his voice to a grave tone. "So we no longer consider Mrs. Harris's death an accident. It's now being treated as a murder."

"You don't think *I* did it, do you?"

"Well, some questions have arisen that need answering."

Now came the tightly scripted part. We had to hammer her with one thing after another and hope she'd break.

Trav held up the evidence envelope. The peanut butter jar was visible through the clear plastic.

"We found this in your trash."

"*My* trash? What right do you—?"

"Perfectly legal. Once you put it out for pickup it stops being private property."

My turn: "Tests were run on the peanut oil in the peanut butter. The DNA signature of the oil on Mrs. Harris's envelope is a perfect match to the sample from your trash."

I didn't know if it was even possible to match samples of peanut oil, but it sounded good. And it seemed to work: Alison's already sallow skin grew even paler.

"But—"

Trav jumped in. "Fingerprints on the peanut butter jar *and* a fingerprint inside the flap on the doctored envelope match yours—we compared them to prints obtained when you were booked on that shoplifting charge."

Trav had come up with that piece of fiction and it was a beaut.

My turn again: "You first became a suspect when one of my patients mentioned that she'd seen you and Stanley Harris pulling out of the Starlight Motel."

"So," Trav said, barely letting her draw a breath, "you have motive, you certainly had opportunity, and there's a ream of hard evidence against you. Do you have anything to say in your defense?"

Alison Crowley burst into tears. "I didn't do it!"

I sensed she was teetering on the edge of confessing. All she needed was a little extra push.

"Come on, Alison. That jar of—"

"That's not my peanut butter!" Her voice rose toward a scream. "I *hate* peanut butter!"

Trav said, "It was in your trash, and had your fingerprints on it. How do you explain that?"

"I found it in my front yard yesterday! I don't know how it got there, and I didn't want it, so I tossed it in the garbage can. *That's* why it's got my fingerprints on it!"

Good one, I thought. And pretty quick.

"Then you deny that you had anything to do with Marge Harris's death."

"Absolutely!"

"Do you also deny that you were having an affair with Stanley Harris?"

She dropped into a chair and pressed her face into her palms.

"No. That part's true. Me and Stan been going out for a while now. He kept saying he wanted to split from her but she has some sort of interest in his business and he was trying to fix that and as soon as he got it worked out he was going to file for divorce. After that it was gonna be me and him."

You poor, stupid kid, I thought.

I'd been there…t he affair with the married man… the lies…

"So I was waiting, y'know? We'd meet at the motel when he could get away. Couple times we even snuck into Bal'more and had a real good time. I was cool with waiting. I knew these things take time. Then she had her attack and that changed everything."

"How?" I said. "You saved her life then."

She looked up briefly. "Of course. I mean, what else could I do, y'know?" She returned to staring at the floor. "But that didn't stop me from wishing later on that I'd got to her too late."

I sensed we were edging toward the truth.

"Why?"

"Because that night, when she was in the hospital, Stan snuck me into the house. We never met at each other's places because of too many chances we'd be seen, but this time he had me hide on the floor by the front seat until we pulled in. And we had a great night. A *great* night. And that was when…"

She fell silent.

"Go on," Trav said.

She took a breath. "That was when I decided I wanted to live there. I'd been through the house like a billion times, y'know? I mean, cleaning it? But this was the first time I'd slept there and ate there and hung out on the couch watching the big TV. I didn't wanna leave. I cried when Stan snuck me back here to this shit hole before he went to the hospital to bring Marge home."

Now I understood why Harris had been so adamant about my keeping Marge for an extra day. He hadn't been concerned for her health, he'd wanted another night of partying with Alison.

Bastard.

"And so I got to thinking. I mean, I wanted to be where Marge was, y'know. And I *had* saved her life. She wouldn't be walking around if it wasn't for me. So I'm thinking maybe I could un-save it, y'know? I mean, she sorta owed me and I'd be sorta collecting."

She looked up, shifting her gaze between Trav and me. If she was looking for understanding, she was out of luck.

"So you murdered her," Trav said.

"No! I just thought about it is all! Even went to the store to pick up some peanut butter, but I couldn't. I just couldn't."

"Why not?"

"Because she was a nice lady—I mean, I really liked her, even if she was standing between me'n Stan."

Trav said, "I guess now there's nothing standing between you and Stan."

She lifted her chin. "Right. But not because of anything I did."

Trav sighed, "Well, if you didn't do it, then it must have been Stan."

Her face took on a scandalized look. "No way! Stan'd never do something like that! He wanted Marge gone, but he was gonna do it the legal way."

I shook my head and stared at her, thinking what a naïve creature she was. As if Stanley Harris had even once considered leaving Marge for her, to be known around town as the guy who'd dumped his popular wife for the cleaning girl. His insurance business would go down the tubes. And now, to imagine that a man of his sterling character and pristine loyalty, as a brand-new millionaire, would take up with a poor, uneducated young woman living in a trailer park…

Pathetic.

Trav kept after her. "You mean he never mentioned anything along the lines of another dose of peanut and she'd be a goner?"

She wiped her eyes and looked up at us. "You mean, like, was he trying to put me up to it? Well… he sorta gave me the idea, but—"

"How did he do that?" Trav said.

"Well, when Marge was in the hospital and we had the house to ourselves, he said something like, 'Imagine if today hadn't been cleaning day. Marge would be gone and every night could be like this one.' Or something along that nature."

"Do you think he could have been trying to get you to do what you did?"

"I didn't *do* anything! And neither did Stan!"

Trav looked disappointed. I knew what he was feeling. He wanted to be able to involve Harris as a conspirator or, barring that, for obstructing justice at the very least. So did I. But I didn't see that happening. The rat was going to walk away with Marge's death benefit and never look back.

Especially not at Alison.

"Not to change the subject," I said. This had nothing to do with Marge, but I had to know. "That was you outside my apartment building the other night, wasn't it."

She stared at me. "How... how did you know?"

"I thought I recognized you." Not true, but I couldn't tell her I'd been hanging around her back door last night. "Why?"

Her expression shifted, the guilt draining away to leave a sullen anger.

"I saw you coming on to Stan outside the hospital."

"*What?* When?"

"Right after you talked to me in the ER. Oh, you were sly, calling me a hero and all that, but all the while you was looking to get your hooks into Stan."

I opened my mouth to reply, but astonishment blocked the words. How do you respond to something so absurd?

She sneered. "Whatsamatter? Cat gotcha tongue? And then you come by the house pretending to be helping the police, but I wasn't fooled. You were really trying to move in on Stan. I mean, with his wife gone it's soooo obvious."

"So that's why you came after me with a knife?"

"I was going to slash your tires, but I couldn't find your car. Then I saw you..."

"And decided to slash me instead?"

"Yes!" she hissed.

Trav, apparently, had heard enough. He reached for the handcuffs in their leather belt pouch.

"Well, Ms. Crowley, you'll have some time to think about that—"

"But I didn't kill no one!"

"That'll be for the court to decide. Please stand up and turn around."

She stood but didn't turn. Rage twisted her features as she looked at me.

"Bet you think you'll have a clear field with Stan once I'm gone. Well, think again, bitch!"

"Please turn around," Trav said. "You've already admitted to assault with a deadly weapon. Terroristic threats won't help your case."

This time she turned, saying, "I don't *have* a case. I'm being framed and *she's* doing it!"

But instead of putting her hands behind her, she grabbed something from between the cushions and whirled.

A flash of steel—her big kitchen knife—raised—slashing toward my face as she screamed, "*But it's not going to work!*"

I yelped and reacted instinctively, ducking and swatting at her arm as it flashed forward. It was enough to make her miss, and then Trav had her, was twisting her arm, forcing her to drop the knife...

# 5

A lison looked miserable as she sat in the locked rear compartment of Trav's cruiser. He'd read her the Miranda thing and left her knife inside on the living-room floor.

The two of us stood by the front fender.

"My God," he said. He looked a little shaken. "That was too close. If anything had happened... you all right?"

I nodded but I could feel my hands trembling with fading adrenaline. "I think so. It happened so fast. If you hadn't been there—"

"You move pretty fast yourself."

"Self-preservation reflex."

He looked at Alison through the windshield and shook his head. "This whole thing... all so damn unnecessary. What a waste. But at least we've got her."

I wasn't so sure.

"I've got to tell you, Trav, I'm having second thoughts about this."

"Oh, no. What now?"

"Alison... what she said when she slashed at me. I think she really believes she's being framed."

Trav stared at me. "Come on, Norrie. She's just trying to save her butt. We're first-hand witnesses to her violent streak— I mean, she tried to *kill* you—and we've got a mountain of evidence—"

"As you said before: all circumstantial. And a violent streak doesn't necessarily go with well-planned, premeditated murder. One's hot blooded, the other's cold-blooded. We saw some very hot blood. For some odd reason she sees me as a rival trying to steal Stan and so she lashed out."

Trav's lips twisted. "Look, if Stan's the one you really want, I'll step aside and—"

I pointed my finger at him. "Another word along that line and I'm going back inside for Alison's knife."

He laughed and held up his hands. "Sorry, sorry!"

God, the thought of being with Stan... my skin crawled.

Trav removed his Stetson and wiped his forehead with his sleeve. "Okay, let's say, just for the sake of argument, she's telling the truth about being framed. That brings us back to square one."

I nodded. "Good old Stanley Harris."

"But all the evidence points to Alison."

"Maybe it's supposed to."

I let that sink in awhile as I tried to arrange all the pieces into a new shape.

"Consider the possibilities," I said. "Marge has a near-fatal reaction. This puts an idea in Stan's head. He tries to nudge Alison into doing the deed but she's not the type. So he doses Marge's envelope himself and leaves for New York. On his way he swings by Alison's and tosses a carefully wiped jar of peanut butter into her front yard. Alison does just what she said she did: Picks it up and tosses it in the garbage can. Stan probably figures he's so clever that no one will suspect foul play, especially with the misdirection of pointing the finger at me. But if it should come to that, he's left someone looking very guilty."

"Alison."

"Right. And with her in the pokey he winds up a millionaire who's free of a wife and a down-market mistress."

Trav shook his head. "I can't believe we've been played so badly... so completely. Like hand puppets."

"Maybe it's time to play him."

"Yeah? How?"

"I think we can come up with something."

# 6

We did. Sort of.

On the way to taking Alison to the sheriff's department, I suggested we swing by the Harris place for a little visit.

"I don't think that'll be kosher," Trav muttered.

We were keeping our voices low because of our passenger.

"Why not?" I whispered. "We'll drop the news that Alison has admitted to an affair with him—truth, right?—and then we'll fabricate a little and tell him a modified version of what we told Alison, saying his prints were found on the jar along with hers."

"And what'll that accomplish?"

"Maybe he'll blurt out something incriminating."

Trav shook his head. "I wouldn't count on that."

"If nothing else it will rattle his cage, give him a few sleepless nights."

I wanted Stanley Harris to have *lots* of sleepless nights.

We pulled into the Harris driveway and Trav got out. I stayed with Alison.

From the back seat she said, "You're not going to fool him, you know. He's way too smart for you."

Obviously she'd overheard us.

"Well, we'll just have to see about that, won't we?"

I watched Trav knock on the door, then ring the bell, then knock again. He turned toward me and shrugged.

Odd. Stan's Mercedes was parked in the driveway.

I got out and went to the nearest window. I peeked in and realized I was looking at the study. Nothing moving there, so—

Then I noticed something on the floor on the far side of the desk: a pair of trousered legs... black shoes...

"Trav!" I shouted as I raced toward him. "Someone's hurt in there. We've got to get inside!"

He tried the handle but it was locked. He threw his shoulder against the door but only bounced off.

"Should we break a window?" I said.

"Let's try something else." He stepped back and lifted the mat. "People with cleaning girls often leave a—here!"

He reached under and came up with a key. It fit the lock and seconds later we were in.

I rushed into the study and found Stan Harris lying on his side in a pool of blood.

Trav said, "Oh, shit! Is he dead?"

From his color and his glazed eyes—no question. But for the sake of appearances more than anything else I pressed two fingers against his throat to check for a carotid pulse. Stan Harris was not only pulseless, he was cold.

"Been dead awhile."

I'd immediately suspected suicide, but then I saw his chest: six wounds, knife stabs from the look of them. No way could they be self-inflicted.

I've never been the victim of violence—although Saturday night was a near miss—and I've never witnessed much, but I was a pro at attending to its consequences. I've done my share of moonlighting the graveyard shift in any number of inner city emergency rooms, and let me tell you, you pretty quickly get used to punctured, battered, broken bodies. You don't have a choice.

I crouched and looked around, searching for the knife, but didn't see one.

I backed away, not wanting to contaminate the crime scene any more than I already had. Trav was on his two-way, calling in the murder.

# 7

Later, we stood out on the sidewalk, watching them cart Stan's bagged body out on a stretcher.

Trav said, "A preliminary analysis of the scene says it looks like he was first stabbed in the kitchen—there's some sliced pepperoni on a cutting board there but no knife—then pursued down the hall to the study. Backing away, most likely. At least that's what the defensive wounds on his hands indicate."

"Who?" I said for maybe the hundredth time.

"My bet is Alison," Stan said. "I mean, we know she's into knives."

Alison had been taken away by one of the other deputies, but I remembered her stricken face when she heard the news: shock, anguish... all very real.

I turned and looked down the street.

"You know, the killer had to arrive, then leave. Don't we know someone who keeps track of all the comings and goings on this block?"

Trav's eyebrows lifted. "Beth Henderson!" He looked around. "Funny she's not here asking a thousand questions."

"Probably at the hospital. I scheduled her mother for discharge today. But still..."

"What?"

"Too early for discharge."

"Yeah? Let's go down and take a look."

We did just that. We found the glass storm door closed but the inner door open. Trav ran through the same knocking-ringing process as on the Harris door, with the same result.

"Something's not right here," I said, playing Mistress of the Obvious.

"Yeah. Let's go in."

He stepped through the door, calling for Beth. No answer, so we checked the rooms.

I found her face up in the tub, fully clothed, floating in red water. Beside the tub lay a black-handled kitchen knife with a bloody blade.

I rushed in and knelt beside the tub. I grabbed one of her wrists and saw a bloody slit, still oozing. Her flesh felt cool, but not as cold as Stan's. I felt for her carotid and found a weak pulse.

"She's alive! Call those EMTs back!"

While Trav fumbled for his two-way I stepped into the hall, found the linen closet, and grabbed a pillowcase. I tried to rip it but it was too strong. So I ran for the kitchen and started going through the drawers until I found a pair of scissors. I used them the cut through the seams. After that it was easy to tear the cloth into strips.

Back at the tub I tied a strip around each arm just below the elbow as tight as I could to act as tourniquets, then I tied strips around the gouges on Beth's wrists as pressure dressings.

She was in shock from loss of blood but she had a chance if the EMTs got here in time to hook up an IV.

# 8

Once again we watched a stretcher being wheeled toward an ambulance, except this time its occupant wasn't in a bag. Beth was alive but still unconscious. Her IVs were flowing wide open and her pressure was rising. She'd make it.

Travis rubbed his eyes. "Why would Beth Henderson try to kill herself?"

"We don't know that she did," I said. "It only looks that way."

"You think she saw something she shouldn't have?"

"I don't know. A successful murder and a botched suicide attempt... on the same day, on the same block. They've got to be connected, don't you think?"

He nodded. "Absolutely."

"This may sound crazy, but I think they'll find Stan Harris's blood on the knife Beth used to slit her wrists."

He loosed a little laugh. "Then we're both crazy. Because I've been thinking the same thing."

"I'll see you and raise on craziness: What if the same person killed Stan and tried to kill Beth and make it look like a suicide. And..." My mind was racing here, going off track left and right. "We've got two and a half dead people here, but what if Beth had been the intended victim all along?"

He laughed. "Maybe you missed your calling. You should be a mystery writer."

"I'm serious."

He shook his head. "That stuff only happens in books and movies. Murders tend to be very simple and straightforward, and the perp usually winds up being someone close to the victim. If Stan's blood is on that blade, dollars to donuts—and we cops do love our donuts—it's because Beth killed him with it."

"But why? She had no relationship with Stan beyond the fact that she knew he was cheating on Marge." I started to riff again. "Maybe Beth and Marge were lovers! Maybe that's why Stan was fooling around—Marge wasn't interested in him. And then Stan kills Marge with the peanut oil and Beth takes revenge."

Another laugh. "Forget books—go straight to Hollywood."

"It's a possibility, isn't it?"

"A very remote one. In most murder-suicides, the murdered party is usually someone the murderer loves. The killer either plans the suicide ahead of time, or can't live with himself afterward—*her*self in this case."

"Stan and Beth… lovers?"

Trav removed his Stetson and scratched his head. "I can't see that either. Alison proves he likes young stuff. Beth Henderson is anything but. Don't know her age, but she looks older than Stan."

"Doesn't mean she's not hot between the sheets."

Trav shook his head. "That's quite a stretch."

I had to agree. As if on cue, we both looked at Beth's open front door, then at each other.

"Can we?" I said.

He hesitated, then nodded. "Okay. Just a quick look."

Another deputy crouched inside the door, fiddling in a vinyl toolbox. He looked up as we entered.

"Hey, Trav. Some morning, huh?"

Trav nodded. "You said it."

He introduced me as Dr. Marconi and I learned the other deputy's name was Hank.

Hank fished in the box and came up with a roll of yellow crime-scene tape.

"What do you think?"

"Better safe than sorry, at least until the photographers finish up at the Harris place and start here. But give us a moment to look around first."

"Sure."

Trav lowered his voice as we moved away. "Just stay out of the bathroom."

We split, Trav taking the front of the house—living room and kitchen—and I the rear.

Everything looked neat, orderly, immaculate. Beth obviously took as much care with the house as she did with her mother.

I froze. Amelia! I'd scheduled her for discharge this morning. I'd have to cancel that and hold her a few more days. The utilization committee would howl, but what could I do? I couldn't send her home to an empty house—the house where her daughter had tried to end her own life that morning.

And worse, I'd have to be the one to tell her *why* I couldn't send her home.

Pardon my French, but *merde*!

One bedroom was obviously Amelia's—fussy, busy, old-fashioned lace, photos of her late husband. The other was spare, with darker furniture, and no photos of anyone.

The only thing out of place was a University of Maryland yearbook, butterflied open, face down on the bed.

"Trav?"

He appeared seconds later and knew immediately why I'd called him. He fished out a pair of latex gloves and turned the yearbook over, revealing a photo of a couple of college kids in formal attire, embracing and smiling for the camera.

The girl was a very young and surprisingly attractive Beth Henderson. The guy, despite a full head of hair and droopy mustache, was unquestionably Stan Harris.

# 9

I reached the office fifteen minutes late, and glad that was all. It could have been so much worse. I'd gone to the hospital first. After checking on Beth who'd regained consciousness but was still disoriented, I'd gone to Amelia's room and broken the news. Gently. I told her that Beth had been "seriously hurt" and hospitalized, but would pull through just fine.

I escaped without having to answer too many questions. I took my Tezinex dose on the way to the office. No video for me today.

The rest of the morning passed with no new drama. And that afternoon Trav showed up an hour late for his appointment. At least he'd called ahead to let me know. I squeezed him in.

"Sorry," he said. "Things are crazy today."

"I'll bet. What about the local crime wave? Is Beth talking?"

He nodded. "Oh, yeah."

"Admit she killed Stan?"

"And Marge too."

That jolted me.

"Marge? She killed *Marge*? But I thought—"

"*We* thought—and we thought just what she wanted us to think. You had it right about framing Alison, but it wasn't Stan doing the framing, it was Beth."

Slightly dazed, I leaned back against the counter.

"Explain. Please."

He pointed to his Band-Aid. "Can we talk while you work? I've got to get back to the station."

"Sorry."

I peeled off his Band-Aid.

"How's it look?"

Not only had the laceration healed into a tight pink line, the eight close-set sutures were loose. A sure sign they were ready for removal.

"Great. Those sutures will be history in a few minutes. But keep talking."

I dabbed the area with Betadine, then pulled open a sterile suture-removal kit.

"Okay. Seems Stan and Beth were a hot couple during college and for a while after. But then Stan met Marge and dropped Beth."

I used my forceps to grasp a strand of the first suture and pull it taut.

"And she's never forgiven her?"

"Never. And never stopped carrying a torch for Stan."

I slipped the hooked end of my scissors under the suture knot and clipped a strand. The severed loop of fine nylon thread popped free of Trav's skin.

"One down, seven to go."

"Didn't even feel it."

"Not supposed to." I started on the next. "Hard to imagine Beth carrying a torch for anyone, let alone Stan Harris. She sort of struck me as asexual."

"I don't know the psychobabble, but I do know what she told us. She said when she heard about Marge's reaction, she saw a way to eliminate her from Stan's life. She sneaked into the house on Wednesday morning after Stan left to take Alison home. She—"

I snipped another suture.

"How'd she get in?"

"Same way we did: the key under the mat."

"But how'd—? Never mind. Miss Neighborhood Watch would have seen Alison lifting the mat twice a week."

"Exactly. She entered with a little container of oil she'd poured off the peanut butter and looked for something to dose. She spotted the bill envelopes and made her decision."

Another suture bit the dust.

"Did she say she saw it on *Seinfeld*?"

"As a matter of fact, yes."

I *had* to catch that episode.

I said, "But that didn't remove Alison from the picture, so she framed her. Pretty smart—get rid of two rivals at once."

Snip.

"Except that wasn't her original plan. Beth had this crazy idea that with Marge out of the way she and Stan could pick up where they'd left off."

"Crazy idea is right."

"But when she saw police activity at the Harris place—namely me—she feared we might suspect foul play. So she wiped down her peanut butter jar and tossed it into Alison's front yard. Then she revealed that Alison was Stan's 'paramour.'"

"So Alison wasn't lying."

"No, but she's still guilty of assault."

Snip.

I said, "Back to Beth. If she had this thing for Stan, why'd she stab him?"

"How's that go? 'Hell hath no fury like a woman scorned'?"

"Something like that." Not exactly correct but close enough. "Which I take to mean that she offered herself to him and he rejected her."

"Uh-huh. Went over there with this crazy idea that he'd fall into her arms, but Stan wasn't buying. According to Beth, he laughed in her face and she lost it. They were in the kitchen. He'd been slicing some pepperoni before she arrived. She grabbed the knife and started stabbing."

"And then tried to join him in death."

"Right. Says that when she cooled down she was so horrified by what she'd done that she couldn't go on living."

I shook my head. Like a Shakespearean tragedy.

"Any other tidbits?"

"No. Her attorney stepped into the picture. Now she's lawyered up and she's shut up. The guy's already talking about getting Beth's confession thrown out."

I paused as I pulled suture number six.

"Can he do that?"

Trav shrugged. "Maybe. Who knows? He's saying she was dazed and confused from the trauma and the blood loss and didn't know what she was saying."

"Are you telling me she may walk? After all we went through, she might still get away with murder?"

"Can we discuss this after you finish?"

"Why?"

"I don't think I want you upset while you're holding scissors so close to my eye."

"Oh. Right."

I quickly removed the final sutures.

"Okay," I said as I gave the area a last daub of Betadine. "How do you think this is going to play out?"

"Well, according to the prosecutor I spoke to, she won't be charged with murder one."

"But it was premeditated! She deliberately poisoned that envelope. You don't get much more premeditated than that!"

"Easy now. The problem is hard evidence—we don't have any. But the good news is that all sorts of folks have heard the tape of her confession and everybody knows she did it. And she and her lawyer know that everybody knows. She'll probably plead temporary insanity in Stan's case. The prosecutor thinks Beth's attorney will try to cut a deal, and he'll be receptive—up to a point. Bottom line: Beth Henderson is going to do some kind of time."

"But not life."

Trav shook his head. "Not life."

"Damn."

"Hey, look on the bright side: If not for us, not only would she be free, but no one would know that Marge was murdered. We did good work, Norrie. And because of it, I'm seen as having real detective potential."

He was right. We'd made a difference in Marge's death.

"I'm glad for you, Trav."

"And I owe it all to you."

The unguarded, heartfelt gratitude in his look made me a little uncomfortable. Whatever I'd contributed hadn't been simply and solely for his sake. I'd had my own issues.

"Does that mean two dinners? I haven't collected on the first yet."

"Two dinners, three, a dozen—whatever you want. I—"

"Trav, it's okay. Really. I wanted Marge's killer as much as you."

He gathered me in his arms and we kissed, and kissed again. And once more before I broke free. All I needed was for Harriet to walk in and I'd never hear the end of it.

"Mmm," he said. "That was nice. Let's try again soon."

"Yes." I felt flushed and my voice sounded a little hoarse. "Let's."

"Look, I know you've got patients backed up, and I've got to run. That dinner I owe you—is tonight okay?"

"Tonight's great—no, wait." I remembered my promise to Donna. "I've got a dinner meeting in the city. Tomorrow's better."

"Tomorrow night then." He was looking into my eyes. "And after dinner… some more of this?"

I smiled. "Depends."

"On what?"

"Just… depends."

"I'll call you." He gave me a peck on the lips. "You're the best, Norrie."

And then he was out the examining room door and heading down the hall.

I felt a little lightheaded, and I must have been grinning like a fool as I brought Trav's chart out to the back desk, because Ken was there, giving me a strange stare.

"What are you so happy about?" he said with his perpetual scowl.

"Nothing," I said. "What's there to be happy about?"

What indeed? I'd helped catch a murderer, my first love was circling back to me, and I could talk to my dad at night. None of which Ken had a right to know.

But on the other hand, I still had a malpractice suit to deal with, and I had to find out what had happened to Uncle Corry or my father would be stuck in that house forever.

And what neither Ken nor I knew was that all too soon we'd both have plenty to be unhappy about.

Look for the next Nina Abbott mystery

## *Rx Mayhem*

Coming in early 2022

# About the Author

F. PAUL WILSON is an award-winning, bestselling author of sixty books and nearly one hundred short stories spanning science fiction, horror, adventure, medical thrillers, and virtually everything between.

His novels *The Keep, The Tomb, Harbingers, By the Sword, The Dark at the End,* and *Nightworld* were *New York Times* Bestsellers. *The Tomb* received the 1984 Porgie Award from *The West Coast Review of Books. Wheels Within Wheels* won the first Prometheus Award, and *Sims* another; *Healer* and *An Enemy of the State* were elected to the Prometheus Hall of Fame. *Dydeetown World* was on the young adult recommended reading lists of the American Library Association and the New York Public Library, among others. His novella *Aftershock* won the Stoker Award. He was voted Grand Master by the World Horror Convention; he received the Lifetime Achievement Award from the Horror Writers of America, and the Thriller Lifetime Achievement Award from the editors of Romantic Times. He also received the prestigious San Diego Comic-Con Inkpot Award and is listed in the 50th anniversary edition of Who's Who in America.

His short fiction has been collected in *Soft & Others, The Barrens & Others,* and *Aftershock & Others.* He has edited two anthologies: *Freak Show* and *Diagnosis: Terminal* plus (with Pierce Watters) the only complete collection of Henry Kuttner's Hogben stories, *The Hogben Chronicles.*

In 1983 Paramount rendered his novel *The Keep* into a visually striking but otherwise incomprehensible movie with screenplay and direction by Michael Mann.

*The Tomb* has spent twenty-five years in development hell at Beacon Films.

Dario Argento adapted his story "Pelts" for *Masters of Horror*.

Over nine million copies of his books are in print in the US and his work has been translated into twenty-four languages. He also has written for the stage, screen, comics, and interactive media. Paul resides at the Jersey Shore and can be found on the Web at www.repairmanjack.com.

### Repairman Jack*

*The Tomb*
*Legacies*
*Conspiracies*
*All the Rage*
*Hosts*
*The Haunted Air*
*Gateways*
*Crisscross*
*Infernal*
*Harbingers*
*Bloodline*
*By the Sword*
*Ground Zero*
*The Last Christmas*
*Fatal Error*
*The Dark at the End*
*Nightworld*
*Quick Fixes—Tales of Repairman Jack*

The Teen Trilogy*
*Jack: Secret Histories*
*Jack: Secret Circles*
*Jack: Secret Vengeance*

The Early Years Trilogy*
*Cold City*
*Dark City*
*Fear City*

The Adversary Cycle*
*The Keep*
*The Tomb*
*The Touch*

*Reborn*
*Reprisal*
*Nightworld*

## Omnibus Editions

*The Complete LaNague*
*Calling Dr. Death (3 medical thrillers)*
*Ephemerata*

## Novellas

*The Peabody-Ozymandias Traveling Circus & Oddity Emporium*\*
*"Wardenclyffe"*\*
*"Signalz"*\*
*The LaNague Federation*
*Healer*
*Wheels Within Wheels*
*An Enemy of the State*
*Dydeetown World*
*The Tery*

## Other Novels

*Black Wind*\*
*Sibs*\*
*The Select*
*Virgin*
*Implant*
*Deep as the Marrow*
*Sims*
*The Fifth Harmonic*\*
*Midnight Mass*

Collaborations
*Mirage* (with Matthew J. Costello)
*Nightkill* (with Steven Spruill)
*Masque* (with Matthew J. Costello)
*Draculas* (with Crouch, Killborn, Strand)
*The Proteus Cure* (with Tracy L. Carbone)
*A Necessary End* (with Sarah Pinborough)
*"Fix"*\* (with J. Konrath & Ann Voss Peterson)

The ICE Trilogy\*
*Panacea*
*The God Gene*
*The Void Protocol*

## Other Novels Cont'd

The Nocturnia Chronicles (with Thomas F. Monteleone)
*Definitely Not Kansas*
*Family Secrets*
*The Silent Ones*

Short Fiction
*Soft & Others*
*The Barrens and Others*
*Aftershock and Others*
*The Christmas Thingy*
*Quick Fixes—Tales of Repairman Jack**
*Sex Slaves of the Dragon Tong*
*Secret Stories*

## Editor

*Freak Show*
*Diagnosis: Terminal*
*The Hogben Chronicles* (with Pierce Watters)

Curious about other Crossroad Press books?
Stop by our site:
http://www.crossroadpress.com
We offer quality writing
in digital, audio, and print formats.